Confessions of a
DANGEROUS
DUKE

ON HIS MAJESTY'S SECRET SERVICE
BOOK 3

PATRICIA BARLETTA
patriciabarletta.com

Published Internationally by Patricia Barletta
Boston, MA
Copyright © 2020 Patricia Barletta

patriciabarletta.com

Exclusive cover © 2020 inputux.com
Interior book design by Tamara Cribley www.deliberatepage.com

PRINT ISBN 978-1-7355994-1-0
EBOOK ISBN 978-1-7355994-0-3

Editor: Joanna D'Angelo
Copy Editor/Proofreader: Amy Smart

This is a work of fiction. Names, characters, places and incidents are either the product of the author's imagination or are used fictitiously, and any resemblance to any person or persons, living or dead, events or locales is entirely coincidental.

ACKNOWLEDGMENTS

Writing a book during a pandemic is a strange thing. On the one hand, it's not much different than writing at any other time, because most authors usually work from home anyway. On the other hand, a stay-at-home order keeps us from going out when we're not writing. It prevents us from mingling with people, traveling for research, and absorbing the world so we can portray it in our books. What's a writer to do to stay sane and connect? Zoom and Skype meetings were essential, so I am grateful for those platforms. Without those meetings, I would have been talking to myself much more than I did. And of course, I am grateful for the people on the other end of those meetings: my adult children and my grandkids, my local chapter of RWA, my critique group, and my author assistant/editor/ombudsman, Joanna, who helps me in countless ways. Once again, Steve Coppola created a fabulous cover; Amy Sharp pointed out all my silly grammatical and punctuation mistakes; and Tamara at The Deliberate Page formatted the book to perfection. My thanks to all you wonderful people.

Because my heroine is a modiste, I consulted several fashion and costume books. Even though I used them for research, they were just great fun to look at. Here are a few:

Costume Reference 5: The Regency, by Marion Sichel.
Fashion in the Time of Jane Austen, by Sarah Jane Downing.
Fashion: A History from the 18th to the 20th Century (The Collection of the Kyoto Costume Institute), by Akiko Fukai, et al.

And because Arianne sends secret messages in her dress designs, this one was invaluable:

Codes and Ciphers: Secret Writing Through the Ages, by John Laffin.

PROLOGUE

April 1811, The Coast of France

Almost there.

The words were a litany inside her head. Arianne de Vouvret hurried across the uneven ground beside her husband, Jean-Paul, and her father, François Chiasson. The chill night breeze cut across the empty landscape around them. She hugged her cloak close and was glad for the woolen stockings she had donned. The clouds, running before the wind and scudding across the moon, created shadows that helped to hide them in their flight. She was thankful for those, too.

Dislodged pebbles clattered behind her. She halted and turned, searching the dark. Was someone there? Or had it only been her imagination? All she could hear was the wind, toying with the branches of trees and sending loose leaves into giddy flights. She could see nothing but moonlight and shadows as the silent, swift clouds sailed far above them in their nighttime game.

"Arianne, what is it?" Jean-Paul stopped and turned back to her.

She listened a moment longer, then shook her head. "It is nothing." She smiled reassuringly at her husband, even though he probably could not see her in the dark. "Hurry along with Papa. I am coming."

She watched Jean-Paul take her father by the arm once more to guide him across the uneven ground. Papa had been ill and was still weak, but they'd had to flee. Their hiding spot, a tiny farm not far from the northern coast, had been discovered. And so they had run.

Only a little farther, she thought, and they would reach the beach where the boat waited to take them to safety.

Almost there.

1

"Hurry, *chérie*," Jean-Paul urged.

She picked up her skirts and hastened after the two men in her life who were more dear to her than anything on earth. They wended their way through the copse of trees that curved back from the shore. Beyond that was a narrow strip of open grass, a small sandy cliff, and then the beach below and the sea. As they cleared the woods, Arianne knew they were the most vulnerable, for then they were silhouetted against the expanse of water. Her spine tingled with the touch of imagined eyes watching. She linked her arm through her father's.

"Just a little farther, Papa," she encouraged.

His labored breathing told her how much of a toll this flight had taken on him. He did not waste breath on an answer, but patted her hand reassuringly. She worried about his strength.

On her father's other side, Jean-Paul slowed and turned his head to listen. His hurried footsteps faltered. "We're being followed! Quickly! To the boat!"

As they broke into a run, the explosion of a gunshot swept to them on the night wind. Jean-Paul grunted and stumbled. Arianne cast a worried glance at him. He took four more steps, then collapsed to one knee.

"Jean-Paul!" she screamed and reached out to help him.

"Go on," he urged, pain lacing his voice. "Take your father and run."

Fear clutched at her as she knelt beside him. "I won't leave you."

"Arianne, you promised you would stay safe," Jean-Paul scolded gently, his words weaker than normal.

"You promised the same," she said, then turned to her father. "Papa, take the boat, cross La Manche to England. I will come to you when I can."

"What kind of father abandons his children?" Her father waved away her suggestion. "Come, we will cross the water together." He took Jean-Paul's arm and tried to help him to his feet.

After an unsuccessful attempt to stand, Jean-Paul shook his head. As he coughed up blood, Arianne and her father carefully laid him on the cold, rocky ground. She felt the warm wetness on his back and the rough-edged hole in his coat. The shot had found its mark in her husband. She tried to staunch the flow of blood with her hand and fought the terror that erupted in her chest.

"I can't go on," he struggled to tell them. "You must leave while… you have…the chance."

"I'm not leaving you." Her arms tightened around him.

She looked up, across her husband's prone body, to the edge of the woods where five dark figures emerged. *Too late*, she thought. *Too late for escape.* They would be taken together. She would plead for help for Jean-Paul.

Turning back to her husband, she smoothed his brow. "I will get help for you. They don't want your death, only our lives."

With a smile, he touched her cheek. "You are dearer to me than life, *ma chérie*," he whispered. A gurgling cough twisted his face in pain. A dark line of blood dribbled from the corner of his mouth. Delicately, Arianne wiped it away with her skirt. Again his words came, tortured and barely audible. "Run, my flower. Run and live. I love you."

His breath ended with his words. His eyes stared beyond her at something only he could see. He was gone.

"No!" she denied. "No, no, no, no!" Arianne bent over him, hugged him, tried to love some life back into his body.

Her father knelt beside her and placed a comforting arm around her shoulders.

A heel grinding against stone announced the arrival of their pursuers. Their footsteps had been hidden by the wind and her own wailing. She knew who they were—one of them even by name.

"Madame de Vouvret, Chavalier Chiasson," Henri Pinard greeted them amiably. The black patch over his left eye gave him a rakish appearance, but beneath his debonair exterior lay a heart as cold as Hades. His single-eyed gaze swept over them. He smiled with chilly satisfaction. "We are well met. Were you planning a midnight sail, perhaps?"

Arianne heard the mocking words, and her grief turned into a cold, hard rage. Immediately, her tears dried up. Her lips drew back in a feral snarl.

"You killed him." Her low tone was more deadly than any screech of anger. "You killed him when he had done nothing more than try to save his family."

"A pity," Pinard acknowledged as if he were lamenting the lack of wine at a picnic. "A tragic accident, but then, he was of little use to us."

"Pig! Snake! Monster!" The words erupted in a growl from her deep, visceral hatred of the man. She would have gone on with her name-calling, but grief choked her and made her thoughts spin off into a void.

Arianne's father rose to his feet. "You will leave my daughter out of your scheming, Pinard. Take me and let her go."

Pinard crossed his arms. "I will certainly take you, François, but I have found that the lovely Madame de Vouvret has become rather valuable."

"You are vile, Pinard." Arianne spat onto his shiny boots.

Pinard's mouth twisted in distaste. "Fortunately, madame, I am not easily insulted, and both you and your papa are too valuable for me to do more than admonish you to mind your manners and keep a civil tongue."

A furtive movement from Arianne's father made Pinard's henchmen swing pistols and swords around in his direction.

"You are too wise to do something so foolish, Chavalier Chiasson." Pinard nodded at the knife in the man's hand. "And you should know after our long association that I do not tolerate insubordination from those in my employ." At his gesture, one of his men wrenched the knife away.

Arianne's father stiffened his spine. "I am not in your employ any longer, Pinard."

Pinard glared with his single eye. "You are in no position to refuse, François, unless you would care to see your daughter come to harm." The pistols and swords swung in Arianne's direction.

"No!" Chavalier Chiasson's shoulders drooped. "I will go with you."

"Good. Now," Pinard went on, "presuming that neither one of you has any more objections or trinkets to show us, we'll be off. I do wish to be back at the inn by morning for croissants and hot chocolate." He spun away as he motioned for his henchmen to bring the prisoners.

"But my husband—" Arianne tried to twist free of the two men who had pulled her to her feet. "You cannot just leave him here!"

Pinard turned back to her with an annoyed scowl. "Of course I can." One of his men whispered something to him. Pinard sighed with irritation. "Well, perhaps you are right. Questions are bound to be asked." He pointed at two of his men. "You and you. Bury him. The rest of us will be off."

Arianne realized it was useless to protest as she was hauled after Pinard. When she glanced at her father, he gave her an imperceptible shake of his head in warning. Pinard could turn cruel at the slightest provocation.

Too late, she thought again with a longing glance back at the dear form of Jean-Paul, now an indistinct, dark shape on the ground. Her heart twisted painfully. Too late to tell him her secret, the one she herself had just discovered. Instinctively, she placed her hand over her womb, then realized she should not make such an obvious, protective movement. She turned the motion into a nervous gesture. If she were very careful and very lucky, she would be able to keep her secret to herself, and Pinard would never discover it.

She went quietly with her captors. Her husband's blood stained her hands and she wiped them on her skirt. But she would never wipe his memory from her heart, nor forget the evil man who so casually stole her dear husband's life. She stumbled along, passive now in Pinard's custody, an icy stream of tears flowing down her cheeks. She vowed that someday she would wreak her revenge. Glancing up at the sky, she called on the moon and clouds and the heavens themselves to witness what had occurred in their presence, and allowed the wind to entwine her heart in its cold embrace.

CHAPTER 1

Five years later, August, 1816, Bath, England

Cameron West, Duke of Lythmore, stepped down from the coach and surveyed the building before him. It was a grand sweep of a crescent, housing numerous political figures and society people when they made their summer sojourn to Bath, this fashionable watering hole of the *ton*. He had secured a luxurious townhouse here for his stay in the city. But he had not come to Bath for the curative powers of its waters, nor to mingle with society during their summer escape from London. He had come to seek out the person who had destroyed his younger brother.

"Darling," a sultry voice beckoned from behind him. "Are you going to stand there all day, or will you hand me down from the coach?"

Cameron turned with a grin to his former mistress, Sally Turner, and held out his hand. "My apologies, sweetling."

In a flurry of striped muslin, its severity alleviated by a multitude of bows down the front, a young woman with bright blonde curls stepped daintily down to the street. Opening her parasol with a snap and holding it just so above her head, she turned her perfect profile to Cameron and gazed up at the building before her.

"Gaw," she breathed, "that's a bit of all right now, ain't it?"

Cameron chuckled as Sally reverted back to the gutter accent of her childhood. Very few people realized her origins, but Cameron had been her first protector. That had been long ago, before she had become an actress at the Drury Lane Theater where she appeared on a regular basis.

Reverting back to the cultured English that was now her habit, Sally went on, "I never knew Bath could be so grand. I will no doubt embarrass you with all my gawking."

"You may gawk all you wish," Cameron told her fondly. "I brought you on holiday just for that reason."

"Oh, darling, is that the only reason?" Sally turned her winsome blue eyes on him and outrageously fluttered her lashes.

Cameron chuckled, knowing she only played a part, but he enjoyed the attention of this attractive woman nevertheless. Besides being his former mistress, Sally had also become one of his most talented spies, able to pry secrets from the most reluctant sources.

"Do you know," Sally commented as her attention wandered from Cameron to the city around them, "I believe I will avail myself of several new frocks while I am here. I have heard there is an outstanding modiste who runs a shop in the city. I do wonder why she does not move to London. Now, what is her name? Villards? No, that's not it. Villiers? No, that's not it either. Hmm. I know! Vouvret! Madame de Vouvret! That's it!" She cuddled against Cameron's arm. "You must open an account for me at her establishment, darling. I simply must have new gowns before I am seen anywhere in this place."

Cameron's brows rose. "New gowns? I don't remember mentioning a new wardrobe in my invitation to you."

Sally's pink little mouth pouted. "Your invitation was more like a command, darling." Then she dimpled attractively. "Consider the purchase as costumes for the part I must play as your cousin, the woeful widow, just emerging from her mourning." She cuddled even closer.

"You will make a pauper of me," Cameron complained good-naturedly.

"Hardly that, darling." Sally's tone was dry. "I've seen your grand Lythmore Manor in Surrey. You could support three mistresses and still not know what to do with the rest of your income."

With a smile, Cameron escorted her through the doorway and into the dim interior of the building. A grim excitement took hold of him as he realized he was moving ever closer to his quarry. Soon, he promised himself, the monster who had destroyed his brother would be in his grip—begging for mercy.

Arianne let out a sigh of relief at seeing the last of her guests leave. Her regular Tuesday afternoon salon was interesting, but always a drain on her energy. Glad that it was over for another week, she was about to close the door when a gentleman stopped on the walkway and tipped his hat.

"Pardon me," he said. "Is this the establishment of Madame de Vouvret, the modiste?"

Arianne was too tired to entertain any business. "It is, monsieur, but Madame de Vouvret is closing for the day. You may come back tomorrow if you wish. Madame will see you then." It amused her to speak of herself as another person when dealing with unknown customers. The confusion could always be cleared up later with a charming apology.

The man stepped closer. "I'm afraid that's impossible. You see, I will be unavailable tomorrow, and my cousin is determined to engage Madame de Vouvret for several gowns. She is just coming out of mourning for her late husband. All I wish to do is establish credit."

"I see." Arianne studied him a moment as she wondered if indulging him would be worth the effort.

He was quite handsome. His eyes were an unusual blue, so dark they were nearly black. His nose was straight, and his chin square. His mouth was chiseled perfection. When he tipped his hat, Arianne saw dark hair with bright highlights, barbered and neat. His clothes were fashionable, well cut, but not ostentatious. Obviously, he was prosperous, perhaps even wealthy. Something about him was vaguely familiar, but she could not pinpoint what it was.

When he smiled, two deep dimples appeared in his cheeks and transformed his face from handsome to beautiful. Arianne found herself dazzled. Forcing herself not to swoon like some love-smitten young lady in her first season, she stepped back and opened the door wider. "Come in, monsieur, and I will see what I can do."

As she led him through the front room and stepped around the servants cleaning up after the departure of her guests, that vague familiarity nagged at her. For some reason, it made her apprehensive, that perhaps she was in some danger. But the gentleman certainly did not appear threatening in any way. Nonetheless, she should have remained firm and had the gentleman return the next day as she had first told him. Then she would have had time to figure out why his appearance unnerved her. She castigated herself for allowing a dazzling smile to make up her mind.

Entering the tiny room that served as her office, she waved to a small, comfortable chair in front of the desk. "Please, have a seat, monsieur, while I have some refreshment brought. Tea, perhaps, or would you prefer something stronger, such as port?"

"Tea will be fine," he answered.

After ringing for a maid to bring the tea, Arianne seated herself behind the desk and picked up her pen. "Now, then, monsieur, how may Madame de Vouvret be of service to you?"

The gentleman smiled, again taking Arianne's breath away. "Let us not play games, shall we? You are Madame de Vouvret, the famous modiste. Am I not correct?"

Arianne bowed her head to hide her blush, and a guilty smile pulled at her lips. "You are quite correct, monsieur. Forgive me for my little charade. How did you guess?"

"You have the air of a woman who knows her own mind, someone who has been in control of her life and must be in control of others," he answered truthfully. "It was a natural assumption, madame."

If only she were in control of her own life. If only — Arianne halted that thought immediately. No good could come of wishing for something that might never happen. The maid arrived at that moment with the tea tray, and Arianne was grateful for the distraction. Pouring for the gentleman, she handed him a cup. "You seem to have me at a disadvantage, monsieur, since you know my name but have not yet revealed yours."

It was the gentleman's turn to be embarrassed. Standing swiftly, he bowed and said, "Forgive me, madame, for my rudeness. I am Cameron, Duke of Lythmore. I have taken up residence in the Royal Crescent while my newly acquired property is refurbished. Perhaps you know something about it? Shipley Hall. It…"

Shipley Hall! Arianne heard nothing after those words and felt the blood drain from her face. No! It could not be! She thought she would never again hear the name of the place that made guilt twist within her like some writhing serpent.

"Madame! Madame de Vouvret!" The man's voice seemed to come from a great distance. "Madame, are you unwell?"

A touch on her arm made her jump, but it also brought her back to her senses. Arianne drew a deep breath and forced herself to smile up at the Duke as he stood over her in concern. "I must apologize, monsieur. I have had a long day, and I suffered a bit of faintness. It is gone now, and we may conclude this matter."

The duke bowed. "Forgive me, madame. I have been rude for forcing my business upon you at this hour. I will rearrange my schedule and return tomorrow."

He started for the door. Arianne was tempted to let him go, to allow herself time to recover from the shock she had just received, but her curiosity was too strong for that. "Wait, please, monsieur," she said as he reached the doorway. He turned back to her and she waved to the chair before her. "Please, your grace, let us conclude our business now. I could not forgive myself for forcing you to return because of my silliness. The tea will refresh me." To prove her words, she smiled and sipped from her cup.

"As you wish." He nodded and returned to his chair. Before seating himself again, he passed a letter across to her. "This is a letter of introduction from my London banker. I trust that will be sufficient for your needs."

Arianne scanned the letter and hoped it might give her a bit more information about the man before her. She was disappointed to discover it did not. The urge to question him about how and why he had come to acquire Shipley Hall expanded within her until she thought she might burst. With an effort, she repressed the impulse. She could not reveal that she had any knowledge concerning the place or its former residents. That would be far too dangerous.

As she forced a smile, she handed his letter back to him. "That is quite acceptable, your grace. May I make an appointment for your cousin?" She scanned her appointment book. "Tomorrow seems to be filled, but the next day I am free in the morning."

"That would be fine." He took a sip of tea. As he placed his cup back in its saucer, he said, "And Shipley Hall? Do you have any knowledge of the place?"

"Unfortunately, I know very little about it," she glibly lied, as she wrote down the appointment in her book.

She wondered why she had never heard of the Duke of Lythmore. And why he had suddenly shown up on her doorstep. And the coincidence of his purchase of Shipley Hall. That guilty serpent in her gut writhed as she considered the only possibility she could think of — he knew what had occurred at Shipley Hall almost two years before. His question about the estate could have been a ruse to discover what she knew. Perhaps, he suspected she had some connection to it. Improbable, yet not impossible. But how could he possibly know what had taken place? Why would he care? And how could he know she had been involved? She could not dwell on that now. She had done what she had to at the time. It was over. Done. Finished.

Forcing herself to remain calm and business-like, she decided she would make inquiries of her customers to see if she could gain any more information about him. When she had finished entering the appointment in her book, she escorted the duke back through the front room, deserted now and put back to rights, to the door. As she offered her hand, she said, "Thank you for your patronage, your grace. I look forward to meeting your cousin."

Bowing gallantly over her hand, he smiled. "Until we meet again, madame."

Arianne coolly disengaged her fingers from his grasp as she steeled herself against the dazzle of that smile. "*Au revoir, monsieur.*" Forcing her lips to curve up at the corners, she nodded and closed the door. She pulled the drape across the front window to indicate that her establishment was now closed for the day.

Stepping back from the door, she drew a deep, calming breath. *A coincidence*, she told herself. Lythmore said he had only recently purchased Shipley Hall. The tragedy had occurred two years ago, and the property had been vacant since then. It was merely coincidence that the Duke of Lythmore had purchased the property and turned up on her doorstep. She was, after all, the foremost modiste in Bath, and Bath was a favorite retreat of the *ton*. It was only logical that he should come to her to have gowns made for his cousin.

After reassuring herself, the serpent in her gut was silenced. She turned her thoughts to the duke. He was by far the most charming, unnerving man she had ever met. Never had she been so disturbed by the attention of a gentleman. His smile alone could cause a woman to dissolve into a puddle of quivering jelly, and the gentle grasp of his hand on her fingers had done odd, jittery things to her insides. She closed one hand about the other and stared down at those append-ages as if they had betrayed her somehow.

If she were any ordinary single woman, she could have been smitten by him immediately. But she was no ordinary, single woman. She was Madame de Vouvret, modiste, with an obligation to perform and a terrible secret to hide. She had no time for the silliness of infat-uation. Jean-Paul still resided in her heart. He always would. There was no room for any other man. She had other, more pressing mat-ters to which she must attend. She dropped her hands to her sides.

With a determined step, she returned to her office, sat down at her desk, and pulled out a piece of foolscap and a stick of charcoal. Using swift, sure strokes, she sketched out a dress design. When she had finished the basic outline, she created shadings and shadows, darkening certain aspects of the design with curving lines and curli-cues. Holding up the completed drawing, she scrutinized it, finally nodding in satisfaction. She placed it flat once more, wrote a list of materials and colors across the bottom, then signed it with a flourish.

Putting down the stick of charcoal, she stared at the foolscap. All the information — social gossip, political rumors, financial deals and enterprises — that she had learned from her weekly salon had been condensed down to the sketch that lay before her. Yet, she had neglected to include one bit of information — the fact that the new owner of Shipley Hall had arrived on her doorstep. *A coincidence,* she told herself again. She did not need to pass that along to Henri Pinard until she could discover more about His Grace, the Duke of Lythmore. For some reason, she wanted to shield him from her oppressor's gaze.

Feeling better that she was able to be Pinard's conscience, at least for a little while, she wiped the charcoal off her fingers.

Tomorrow she would transpose the sketch into a watercolor on parchment that would hold up better to the grasp of many hands. Until then, she placed it carefully within a portfolio containing several other sketches and drawings. Her job was finished for now. In a few days, it would find its way to its final destination where her father would decipher her shadings and curlicues back into the information she had learned. And then he would hand that to his jailer, Henri Pinard.

With a tired sigh, she sat back in her chair and allowed her thoughts to dwell once again on the Duke of Lythmore. She wondered why she had never heard any rumors or gossip about him. He was a very charming gentleman and probably had every young lady in London swooning at his feet. No doubt those in Bath would follow suit. His dazzling smile would guarantee that.

Her lips curled up into her own smile, one of cynical detachment. She had no time to indulge in daydreams about the handsome duke. But she would like to discover more about him, particularly his connection to Shipley Hall. Perhaps his cousin, who had an appointment in two days, might divulge more information about His Grace, the Duke of Lythmore.

As she stood to change for the concert and supper she was to attend that evening, she wondered what the duke's cousin looked like. She decided the woman was most likely beautiful. Not like her. She stopped before the small looking glass in the front room and nodded approval at what she saw. As a modiste, she wanted to be inconspicuous, for her goal was to make her customer the most attractive one in the room. Feeling more secure, she climbed the stairs to her rooms and called her lady's maid to attend her.

Two days later, Cameron handed Sally out of the carriage before the establishment of Madame de Vouvret. His decision to accompany her this morning had been an impulse of the moment. In truth, the idea of sitting with her while she chose her ensembles, while she considered this voile over that lawn, this color blue over that rose, bored him silly. The true reason he was walking beside her into the establishment of the modiste was because something about Madame de Vouvret fascinated him.

They entered the front room, decorated in pale green and ivory, with an Aubusson carpet spread across the floor and comfortable chairs scattered about. Gauzy curtains covered the bottom half of the windows, allowing in light but preventing the prying eyes of those passing on the street to see anything. He had seen the room before when he had come to arrange credit for Sally, but he had not really paid attention as he had been whisked through by the modiste. Surveying his surroundings, he was impressed with the quiet elegance of the decor, a reflection of the owner of the establishment. A young girl, obviously an apprentice, greeted them and informed them Madame de Vouvret would be with them shortly. After only a very short wait, the woman herself entered the room.

Cameron studied her as she greeted them and he introduced her to Sally. She was a very striking woman, lovely in fact, perhaps a year or two younger than himself, making her a score and four or five. Her hair, a rich coppery color, was pulled up into a topknot and only tiny love locks before her ears relieved the severity of the style. He wondered what that hair would look like if it were let loose from its confines and allowed to tumble in abandon about her shoulders. Her eyes, as changeable in different light as jewels, were sometimes blue, sometimes green, sometimes smoky gray, and were surrounded by a thick layer of dark lashes. Her nose was straight and sat well between her high cheekbones. He watched her lips, smiling now with professional courtesy at Sally, and saw beyond the practiced exterior to the woman beneath, for her mouth was full and rosy and promised passion to a man who could unlock its fire. He wondered what man, if any, had done that, for women who took up the trade of modiste were usually widows or spinsters. The title *Madame*, implying her wedded state, could be merely artifice to protect herself. He wondered if she had a man in her life. Settling himself in a chair, he sat back and contented himself with observing the intriguing Madame de Vouvret.

After an hour of remembering to nod and comment in all the correct places, Cameron found himself engaging in flights of fancy concerning Madame de Vouvret, of how she would look in a low-cut evening gown of filmy, flowing material the color of old gold instead of the prim, high-necked, long-sleeved charcoal-colored gown she wore at present, of how she would look in only her corset and petticoats with her hair disheveled, of how she would look in the moonlight, naked and passionate. Realizing he was being absurd, he attempted to pay more attention to Sally.

His relationship with Sally was a comfortable friendship. They had explored the avenues of passion when they had both been much younger and had developed a mutual trust. Having moved in separate directions in their amours, they had retained their friendship and established a fruitful working relationship. Sally wanted a husband and children when she tired of her career in the theater, and Cameron was perfectly content to remain single and work as a spy for His Majesty's government. Sally was presently looking about for a man who would offer her a more permanent position as his wife. Until she found that man, they would enjoy each other's company. And she would continue to gather secrets for Cameron.

"I believe I have just the gown for you," Madame de Vouvret said. She turned to the young apprentice who had first greeted them. "Marie, please fetch the portfolio on my desk." The young woman vanished and Madame de Vouvret turned back to Sally. "This is a new design of mine, and I have not yet made a sample." The girl returned and handed the portfolio to the modiste. She opened it and shuffled several papers. "*Voilà*," she said, handing the watercolor to Sally. As she pulled it out, another design fluttered to the floor at Sally's feet. Both women bent down to retrieve it, but Sally's fingers grasped it first.

"Oh, this is divine!" she exclaimed. "Look, Cameron, don't you think this will be perfect for my first ball of the season?"

He had a quick glance at a watercolor sketch of a fanciful gown of flowing lines decorated with flowers and lace. At the same time, he sensed Madame de Vouvret stiffen with some sort of emotion entirely out of place in the situation. He did not know why, but he thought it might be fear.

"I am sorry." She eased the piece of parchment out of Sally's fingers. "I designed that specifically for someone else."

"Someone else?" Sally echoed. "No, I must have it."

"That is quite impossible." Madame de Vouvret put the design back inside the portfolio and closed it decisively.

Sally turned beseeching eyes on Cameron. "Darling, I must have this gown. Please, convince Madame de Vouvret I must have it. It is perfect for me."

Cameron smiled indulgently at Sally. "If Madame de Vouvret says she has designed it for someone else, then it is not for you, dear cuz."

"Oh, Cameron, please?" she begged. "You can always change anyone's mind."

He knew he could offer the modiste a staggering sum for the gown, and she would more than likely capitulate, but for some reason he did not wish to force her to give the design to Sally. The odd emotion that had shown in the woman's eyes and her strange behavior hinted at something more than unease at giving a design to one customer that she had created for another. Perhaps he was being overly suspicious, perhaps his vendetta made him too cynical, perhaps his years as a spy had colored his perception. Yet, he wanted to discover more about this design, and the only way to do that was to allow the modiste to keep it.

"No, not this time," he said. "Perhaps Madame de Vouvret can design something else for your first ball here in Bath." He watched relief flicker across the face of the modiste. His suspicions might be correct.

"Of course," the modiste agreed. "I would be delighted to design something for this event." She tilted her head to one side as she studied Sally. "I have an idea. It will be perfect. This other... Bah." She waved her hand in dismissal at the design. "It is not for you. No, it is too young, too innocent, not at all right for you. You are a woman of refined taste and elegance, a woman who has seen a bit of the world and knows what she wants, *n'est-çe pas*?" The modiste slanted a teasing peek in Cameron's direction.

"Yes, madame." Sally nodded decisively, making her bright curls jump. "That is true."

"There, you see?" Madame de Vouvret smiled. "I will draw the design for this gown and show it to you when you come back for a fitting. Now, come, we must take your measurements."

She stood and led Sally toward the back of the establishment. Before she disappeared, the jingling of the bell over the door announced a new arrival. Glancing with impatience over her shoulder, she sent Sally off with one of her assistants and went to greet the customer.

"You are early," Cameron heard her accuse the man who had entered.

The man shrugged. "It couldn't be helped. I couldn't wait any longer."

The modiste sent a glance in Cameron's direction and covered her quick scrutiny with a smile. "Pardon, monsieur, my messenger," she murmured in explanation, then she led the man out of earshot.

Cameron was intrigued. The messenger was dressed according to his station, with clothes well-used and cut poorly. Yet, his attitude suggested something far different than that of a lowly servant. As Cameron wandered to the window to gaze out at the scene on the street beyond, he strained to listen to the conversation being conducted in hushed but urgent tones. Only a word now and then reached his ears, and those were in French. When he took a peek in their direction, he saw Madame de Vouvret pull the disputed dress design from the portfolio, the design Sally so much desired for her "first ball." He watched the modiste roll it up and give it to the messenger. The man left immediately.

Cameron very much wanted to follow him to discover where this man was delivering the dress design, but he could not leave without seeming to be a complete boor for abandoning Sally. In frustration, he watched the man hurry away down the street. Appearing to be indifferent, he absently strolled about the room to observe the paintings on the wall and hummed a tuneless melody. He heard the swish of skirts as Madame de Vouvret hurried to the fitting rooms where Sally was being measured.

As soon as he was alone, he strode back to the window and gazed out. The man had disappeared. Cameron allowed his thoughts and suspicions free rein as he contemplated the scene he had just witnessed. He had come to the city to discover the identity of the person responsible for his brother's death. Perhaps, he had inadvertently done just that. He turned over the possibility in his mind.

No, he decided, that would be too easy, too much of a coincidence. Madame de Vouvret was a well-respected citizen of the city. Sally had told him she served all the great ladies of Bath—the wives and mistresses of the members of Parliament, of all arms of government, of the nobility and gentry, even, she had heard, those connected with the Prince Regent. A woman with such a clientele would not be a favorite if she conducted scandalous affairs. Yet, a woman had been involved in the scandalous affair surrounding his brother. Could that woman have been the cool, aloof Madame de Vouvret?

Inwardly, he cringed at what he was thinking. The prospect of Madame de Vouvret being the Jezebel did not sit well on his conscience. She was too lovely to be involved in something so ugly. But if she were not involved in treachery, why had she acted so strangely about the dress design? Was it some sort of message to her accomplice about his arrival in Bath? Was the man merely a messenger, or something more sinister? And how could she have put information into the design? That seemed impossible.

With a frown of disgust at his wild imaginings, he turned back to his chair and sat down. The man was probably only a simple messenger, as Madame de Vouvret had stated, and she was more than likely only sending the design to someone for approval before she actually began to create the gown. Cameron's purpose in Bath was making him distrust even the most innocent situations.

Sally and Madame de Vouvret emerged from the fitting room at that moment and interrupted his brooding. "You must come to my salon, Mrs. Turner," Madame de Vouvret was saying. "It is every Tuesday afternoon, and it is for the women only." She winked at Sally and turned a mischievous smile on Cameron.

"Oh, yes, that would be delightful," Sally said, then turned to Cameron. "You don't mind, do you, cuz? You know how you enjoy your game of cards in the afternoon."

"Whatever you wish, sweetling," Cameron concurred lazily as he hid his excitement at the invitation to Sally, a perfect way for her to become better acquainted with the modiste.

They left after Madame de Vouvret made an appointment with Sally to return for her first fitting. As they rode in the carriage back to the Royal Crescent, Cameron gave Sally a pleased smile.

"Why are you smiling like the cat who just ate the sparrow?" she demanded.

"Because I am with one of the most beautiful women in England," he lied glibly. He was thinking instead about the invitation she had received.

Sally made a tiny moue with her perfect little mouth. "You are not thinking about me at all. You are thinking about the lovely Madame de Vouvret."

"Hmm," Cameron responded vaguely.

"She must have had a husband, you know."

"Who must have had a husband?" He was brought back from his musings.

"Madame de Vouvret, silly." Sally slapped him playfully on the arm. "She is addressed as *Madame*. She is probably a widow who dearly loved her husband and will never love again." She sighed dramatically.

Cameron smiled at Sally's romantic imagination. "I'm sure you'll discover the truth for me, won't you?" His gaze turned stern. "I want to know everything. After all, I am giving you a new wardrobe."

Sally grumbled something but agreed to discover all she could about the woman. Cameron only half-listened as he thanked whatever impulse had made him bring Sally to Bath. With her attending Madame de Vouvret's salon, he would be able to find out more about the mysterious woman, who might very well be hiding a dark, dangerous secret.

CHAPTER 2

Arianne, flushed with excitement, drove the pony cart along the narrow lane. *Just a little farther.* The day had begun sunny and sultry. Now, dark clouds threatened on the horizon. She would reach the cottage long before the rain began, but her return trip to the city would be wet and uncomfortable. It did not matter. She would spend a wonderful afternoon with him.

The end of the hedgerow came into sight and with it the entrance to the short drive to the cottage. With gentle pressure on the reins, she slowed the pony and guided it into the drive. At the end stood the cottage, flower-decked and inviting, Even before she reached it, the door flew open, and a little boy came barreling down the drive.

"Mama!" he called. "Mama! Mama!"

Arianne drew on the reins and scrambled down from the cart. Opening her arms, she caught him up and hugged him to her. His sweet scent that was only his filled her nostrils as she buried her face in his dark curls. She wanted so much to have him live with her. Instead, to keep him safe, she was forced to hide him here in the country and could see him only once or twice a week.

"Oh, Luc," she laughed. "Did you miss your mama? I missed you."

Luc wriggled to be put on his own two feet. "I am sorry you missed me, mama," he said solemnly. "I missed you very much."

"How much did you miss me, *mon petit*?" she teased.

Luc spread his arms as wide as he could. "This much." He dissolved into giggles as their customary greeting went exactly as it always did. Taking Arianne's hand, he dragged her down the walk between an herb and vegetable garden toward the cottage where a middle-aged woman stood smiling in the doorway. "Come, Mama,

I must show you what Mr. Inglis has taught me. And Mrs. Inglis made sugar biscuits for our tea." He stopped short, clapped his hand over his mouth, and became wide-eyed at his error. "I was not supposed to tell you that," he whispered dramatically. "It was to be a surprise."

Arianne laughed and whispered back, "I won't let on that you told."

With a conspiratorial grin, Luc turned and pulled her the rest of the way to the front door of the cottage, where Mrs. Inglis was waiting. The plump, older woman in her white mobcap and crisp apron exuded an air of comfort and competence that reassured Arianne at leaving her son here. She always felt a sense of peace whenever she visited. Bess Inglis had been a housekeeper in a large, nearby estate for many years, and George, her husband, had tutored the sons who lived there.

"Welcome, Madame de Vouvret," Mrs. Inglis said with a warm smile. "Little Luc has been a joy all week. Bright as a new penny he is, too, but Mr. Inglis can tell you that." She waved them into the cottage that smelled of freshly baked cookies.

In the parlor just to the right of the front door, George Inglis placed a book on the table beside him and unfolded himself from a padded chair by the window. A tall, broad-chested gentleman, he looked more like he should have been a groundskeeper instead of Luc's tutor. His hair, pulled back into an old-fashioned queue, had turned completely gray in the time Arianne had known him.

He welcomed her with a gentle smile. "Madame de Vouvret, you have a bright young man. Soon he will be doing sums faster than his tutor and reading Latin and French."

"I can count all the way to one hundred!" Luc announced.

Arianne ruffled her son's hair. "That's wonderful, *mon petit*."

"And see what the Countess sent Mr. Inglis!" Luc pointed to a small pile of books on a table by the window. "He can use them to teach me my letters."

Arianne's hand stilled on her son's head. "The Countess?"

In surprise, she looked at Mr. and Mrs. Inglis. The woman her son had named had helped her find George and Bess Inglis four years ago. A French emigrée, the Countess had been the person Pinard had told her to contact once she arrived in England. As soon as the Countess had met her, she guessed Arianne's condition. With cold proficiency, she had whisked Arianne to her estate, sent Pinard a message that Arianne was suffering from a severe illness, and secreted her in her house until Arianne had given birth to Luc. The woman had found a wet nurse for Luc, contacted the Inglises, who were her tenants, and requested that they care for the child. Yet, as soon as Luc had been placed with the couple, the strange woman had severed all ties with them. Hearing that she had sent George Inglis a gift to help educate her son was a shock.

"We were just as surprised as you." George nodded. "We haven't heard from her since she first brought you and Luc to us."

"It's very odd that she should suddenly send you books," Arianne observed.

Luc tugged at her hand. "Mama, come see what the Countess sent to me."

Intrigued, Arianne followed her son to a corner of the parlor. There, propped up on a stand, was a beautifully carved model of a sailing ship. "It's the *Victory*," he told her. "The ship Lord Nelson commanded in the battle of Tra… Tra…"

"Trafalgar, young man." George Inglis helped him out.

"Tra-flay-ger," Luc mispronounced with a decisive nod.

Arianne was bewildered by the sudden generosity of the woman who had announced four years ago that she never wanted to hear from her again. "These are wonderful gifts, but I cannot allow Luc to keep the ship. It is far too precious for a four-year-old boy to play with." She turned to her son. "Luc, we must return this to the lady who sent it to you. This is not a proper gift for us to accept."

As disappointment made the little boy's lower lip start to tremble, George Inglis cleared his throat. "Excuse me for interfering, madame, but the Countess made it clear that she would not take back the items, and, in fact, would be very insulted if they were returned." He lowered his voice. "She even hinted at terminating our lease and doing something worse."

"Terminating your lease! What could be worse than that?" Arianne was shocked and angry that the woman would go to such lengths just to have her gifts accepted.

George Inglis moved away a few steps and beckoned Arianne to follow. His voice dropped to a whisper. "She hinted she might let Luc's existence become known in the city."

"*Sacré bleu!*" Arianne grabbed at the back of a chair to keep herself steady. She could not allow anyone else to know of Luc's existence. Pinard might discover her secret. What would that monster do if he learned she had a son?

"Forgive me for saying so, madame," George told her gently, "but you must accept the gifts. You can do nothing else. The Countess is a strange woman, and I feel she would not hesitate to carry out her threats."

Reluctantly, Arianne agreed, but frustration at the woman's arrogant, highhanded behavior made her angry at the situation. She would like to be able to take Luc into the city and show him off to everyone she met. Instead, she was forced to keep his existence a secret and accept gifts from an odd, haughty, old woman.

Luc tugged on her hand. "Mama, may I keep the ship, then?"

Arianne looked down at her son and saw the hope lurking in his eyes. She had been able to give him so little, and the knowledge hurt. Reluctantly, she gave in. With a smile, she nodded. "*Oui, mon petit.* You may keep the ship."

Luc let out an enthusiastic cry of joy. "Come, Mama, we must take her sailing!"

Arianne reminded him of his manners, but George Inglis told them, "Go on. Go launch your ship, boy."

Arianne scooped up her hat as Luc scampered out the door with the ship model. Despite Arianne's nagging feeling of dismay at the gifts, his enthusiasm was infectious. "We'll be back in time for tea," she called, trailing her son as he skipped toward the tiny pond at the bottom of the meadow.

Back in the city, Arianne steered the pony cart through the alley to the entrance of the mews where a lamp burned brightly. The light was welcome in the decreasing twilight. The storm that had threatened in the afternoon had come and gone, but a fine mist remained after the storm blew itself out. Both Bess and George Inglis had urged her to stay the night, but she had turned down their invitation. She had a great deal of work to do in the morning. Besides, she could not be missed from her usual schedule. That would cause questions, and she could not afford to have anyone curious about her.

Despite the damp weather and the twilight, which was turning to darkness, a smile curved her lips as she thought back over her afternoon. The time spent with Luc had been wonderful, as always. George and Bess Inglis were very special people. She was grateful to the Countess for helping her find them four years ago. Yet, the arrival of the woman's gifts and the conditions she put upon accepting them made Arianne uneasy. Something was not right. Why had the Countess suddenly reached out after so many years of silence? If Pinard ever discovered her son's existence… She did not wish to think about that.

With her thoughts elsewhere, she climbed down from the pony cart and handed the reins to the stable boy. Smiling at him, she hurried back out into the night toward the rear door of her shop. She lived in the rooms above, a comfortable suite but not extravagant. Anticipating the hot cup of tea she would make for herself, she slipped the key into the lock of her door.

"It's about time you returned," a man's voice said from the shadows.

With a gasp, she spun around. A dark figure stepped into the pale light of the alley.

"Courcy," she croaked when she found her voice.

"Where have you been?" Edouard Courcy, Pinard's messenger, took a menacing step forward.

She came up with an answer. "For a ride in the country."

"Alone? And in a storm?" His lips twisted in a sneer. "Not very likely."

"I did not expect it to rain," she said, allowing her irritation to show. "What I do in my free time is none of your concern."

"Oh, it's very much my concern, dear Arianne." His smooth response threatened.

Arianne tried to distract him from his curiosity about her afternoon ride. "What are you doing here?"

"I think we should discuss that inside. I have news that could not wait." He motioned impatiently at the door.

Arianne tried to think of an excuse to make him leave as she turned the key in the lock, but nothing came to mind. His presence was like a shadow that made the twilight darker. He followed her across the threshold and up the stairs to her suite of rooms. Flinging off his wet cloak and hat, he made himself comfortable in a chair near the hearth. He was an attractive man, tall, slim, with brown hair and brown eyes. If those eyes had been kind with a kind disposition to match, she might have been drawn to him. But his eyes were hard, and he was Pinard's watchdog as well as his messenger. His manner always threatened, even when he merely came to collect the dress designs with the encrypted code hidden within them.

She lit the lamps and carefully closed the drapes. She was cold and damp and tired, and she did not relish entertaining this man, but neither could she send him away. At least not yet, not until she discovered what had brought him to her back door at this hour.

As she removed her hat, she asked, "What is this news you have to tell me?"

His dark eyes glittered as he glanced up at her. "Don't you like my visits, Arianne? I thought you could not wait for me to come."

Ignoring his innuendo, she turned away to hang her hat on a hook so he would not see the hatred in her eyes. "You know our arrangement. You must not be seen here other than during the hours when my shop is open. You are supposed to be my messenger. I can't afford any gossip."

He stretched out his legs before the dark fireplace and spoke as if he had not heard her. "It's cold in here. I think we should have a fire."

"Light it yourself," Arianne snapped, her temper overcoming her good sense.

"Tsk. There is no cause to be nasty, madame."

Sighing with impatience, she repeated, "Why are you here, Edouard? What do you have to tell me?"

He cocked his head as if he were listening for something. "Are we alone in the flat, Arianne? Did you give your maid the night off?" His innocent questions became suggestive insinuations in the hushed tone he used.

She had, indeed, given her maid the night off, but she was not about to reveal that to the man seated before her hearth. "I do not think that should concern you."

"Quite the contrary. How do I know whether she might be listening to our conversation?"

Arianne placed her reticule in the drawer of a small table beside the door. Nestled in a corner of the drawer was a sharp little dagger that she had purchased some time ago. She had never used the weapon, had never even shown it to anyone, but something made her wrap her fingers about its handle and hide it in the folds of her skirt. Stepping to put a chair between herself and Edouard, she said, "We are quite alone. Now say what you must and leave. I am tired and wish to retire."

"Ah, Arianne, what a delightful idea!" His eyes lit suggestively.

"Do not be insulting," she snapped. "Besides, Pinard would not be pleased if you disobeyed him. You are his courier, nothing more."

His eyes narrowed. "I am more than that, my little caged bird, much more, and you know that very well."

Arianne gritted her teeth to hold back her invective. What he said was true. He made sure she played the part that Pinard dictated. She wanted to scream her rebellion at him, but more than that, she wanted to stab this man through the heart. She could not do that. Not yet. Not while she had others to protect.

"Pinard holds you responsible for my safety, Edouard." She tried to reason with him. "Would you bring his anger down on your head because of your weakness?"

Edouard's teeth showed in a greedy grin. "Monsieur Pinard would not have to know. He is in France…and we are here." He stood and leaned across the chair separating them. "We would not have to tell him. Besides, he has promised you to me when this is finished."

"I think I might have something to say about who I am promised to. Pinard is no longer an agent for France. He has lost his influence now that Napoleon is in exile. He cannot *give* me to anyone."

Edouard smiled with superiority. "Sometimes, you are so naïve, Arianne. Monsieur Pinard may no longer work for Napoleon, but he still has a great deal of power. You know he has ways of persuading people to do as he wants. It will be much easier for you — and your dear papa — if you agree to Pinard's plans." He reached out to touch her.

Arianne pointed the dagger at him. "Keep your hands to yourself. Now say why you have come and then leave."

Edouard turned back to his chair and shook his head. "You know I am only trying to be friendly, Arianne. A pity you will not allow me that kindness." He sat and waited for her to speak. When she said nothing, he sighed. "Very well. I came to tell you that Cocteau, the fisherman, was stopped and his boat boarded by the English."

Arianne felt the blood drain from her face. Cocteau was the man who sailed between England and France to deliver her messages, secreted in her dress designs, to Pinard. Edouard's gaze was like a weight on her chest.

"The English do not take kindly to spies," he said as if she did not know that spies were executed. "If Cocteau decides to talk to save his own skin…." His words trailed off into a shrug.

Arianne gripped the back of the chair as fear slithered through her. While her past sins could cause her arrest, conviction, and either imprisonment or transportation, spying would mean the end of her life. What would happen to Luc?

When she was finally able to speak, she asked, "What happened?"

"It seems he was sighted by one of the English corvettes that patrol the coast. He was questioned and released," he said. "Evidently, his story about being blown off course was believed."

"The information he had, did they find it?" She had trouble breathing.

"Only a scrap. Not enough to give them a clue as to what they had or where it came from." Edouard scowled. "If anyone becomes suspicious about a fisherman carrying a dress design and the English are able to figure out your code, you could be in danger. Be prepared to leave at a moment's notice."

"But —" She started to protest at the thought of having to collect Luc before she could flee anywhere. Then she realized she could say nothing. Luc was her secret. Edouard knew nothing about him. When the time came to run, she would figure out something, a way to take Luc with her and keep him from Edouard's — and Pinard's — eyes.

"You knew this might happen, Arianne," Edouard admonished. "There is no point in arguing. You could not remain and put the rest of us in danger. Pinard would not be pleased, to say the least."

Damn Pinard! She wanted to scream. Damn Courcy! Damn them all to hell! But she remained mute, meekly bowing her head in agreement.

"Good." Courcy nodded his satisfaction at her acquiescence. "I knew you would understand." He stood and collected his cloak and hat. "You are a clever woman, Arianne. Don't make any stupid mistakes now. I would not like to report to Pinard that the English have arrested you. You know that he would give the order to silence you."

Arianne's chin rose in indignation to hide the terror that clutched at her. "I will not make any mistakes, Edouard. I did not risk anything with this meeting. It is you who should be careful. Don't come here anymore except when I summon you."

Courcy flung his cloak about his shoulders and swept her a bow. His insolent grin mocked the courtesy of his gesture. "As you wish, madame. Until we meet again." He opened the door but stopped and turned back to her. "By the way, I will be returning to France for a while. Pinard needs me there, so I will be unable to act as your messenger. Other arrangements will be made while I am gone to get your dress designs to Cocteau."

"Who will act as my messenger?" Apprehension gripped her, for her new contact could be worse than Courcy.

"You will be contacted." His smile was suggestive. "Will you miss me, Arianne?"

"Get out, Edouard," she said flatly.

He gave her a mocking bow. His menacing chuckle floated back to her as he left and closed the door behind him.

She listened to his footsteps going down the stairs, heard the outside door open and close. Not until she was sure he was gone did she allow herself to relax. Grabbing the chair before her, she leaned against it and let out her breath. Her hand holding the dagger shook, and she quickly put it down. She felt trapped, cornered, nowhere to turn, nowhere to run.

She could not leave England because of Luc, but neither could she stay if she were ordered to go. Papa was in France. With Pinard. Under guard. Papa deciphered her shadings and curlicues, the materials and colors from her dress designs into meaningful information, information that Pinard tucked carefully away and brought out only when he could use it to further his own ends, to destroy those whom he hated. If she refused to leave England when she was ordered, then Papa's life would be forfeit. If she left, then she might never see Luc again.

A trick of fate had placed Papa in Pinard's path. Having been a code-breaker for His Majesty, King Louis XVI, Papa had been coerced by Pinard after the King's beheading to work in the same capacity for the Committee of Public Safety and later the Directory. Then Napoleon established himself as Emperor, and Pinard, under Joseph Fouché, Napoleon's Minister of Police, kept Papa working. No one could make up codes or break them like Papa. That was why Pinard, even now when he was out of favor, kept Papa with him in France, why she was in England to send information to him across the Channel. Pinard had a list of people whom he hated, among them the man who had taken his eye. She was an instrument of Pinard's revenge. But there was nothing she could do to free herself. Nothing.

She sank into the chair before her. What should she do?

I must go on was the only answer that came to her. Go on as if nothing had happened. She must not act foolishly now, not when so much was at stake. Two people who were very dear to her depended on her cool head, her steadiness.

In a fit of weakness, she covered her face with her hands. If only Jean-Paul were alive, he would know what to do. If only there were someone she could trust, someone to whom she could turn for help. But there was no one.

Incongruously, the thought of the Duke of Lythmore entered her head. *Fool!* She berated herself. She could not indulge in such silly daydreams when there was so much at stake. She tried to concentrate on a way out of this mess, but the duke's image seemed to float before her like a persistent and unnerving ghost. Too tired to think, she wearily stood, headed for her bedchamber, and hoped that the Duke of Lythmore would not invade her dreams.

One-Armed Lewis crouched amid the piles of refuse that littered the alley behind the fancy dressmaker's shop. He had been scavenging for bits and pieces of discarded material when the dressmaker arrived at her back door. He kept one eye on the lady and the other on a bit of pink satin that peeked from beneath a pile of refuse in the corner. Mrs. Wiggit's girls would pay a pretty penny for it. Those girls were always looking for ways to fancy up their gowns to impress the gents who paid for their services.

He did not want to be chased off, so he stayed quiet and waited. That was when he saw the cloaked man approach her. He watched as they went inside together, and saw the drapes drawn shut across the windows and the sliver of light that escaped when lamps within were lit. But no fire had been started because no sparks escaped up the cold, dark chimney.

Something, he knew, was queer. Something was happening that he should watch. He waited, and while he waited, he found a good length of linen, one large enough to make several handkerchiefs, and a bit of yellow silk and pale velvet. Soon, the cloaked man came out, and Lewis watched him walk down the darkened street. The man's steps were long and fast. The bloke was angry about something.

One-Armed Lewis watched a little while longer, but nothing else happened. Grabbing the pink satin, he stuffed the bits of cloth inside his shirt to keep them dry and gave one last look at the dark windows above him. Nothing interesting. Time to move on. But what he had seen tonight might earn him a few extra shillings. Information could be sold like cloth. A body only had to know who wanted to buy it.

The night blanketed Cameron as he made his way through the deserted streets of Bath. Sally was sleeping peacefully, blissfully unaware that he'd left the townhouse. If she discovered his absence, he could use the excuse of restlessness and needing some air.

He came to a corner, stood back against the building beside him, and faded into its shadows. Checking in all directions to make sure he was not followed, he waited a moment before he turned left. Another left, a right, a third left, a second right. He was almost back where he had begun, but he had been told the roundabout route was necessary. If he was being followed, he would have lost the person in his meanderings.

He had done this before, many times, in Paris, in Madrid, in Rome and Venice, but never in his own country. Those were times when he had gathered and passed information for his King. But not this time. Tonight, he skulked through the dark for himself—and his brother.

Certain now that no one dogged his steps, he slipped into the shadowed doorway of a rooming house. Noiselessly, he closed the door behind him. A stairway rose to his left, and a dim hallway, barren of decoration, stretched to the back of the building. He picked up the single lit lamp that had been left on the floor and traversed the hallway to a door at the other end. Turning down the lamp, he left it and silently exited the building.

A small, enclosed garden spread out before him. He knew from the directions he had received that there would be a gate in the back wall. The half-moon hung low in the sky, and it threw the flowers and shrubs into ghostly relief. He glanced back up at the building he'd just left, at the dark windows with their drapes drawn like closed eyelids in slumber. What if one or two were not closed? What if someone watched from a slit in a curtain, as though peeking from lowered lashes? He had been assured he would be safe from prying eyes as he crossed the garden. Not trusting anything to chance, he circled the garden stealthily and kept to the shadowy wall.

Upon reaching the gate, he looked back once more at the building. No sign of movement in any of the windows. They were all dark, all shuttered, and those within were all asleep. It did not hurt to be wary. More than once, his caution had kept him alive.

The gate creaked with complaint when he pushed it open. In the stillness of the night, the noise sounded like an alarm bell, but in truth was only a tiny noise. A small dog yapped from the house next door. A window flew up and a man yelled, "Who's there?"

Cameron ducked into a crevice in the wall and froze. Finally, he heard the man silence the dog and the sound of the window being lowered. He waited, counting slowly to fifty to be sure no one else was inclined to investigate. Releasing a quiet breath, he slipped through the gate and found himself in a service alley. Across from him stood a long wall that mirrored the one he had just come through. Gates punctuated it at intervals and marked the back entrances to gardens like the one behind him.

He turned to his right and counted off three gates. One stood slightly ajar. He had almost reached his destination. Pushing the gate open, he was relieved when it moved on well-oiled hinges. He carefully latched it closed behind him. The garden showed signs of neglect, but a row of small fruit trees shaded the path to the back door of the building before him. Windfall fruit in varying degrees of decay littered the ground. Stepping carefully to avoid the mess, he kept to the shadows of the trees, crossed the garden, and entered the building.

The door to the first-floor apartment opened immediately at his knock. No words were uttered until he was safely across the threshold, and the door closed behind him.

"You were not followed?" Adrian Bennett, Duke of Dunbary, queried.

Hiding his surprise at who stood before him, Cameron blinked in the sudden light of many candles and lamps. "No, I was not," he answered stiffly. "And if I had been, don't you think I would have been able to lose my pursuer?"

"You always were an impertinent brat, Lythmore." Adrian grinned.

Cameron returned the smile. "Isn't that why you took up with me at Cambridge?"

"What else could I do?" Adrian shrugged. "Someone had to keep you out of trouble."

"I always thought you took up with him because of the sweets his mother sent along every fortnight," a voice drawled from a corner.

Cameron spun to the voice behind him. Once again, he hid his surprise as he retorted, "I seem to recall that you never passed up those sweets."

Sprawled in a chair, Damien Trevor, Duke of Wyndham, barked a laugh. "They were damned good sweets, too, if I recall." He unfolded his frame from the chair and stood.

Cameron glanced from one man to the other. He was astonished to see both of them here, for the message he'd received had only said that someone would give him information. Both men gave the outward appearance of being settled members of society, happily wed and now raising families. Wyndham, who had once been the notorious spy, Le Chat, had retired, although Cameron suspected he still kept his finger in the pie of foreign service. Dunbary had also officially retired as a master spy who ran a ring of agents, but he secretly advised Lord Castlereagh, Secretary of the Foreign Office. When Cameron had sent a request to them for information, he never expected them to appear in person.

Dunbary waved Cameron to a group of shabby wooden chairs and a rickety table where a beautifully etched crystal decanter and glasses glimmered, incongruous in the seedy surroundings. "Come, have a brandy while we show you what we've discovered."

"I'm very grateful for what you're doing," Cameron said as he took a seat.

"It was the least we could do for a school chum." Wyndham shrugged.

Cameron glanced about at the shabby surroundings while Dunbary poured two fingers of brandy into three glasses. As Cameron accepted one, he indicated the second-rate room. "Your fortunes seem to have taken a turn for the worse."

Wyndham chuckled. "I know this place isn't up to our usual standards, but it does have its advantages in keeping with our need for anonymity. We would prefer no one knew we are in residence here. I'm supposed to be at Wyndham."

"And I'm supposed to be in Cornwall," Dunbary added.

"How long do you plan to stay?" Cameron asked.

Wry humor twisted Wyndham's lips. "Only as long as we must. The beds are lumpy."

"Not to mention cold and lonely, I'd wager," Cameron said wickedly as he took a sip of brandy. "How are your lovely wives?"

"Jillian is a treasure." Adrian sighed. "I can't imagine why I ever avoided marriage. It's the best institution ever invented."

"I'll second that," Damien said. "My wife, Jessica, makes every day an adventure. You should try it."

"Not me, old man." Cameron shook his head. "I'll leave marriage to lucky bounders like you. Besides, I have other matters needing my attention."

Adrian gave his friend a sharp look as he spread a few papers out on the table before him. "Finding and catching the person responsible for your brother's death is not going to bring him back from the grave, Cam."

"No, but it will make me feel a hell of a lot better." Cameron smacked his glass down on the table. Anger shot through him as he thought about the sly betrayer who had destroyed his brother and ultimately caused his death. "What have you got?" he growled.

Damien passed a scrap of torn parchment across to him. "We took this from a fellow who claimed he was merely a fisherman blown off course. Said he was from Querqueville, a village on the coast of France, near Cherbourg. We picked him up off our coast just west of here."

"A bit far from home for him," Cameron murmured. The fisherman would have had to travel around the peninsula of Cornwall and along the coast into the Bristol Channel, very far to be blown off course from where he claimed his home was.

Cameron studied the scrap of parchment. A wash of pale colors—white, yellow, and green—covered one end, and letters trailing off into a tattered edge were written across the other. He could make out *wn*, *u*, and *br*. Water had smeared everything else into a blur.

"What is it?" he asked.

Adrian shrugged. "That's the puzzle. We don't know. We thought you might have an idea. We've heard you're rather good at deciphering codes."

Bewildered, Cameron just shook his head. Yet, something about it niggled at him. It seemed familiar somehow, as if he had seen it, or something very much like it.

Adrian handed Cameron another sheet, this time full-sized and covered with legible writing. "This is a report from the local constabulary." He offered a third sheet. "And this is a report by Castlereagh's aide. We requested he do a bit of digging after you asked us for help. Did you know that your brother had dealings with a Marquis de Pagière and a Mr. Clifford Rathbone?"

Cameron glanced at the two parchments. "I heard him speak of de Pagière. An ex-patriot who has been in this country for some time, I believe."

Adrian nodded.

"But this Rathbone fellow," Cameron went on. "Who is he?"

"The third son of an earl," Damien said. He gestured at the dossier in Cameron's hands. "It's all there, whatever information we could find. Evidently, Rathbone and your brother invested in a small trading company that lost everything just before your brother...just before he died."

"But why weren't any of the investment documents with my brother's papers?" Cameron wondered aloud. His mind raced. Then the answer came in a rush. "It's the woman. She took the documents."

"What woman?" Damien and Adrian asked in unison.

Cameron frowned. "I'm not sure. Someone French, or at least with a French accent. Someone my brother called Marguerite."

"Have you found anyone by that name who might have been connected to your brother in any way?" Damien asked. "Someone of the *ton*? A daughter or sister of an acquaintance? A serving girl? Shopkeeper?"

Slumping back in his chair, Cameron shook his head. "No. I've found several Margarets and a few Maggies and a Meg or two, but they are all either too young or too old or happily wed or just had no occasion to meet my brother." He tossed the papers onto the table. "Did you arrest this fisherman who was so far from home?"

"We let him go," Adrian said.

"Let him go?" Cameron nearly jumped from his chair. "Why? You could have questioned him. He might have revealed some scrap of information."

His two friends exchanged a glance.

Cameron's eyes narrowed in suspicion. "What aren't you telling me?"

"The Foreign Office is interested in your brother's death," Adrian said. "There are too many connections to France for us to be comfortable. It has the feel of espionage."

Insulted, Cameron straightened. "My brother was not involved in any sort of treason."

"Calm down, Cam." Damien poured more brandy into all three glasses. "We didn't mean to imply that he was. If anything, we believe he was an unwitting pawn."

"That makes me feel so much better." Cameron's tone was as dry as stone dust.

"Or perhaps he bragged that his brother had access to secrets," Damien added.

"He would never—" Then he halted as he realized his younger brother might very well have done such a thing. "God's teeth," he muttered.

"Cheer up, Cam," Adrian said as he picked up his glass. "At least you have another two names to investigate. If we come across anything more, we'll pass it along."

Cameron picked up his own glass and held it up to the candle beside him. The brandy sloshed perilously close to the rim. "I have been searching for whoever destroyed my brother for two years, and I'm not any closer now than when I began. I feel as explosive as the brandy in this glass."

"Please don't do anything rash," Adrian warned mildly as Cameron's brandy tipped closer to the flame. "And—uh—we'd prefer you didn't start a fire. We're trying not to be noticed while we're here."

"Ah, bloody hell," Cameron muttered. "Bloody, bloody hell." Then he tossed the expensive brandy down his throat.

Henri Pinard stood on his veranda and looked across his formal gardens, his manicured lawns, his wooded acres, to the sea beyond, shimmering in the moonlight. He enjoyed this view, particularly at this time of night when the moon was high in the sky and the night birds called to each other from the trees. This view had prompted his craving for this estate. When he had seen it nearly thirty years ago, he had determined he would have it, and he had done everything to make his desire become reality.

The people who had once lived in this chateau were descendants of an ancient French family that had been aristocratic before the time of the Crusades. Yet, during the Terror, a few well-placed words in the ears of the right people had been enough to have such an ancient and noble family accused of treason against the Directorate of France.

He had regretted having to resort to such measures. After all, if the daughter of the family had agreed to marry him, they could have fled to England instead of meeting Madame Guillotine and losing their heads. They had all been executed, all except the daughter, the haughty bitch. She had escaped to England with her lover—that English cur of a spy—and married him. Married him! Rage surged through him like a fire out of control, even after all the years that had passed since then.

That did not matter any longer. Calming himself, he breathed deeply of the night air. The English spy and his bitch were both dead now, while he was still very much alive and living in their chateau. After being confiscated, the estate had become his, a gift from Joseph Fouché, his former superior and former head of the secret police. He had heard that Fouché was in Italy now and trying to regain some of his power and influence in the government. Fouché was foolish to try, but then the man had nothing else to occupy himself.

For Pinard's part, he would use the wealth he had acquired while working in Napoleon's secret police to settle some scores. He had already won a victory with the death of Ian West. His next victim was slowly being enticed into his web. Tantalizing bits of information had been laid like a trail of bread crumbs to draw his quarry to the city of Bath. Even now, the news of the man's arrival in the city could be in the recent message that had arrived from dear Arianne.

He heard a step behind him. "Ah, Chevalier Chiasson, come, look at this view. Magnificent, is it not?"

François Chiasson stepped across the flagstones of the veranda to stand at the balustrade. "Beautiful." His one word was a mechanical response.

Pinard ignored his lack of enthusiasm. "Across that water lies England, my friend, and your lovely daughter." He swept his arm wide. "She is not so very far away, eh?"

"Too far away for me to see her," François said flatly.

"Now, now, François, you must not grumble." Pinard was in a mellow mood and so chastised mildly.

"It has been five years, Pinard, five years since I have seen my daughter," François said, his voice pitched low. "I am an old man. How do I know how much longer I have to live? I would like very much to see her again before I die." His hand tightened on the stone of the balustrade.

"*Mon Dieu*, François, I hate when you whine," Pinard snapped. "You know I need you here, and I need Arianne in England in order to accomplish my goal. When that is done, then you may see her."

"When will that be?" Chiasson demanded. "When someone else dies? You have no conscience, Pinard, no conscience at all."

Pinard's patience broke. "This is my conscience, old man! This!" He spun toward Chiasson and pointed to the patch that covered his empty eye socket and the scar running down his cheek. "Until I have wiped out the spawn of the man who did this to me, I will not rest! And until I have done that, you and your daughter will do as I say! Do you understand?" His voice rose with each statement.

Chiasson turned to stare out at the sea. "I understand."

Drawing a breath, Pinard turned to the scene before him as well. He hated losing his temper, but the old man knew just the right words to set him off. He had explained what he wanted to accomplish. Why did Chiasson always question and demand to see his daughter? He breathed deeply once more. Soon enough, his task would be finished, and he would not need the whining old fool. He would let the man set eyes on his lovely daughter once more and then… Well, he would decide what to do when the time came.

Calm again, Pinard said, "I have just this evening received the latest message from Arianne." He picked up a damp, folded piece of parchment from the balustrade with two fingers and held it out. "It seems the fisherman who travels back and forth across La Manche ran into a bit of difficulty. A piece is missing, and the rest is a mite smudged." As he handed it across to François, he wrinkled his nose in distaste. A strong, fishy smell wafted from the parchment.

The chevalier took the message carefully. "Why does it smell so?"

"I believe Cocteau was forced to hide it inside a fish." Pinard pulled a handkerchief from his pocket and carefully wiped his fingers.

Chiasson frowned. "If it is smudged, I may not be able to decode it properly."

"I'm sure you will do your best." Pinard waved away Chiasson's grumble. "After all, you will want to read that your daughter sends you her love." At the man's surprised, wary glance, Pinard raised a brow. "Do you think I am a complete fool, François? I know that the messages we receive contain more than the information Arianne collects." He waved his hand in dismissal. "Be quick, François. I am anxious to hear what our dear Arianne has to report."

Turning back to his view, he heard the man's footsteps retreat to his attic niche where he decoded the squiggles and curlicues in the dress designs. Excitement surged through Pinard while he contemplated the news the message held. Perhaps this one reported that his victim had arrived in Bath. If not this message, then surely the next. And when he learned that his victim was in place, then he would begin the next phase of his plan.

Smiling, he contemplated the satisfying end to this game of wits.

CHAPTER 3

Arianne strolled through Sydney Gardens with her acquaintances, Mrs. Charles Weathersby and her daughter, Miss Barbara, Sir Roderick and Lady Cecilia Crump, and the young widow Baroness Souffant with her little daughters, Laudine and Sandrine. Despite Arianne's being a mere modiste, a few of the society ladies included her in their outings, perhaps because of her salon, or perhaps they did not want to lose their dressmaker. Whatever the case, she was grateful for their generosity.

Since it was Sunday and her shop was closed, she had allowed Miss Barbara to cajole her into the outing. But she wished she had found some excuse to decline the invitation, for she was exhausted. Courcy's visit two nights ago with his threat of flight had unnerved her, and she had slept little since. She could not reveal Luc's existence, but how could she flee without him? And the Duke of Lythmore invaded her dreams, not because he was charming and handsome, she told herself, but because of his connection to Shipley Hall. Her part in the tragedy that had occurred there would haunt her forever.

She tried to concentrate on the chatter going on around her. Did she hear that the gown she had designed for the Countess of Fulcher had been the talk of the Upper Assembly Rooms last week? Did she happen to see the walking dress of Miss Streator? A disaster, and obviously not created by the fabulous de Vouvret. Did she know that the reclusive Duke of Lythmore had arrived in Bath with his widowed cousin?

At his name, Arianne stumbled. Sir Roderick jumped forward to steady her.

"Careful there, madame," he cautioned. "Lady Cecilia would be very upset if her favorite modiste were injured."

As Arianne smiled her thanks, she caught sight of a curricle flash by just beyond the entrance to the park. The conveyance held two passengers, and one of them was Lythmore. Across the distance, their eyes met. She caught her breath. No! That was too much of a coincidence. She must have imposed his face onto the driver because of the ladies' gossip.

"Are you sure you are well enough to continue?" Mrs. Weathersby asked. "Why, my sister suffered the vapors just yesterday. This heat is enough to wear down the strongest soul."

Baroness Souffant sniffed. "You have not felt heat until you have been in Paris in the middle of summer."

"I adore the heat," Miss Barbara gushed.

As Barbara's mother sent her daughter a warning glance for being so outspoken, Arianne said, "I am quite well, thank you." Or she would be if the Duke of Lythmore didn't consume her thoughts.

Satisfied, they continued their stroll. Laudine and Sandrine skipped ahead. Their mother reproached them for unladylike behavior, then sighed.

"I do miss their governess, but I had to leave her behind in France." She turned to Arianne. "Perhaps you know of someone? After all, you work with —" She made a dismissive gesture. " — those people."

Arianne bit back the sharp retort that *those people* had worked long hours constructing the elaborate walking dress the baroness wore. Just as she murmured she knew of no one, the Duke of Lythmore in his vehicle — the very same curricle she had seen flying past — entered the gardens and pulled up beside them.

"Good afternoon, ladies, sir," Lythmore greeted them with a doff of his hat. "I could not help but notice as we drove past that Madame de Vouvret seemed unwell. May I offer my assistance?"

Arianne's companions stared, speechless, for they had just been discussing the duke, and here he was! As if they had conjured him! Arianne's heart fluttered in her chest. Lythmore's gaze settled on her as he waited for an answer. Words would not form on her lips. All she could do was shake her head in the negative. Fortunately, the others did not notice she was speechless.

Arianne found her voice long enough to introduce her acquaintances. Lythmore bowed his greeting, tossed a cocky little smile in Arianne's direction, and then introduced his companion, Mrs. Sally Turner, his cousin, lately widowed. *Fool*, she scolded herself for being such a ninny. The baroness fluttered her lashes, and Sir Roderick and Lady Cecilia expressed their condolences upon the demise of Mrs. Turner's dear husband. Lythmore's attention crept back to her.

Arianne tried to focus on the conversation going on around her, but his gaze drew her in. She felt herself falling into a void, so huge and so expansive, it seemed to swallow her. But his eyes held her softly, safely. Time turned to infinity. Her breathing halted. Her heart, that traitorous, fickle organ, skipped and cavorted wildly in her chest.

Stop, she commanded herself.

Stop.

Now.

She must not.

Could not.

He smiled. She blinked.

That void had a very hard bottom as she landed. She stumbled again. Gasping, she dragged air into her lungs.

"My dear, what is it?" Mrs. Weathersby whispered from her right.

"Is something amiss?" Lady Cecilia Crump demanded from her left.

"I'm terribly sorry," Arianne said. "I am not feeling well. A slight dizzy spell." She watched a line of concern appear between Lythmore's brows. Embarrassed at the commotion she was creating, she said, "I'll be fine after a few moments."

"Oh, you poor dear," Sally Turner exclaimed. "You must have Lythmore drive you home. I feel the need to walk a bit. I will promenade with your delightful companions."

The others enthusiastically agreed, except for the baroness, who sent Mrs. Turner a chilly sideways glare. Arianne tried to decline gracefully, but matters were taken out of her hands. Lythmore nimbly jumped down from the curricle. He helped Mrs. Turner descend. Arianne closed her eyes and wished she could disappear. She did not want to create a disturbance, and she certainly did not wish to have news of her silly weakness spread about. She sensed his presence before her and felt herself teeter on the brink of that void once more. *If I do not look at him, I will not fall.*

"Madame, may I help you up?" she heard him say.

Her eyes snapped open.

Lythmore held out a hand to her.

Arianne forced a smile and kept her gaze focused on his hand, neatly covered in a leather driving glove. Perhaps if that hand had been bare, she might have been all right. She might not have remembered another gloved hand from another time, one that had reached out to her, one that caused guilt to twist in her chest. That other hand floated before her vision and superimposed itself on Lythmore's hand. The sands at the edge of the void shifted. She felt herself falling weightless once more. She swayed. Calmly, Lythmore stepped forward, and without warning, swept Arianne up into his arms.

She blinked. The vision of the hand disappeared, and she found herself inexplicably, mortifyingly draped in the duke's embrace.

"Your grace," she gasped.

"The lady is obviously quite faint," he said. "I will make certain she arrives home safely."

"Your grace," Arianne protested once more as he turned to his curricle. "Please put me down this instant. This is most embarrassing."

"You should hold on, madame, or I will drop you, and then you will be even more embarrassed," he said with a grin.

Arianne could do nothing but take his advice. Slipping her arm over his shoulder, she tried to touch him as little as possible, but even so, she was intensely aware of the muscles rippling beneath his clothing, the easy strength of him, the heat of him. The scent of him, woodsy and rich. If he had not been cradling her in his arms, she certainly would have plunged again into that awful void.

"I am quite all right, monsieur," she protested again and tried to keep her voice coolly impersonal. Instead, she found her throat had become tight, and the words came out breathy and intimate.

He did not look at her, but his lips twitched, and an eyebrow quirked upward. "I am sure you are fine, Madame de Vouvret," he said, and his voice lowered to a murmur, "but what other excuse could I find to hold you in my arms?"

Arianne blushed hotly like an innocent, young girl. The others were standing only a few feet away. Had they heard? She should have reprimanded Lythmore for his outrageous comment. But she found that those words would not form. She felt too comfortable, too safe in the cradle of his arms. He turned to look at her, and their eyes met. Something, a spark, a flash of lightning passed between them. Her gaze fell to his mouth. Perfect. The top lip sculpted, the dip in the middle well-defined, the bottom lip a bit plumper. Sensuous. She wanted to kiss that mouth, to taste it, lick it, devour it. Without thinking, she touched those lips with her fingertips. His eyes blazed hot. His mouth quirked with the hint of a smile.

Reality intruded when he stopped beside the curricle. She snatched back her fingers, curling them into her palm. She could not kiss him. And she certainly should not be touching him so intimately. She hardly knew him. She couldn't allow anyone into her life, not with Pinard's threat hanging over her. And she could never allow him to learn anything about the tragedy at Shipley Hall. She forced her concentration away from his lips. He lifted her onto the seat as if she weighed nothing, then climbed up himself. With a snap of the reins, they set off.

They drove out of Sydney Gardens, down Great Pulteney Street, around Laura Place, to Argyle Street and the Pulteney Bridge. He attempted to make light conversation, first about the unusually hot weather, then about various new buildings they passed, and finally, the Monday morning breakfasts held outside in the gardens surrounding Sydney Hotel. Arianne's answers were short and nearly impolite. She could not encourage him.

As they turned into Milsom Street, where her shop was located, she felt she should voice her gratitude. "You are very brave to allow me to ride with you, your grace, for I am far below your station, but I do thank you for your concern."

"Nonsense," he declared. "You have honored me with your presence, Madame de Vouvret. I'm sure every gentleman we passed was envious that I had such a beautiful companion."

Heat bloomed in Arianne's cheeks, and she ducked her head. "You are too kind, your grace," she murmured.

He pulled up before her shop, then turned to her with a smile. "I am being truthful."

His gaze seemed to sear her soul. His words flustered her. Then he tied off the reins and jumped down to the street. Arianne drew a breath to regain her equilibrium and reminded herself once again she could not fall under this man's spell.

He came around to her side of the curricle to help her down. She placed her foot on the step and took his hand at the same time. For some reason, she lost her balance and found herself caught up in his arms once again.

She cast a wild glance around to see if anyone noticed. The street was unusually quiet with only two women, far at the other end, walking in the opposite direction. They couldn't possibly have noticed the impropriety of her in the duke's arms.

"Please, release me, your grace," she murmured.

"On one condition," he said. He turned to her, and their eyes met. Again.

She felt that spark pass between them. Again. Swallowing, she looked away at anything else besides those seductive eyes. "What condition?" she asked, her voice sounding high and tight in her throat.

"That you stop calling me 'your grace.' I have a name." His demand held an edge of laughter.

She cleared her throat. All she wanted was for him to put her on her feet so she could disappear into her shop. "Lythmore," she whispered.

"Hmm. That will do for now." Then leaning close, he whispered, "May I call you Arianne?"

The intimacy that his words implied, the seduction of his tone, frightened her. She gasped. "No. Absolutely not."

His lips tipped up in an impudent grin. "As you wish, Madame de Vouvret." Removing his arm from beneath her knees, he plunked her down on her own feet. "Until we meet again. Arianne." He bowed as he murmured her name, then swung about, climbed up onto his curricle, and drove off.

Arianne felt as if she had abruptly landed on solid ground after falling from a distant height. The earth beneath her feet was reassuring, and her equilibrium and good sense returned. She had an overwhelming urge to stamp her foot in outrage at the audacity of the man. He had put her in an embarrassing situation. Not only had he set her beside him on the seat of his curricle and ridden with her through the city streets, but he had also literally swept her up into his arms. He was titled, while she was in trade, a mere seamstress.

With his arrogant gesture, he had placed her in an untenable position, giving the impression that she was his mistress. Everything he had done in the past hour could ruin her. If she were ruined, her business would die, and she would not be able to gather information to send to Pinard. Her father's life would be in danger. And how would she be able to protect dear little Luc?

She ground her teeth together and silently called the handsome, suave, infuriating Duke of Lythmore every insulting name she knew. The man was a rogue, a rake. If she did not need the business, if she were not caught in a desperate situation, she would tell his cousin to have her gowns made by someone else.

But no other man had ever made her feel like Cameron, Duke of Lythmore—not even Jean-Paul with his good heart and gentle ways. No other man had caused that frightening void to open at her feet, and no other man had held her suspended above that void and made her feel safe at the same time. No other man.

Yet, he had brought back the memory of Shipley Hall. Shipley Hall and the terrible, tragic, evil events that had taken place there that caused the guilt to writhe within her. Pinard had forced her to beguile and then destroy a man by holding her father's life hostage. Ian West. She had been fond of Ian with his teasing smile and easy manner, and she hated herself every time she had flirted with him. She had watched him fall in love with her. Never again would she allow another man to get that close. She could not allow herself to feel. She was Pinard's weapon. Cameron, Duke of Lythmore, would not be another casualty. She would not, could not, allow him into her life.

Tomorrow, she would write a cool note of thanks and let him know she was unavailable. She could not afford to have these uncontrollable feelings about a man—about *that* man. Her life centered around keeping Luc and Papa safe. She had to wall off her heart. Resolving to think no more about him, she entered her shop, closed the door, and turning the key in the lock, shut out the dangerous world that contained both Henri Pinard and the Duke of Lythmore.

Late that night, Cameron prowled the library in the townhouse he had taken in the Royal Crescent. He could not get the lovely Arianne de Vouvret out of his mind. When he had driven past Sydney Gardens and seen her stumble, he had wanted nothing more than to help her. Violating propriety, he had turned his curricle around and driven into the gardens. Once there, her eyes had drawn him in, so he reached out for her as she swayed unsteadily on her feet. And then in a lapse of good sense, scandalously, he had lifted her in his arms. As he held her, he wished he would never have to release her. At the same time, he wished he had never touched her. The feel of her lithe curves nestled snugly against him had swamped his senses. Her scent, something spicy yet sweet, like a peony, was intoxicating. He had never been so strongly affected by a woman.

He had thought of her often since their first meeting when he had gone to her shop to establish credit for Sally's purchases. Her reserve and dignity intrigued him, especially when he contrasted those qualities with her expressive eyes and lush mouth. He had thought that she was unattainable because of her married status, but Sally had returned from her afternoon salon with the news that Madame de Vouvret was a widow and alone in this country with few friends and no relatives. With that information, his interest grew.

He could not allow his attraction to interfere with the reason he had come to Bath. The circumstances surrounding the dress design the day he had accompanied Sally to the modiste's establishment had been suspicious. Was she a spy? Had she been involved in his brother's death? He had no evidence to support his impression, only something in his gut that warned him to be careful. Her name was not Marguerite, the one that had been connected to his brother, yet she had the most delightful French accent. A name could be assumed and false. Her accent, he was sure, was real.

Since he had been in Bath, he had attempted to meet anyone who would have conceivably been acquainted with his brother when he had been in the city. He had been to the Pump Room, had attended the Upper and Lower Assembly Rooms, had strolled Milsom Street, and generally been introduced to the society of Bath. He had met the two men whom Dunbary mentioned that had business dealings with his brother: Mr. Clifford Rathbone, the third son of an earl, and the Frenchman, the Marquis de Pagière. Both seemed pleasant enough fellows and appeared harmless, but, of course, one never knew what hidden intentions men held. There were also two others whom he suspected: a Prussian, Baron Wilhelm Volks, who had boxed frequently with his brother, and an impoverished baronet from the north country, Sir Lindsey Wooten, who had regularly played Whist with him. Each of them might have some reason to dislike his brother, but none strong enough to want to destroy him.

He had met several women, as well. A few French emigrées had caught his attention as possible suspects, but he had dismissed them all for one reason or another. But the Baroness Souffant, whom he had met only that afternoon, might be someone he would need to investigate. She was an attractive woman with dark hair and flashing dark eyes, and she might have interested his brother. But as a widow, why would she want to destroy a man who could possibly become a husband? Unless another hand guided her. Dunbary had mentioned that the circumstances surrounding his brother's death had the feel of espionage. But his brother had never been involved in that. Or had he?

Shaking his head to clear his thoughts, Cameron stopped before a window and stared down at the dark street. Then there was Arianne. He could not erase the image of her face nor the memory of the feel of her from his mind. Becoming infatuated with a woman who might have been involved with destroying his brother was sheer lunacy. From the few encounters he had with her, he did not think her to be ruthless enough to be a destroyer of men. There was a gentleness about her that contradicted what that woman would have to be. In comparison, the attractive Baroness Souffant had a hard glint to her eye, despite her charming smile. Which woman had beguiled his brother?

Walking to his desk, he pulled out the small scrap of paper with its wash of colors and smeared letters that Dunbary had given him.

Again, something about it niggled at him. It seemed familiar. Turning it this way and that, he tried to make out what the bit of color signified. Nothing came to mind. He left that part of the message and worked on the letters written across the bottom. Trying to manipulate them into words, he only succeeded in becoming frustrated at his efforts, for nothing he thought of made any sense. With a sigh of frustration, he threw down his quill, jumped from his chair, and began pacing again.

The door opened, and his former mistress stood silhouetted by the candles behind her. "Darling," Sally purred, "whatever are you doing prowling about like some ferocious animal?"

Cameron stopped and regarded her from beneath lowered lids. She was a beautiful woman, smart, resourceful, and practical, all qualities that made her a perfect spy. She was also quite inventive between the covers. They had enjoyed more than a few frolics when they had been younger. But that was years ago.

"I could not sleep." He gave a negligent shrug.

Sally's eyes narrowed thoughtfully. "It's that woman, Madame de Vouvret, who makes you sleepless," she said as she crossed the floor.

He frowned. "Why should that concern you when you had the attention of the Marquis de Pagière at the concert this evening?"

Her chagrined little laugh tinkled. "Guilty as charged." With a teasing smile, she sashayed toward him. "You know I am jealous whenever I see you with another woman." She rested her hand on his chest.

"Truly?" He raised a skeptical brow. "I seem to remember you encouraged me to drive Madame de Vouvret home from Sydney Gardens."

She shrugged a bare shoulder. "I had my part to play as your cousin, and I was only concerned for the poor woman's health. She turned a most dreadful shade of pale." Her fingers made light circles against his chest. "But I was disappointed we did not conclude our outing."

He ignored her caress. "It was over between us long ago, Sally."

"I know." She sighed dramatically. "I was in love with you back then."

A bit taken aback at this pronouncement, Cameron could not be sure if she was being truthful or playing. As he patted her hand, he was surprised to see her eyes misted over. "You will always have a place in my heart, Sally."

"Oh, Cameron, you're such a kind man. I think that is why I fell in love with you." Standing on tiptoe, she brushed her lips across his. "But I know that you never loved me, and a girl must be practical. De Pagière appears so very wealthy and is quite charming and handsome despite his age. He could make a girl like me very content. I believe it's time for me to settle down and become a respectable married lady."

Worry about Sally's attraction to a man who might have been involved with his brother's destruction made Cameron caution her. "Be careful, Sally. You don't know him very well. Stay under my protection until you are sure of him and his intentions."

Sally dimpled. "Don't fret so. You know that I have taken care of myself since I was a girl."

Cameron's eyes narrowed thoughtfully as an opportunity presented itself. "If you are going to lure de Pagiére into your sweet web, perhaps you could discover more about him for me."

Sally tilted her head, and her gaze turned crafty. "Only if it does not interfere with my plans."

Cameron smiled indulgently. "I would never do that. Just be safe for me, please."

With a nod and a sly grin, she glanced down at the scrap of parchment lying on the desk. "What's this? Some secret love letter from Madame de Vouvrct?"

The mention of the modiste's name arrested him. "Why do you say that?" His suspicions of the woman took hold of him again.

"Because it looks like a piece from one of her dress designs." Sally tilted her head thoughtfully. "Yes!" she cried out in delight. "Of course, it is! Look! Here, this is the hem of a gown." She pointed to the wash of green and a dark, curved line that could have been brown or black. "And here is the petticoat." Her finger moved to the shading of yellow. "And these letters—*wn, u, br*—they are from the words for the colors and types of materials to be used, like lawn, blue, brocade." Sally emitted a tinkling, amused laugh as she handed the bit of parchment to him. "Oh, Cameron, darling, what secret message of love did you hope to find in a dress design?"

Something sank within him at the information. A dress design? Now he knew why the damned thing had seemed so familiar. He had caught a glimpse of it at the modiste's shop. Why would a French fisherman who had been "blown off-course" have a dress design from Madame de Vouvret? The answer was obvious. Neither the fisherman nor the modiste was who they claimed to be. But he needed proof. The design and the fisherman could be completely innocent, despite the suspicions of his friends. He could not accuse Madame de Vouvret of spying from a vague notion, and he still could not connect her or anyone else to his brother's death. He needed to investigate the Baroness Souffant, as well as the other French emigrées in Bath.

Not willing to share his disappointment, he pasted a chagrined smile on his face and tossed the scrap down as if it meant nothing. "Only a dress design? I had hoped to learn of the lady's undying love for me, but I find I am only a fool." He chuckled. "I seem to be losing my wits."

"Oh, Cam." Sally laughed as she tugged on his arm. "Come to bed, darling, and I will make you see you are not the fool you believe. Once more, in honor of past memories."

At one time, Cameron would have gone willingly to Sally's bed. Now, he found no excitement in the idea. Patting her hand, he said, "I don't think I would make a good bed partner for you tonight, Sally. Perhaps some other time."

"Ah, well, good night, darling." Sally smiled bravely.

As she moved away from him, he caught her hand and raised it to his lips. "You are a true and good friend, Sally Turner."

"Well, now, that's sumpthin', ain't it?" she mocked good-naturedly. "A girl like me always needs a gent wot thinks of 'imself as a friend."

Cameron winced at her barb. "You know I'll always be around to help if you need it, Sally."

She disengaged her hand from his grasp. "Good night, Cam," she said and walked into her room.

Cameron watched her go, then turned back to the scrap of parchment before him on the desk. Although it was merely a torn piece from a dress design, he felt it was far more significant than he could figure out at the moment. Perhaps, if he stared at it long enough, something would occur to him that might give him a clue to what it meant. Something that would not connect it with the bewitching Arianne.

Sleepless, Arianne stared up at the canopy above her head. The afternoon stroll, which she had at first thought would be a delightful diversion from her work and her worries, had turned into a disaster. Once again, that roguish Duke of Lythmore had appeared as if conjured from her thoughts. What devil dogged her steps to create such havoc in her life?

The feel of his arms hugging her close to his body still remained with her. She couldn't wipe the memory of his eyes from her mind. His devastating smile and soft words still made her flush with heat. Squirming, she tried to forget her brazen act of touching his mouth. How could she have acted so foolishly? How could she have forgotten that she had a reputation to uphold? How could she have forgotten that Jean-Paul still resided in her heart?

Throwing off the covers, she slipped from the bed and pulled a dressing-gown about her shoulders. She knew sleep would not come for a long time, if ever, this night. The pale moonlight beckoned her, and she wandered to the window to look out. Somewhere out there, across the rooftops and through the gardens, Cameron, Duke of Lythmore, lay sleeping.

She made a small sound of disgust at herself and turned away from the scene of silvery light and black shadows. Stupid. Crazy. Witless. That was what she was. Lythmore owned Shipley Hall, the site of her sin, her guilt. What if he discovered what she had done? She could not let that happen. She had too much to lose if she should make a mistake.

Concentrating on the fact that he was a forbidden temptation, she thought back to this evening's concert. Lythmore had attended with Mrs. Turner, and for once, the fates had smiled on Arianne by keeping him occupied and far away from her. But she was very aware of him as she tried to concentrate on the music.

She had watched Sally Turner flirting with Monsieur le Marquis de Pagière, who had sat in Lythmore's box. De Pagière could be a charming man when he wished, and he had, from time to time, passed along interesting bits of information to her that she sent to Pinard. He had been involved with the affair at Shipley Hall. She wondered at the fact that de Pagière was in the same box with Lythmore but then dismissed her suspicion that there might be any connection other than social between the two men. Monsieur le Marquis de Pagière enjoyed the company of many people.

A noise in the alley beneath the back window made her stop and listen. Muffled curses and the complaint of a stray cat disturbed the night silence. She flung open the window and leaned out. The dark shape of a scrawny man clambered from beneath a toppled pile of refuse.

"Who is there? Get away from here, or I will shoot you," she bluffed.

The man looked up and scrambled back into the alley. "Don't shoot," he whined. "Ain't nobody but me, One-Armed Lewis. Don't mean no harm. Jus' lookin' for some bits o' cloth. I'll be goin' now. Don't shoot."

Arianne watched as he limped quickly down the alley and disappeared into the shadows. With a shake of her head, she closed and latched the window. She had seen One-Armed Lewis before as he rifled the scraps her seamstresses tossed out, and she knew he sold them for much more than they were worth. Usually, she did not chase him away, but tonight, every one of her nerve endings seemed to be on edge. She wanted no one sneaking up on her from the back alley.

She froze as a terrible idea entered her head. What if One-Armed Lewis had seen Edouard Courcy that night he came to tell her that the authorities had boarded the boat of Cocteau, the fisherman? Would Lewis think it odd for a man in a cloak to enter her rooms? Would he sell that information, as well as his scraps of cloth? Would Lewis know who would want to buy such information?

A chill ran through her, and she rubbed her arms. Edouard had been foolish that night. He should have allowed her to arrange the meeting. She would have made certain that no one would see them.

Now, she could be in even greater danger than before. And there was no one to whom she could turn for help. Unless…

Unless the Duke of Lythmore would care to take her under his protection. Just as suddenly as she thought of the idea, she dismissed it. No, she could not invite such complications into her life. The best thing she could do was to keep Lythmore as far away as possible. She did not really know the man, so how could she trust him? Besides, Jean-Paul still resided in her heart.

But the memory of Lythmore's embrace remained with her. And the fantasy of being his lover was very pleasant, despite what had happened at Shipley Hall.

CHAPTER 4

On the Thursday after the disastrous stroll in Sydney Gardens, Arianne sat with Mrs. Weathersby, Miss Barbara, and Baroness Souffant. They were attending the weekly fancy dress ball at the Upper Assembly Rooms. As she gazed at the dancers flowing past, her thoughts were not on the scene before her. Instead, she was thinking of Edouard Courcy and the possibility that One-Armed Lewis had seen him leave her house.

"May I have this dance, Madame de Vouvret?"

Arianne's head snapped up at the invitation. Standing above her, smiling, was none other than the Duke of Lythmore. She had not seen him approach. Dazzled once again by his smile, she sought to give herself some relief by glancing about the crowded hall. The Upper Assembly Rooms were teeming with men and women in their stylish dress. The scene had not changed from just a moment ago before she had been invited to dance. Yet, she felt as if time stood still when he smiled at her. Miss Barbara's nudge reminded her that she had not answered the gentleman's question.

She glanced at her companions. The baroness was fluttering her fan and trying to attract Lythmore's attention. The excited face of Miss Barbara and the curious one of Mrs. Weathersby indicated they were waiting for her response. The man standing before her was waiting for her response. She could feel his presence enveloping her like a warm, soft cloud. It lifted her up and away from the solidity of her surroundings.

"I—ah—I—" she stuttered. She wanted *very much* to dance with this man. She very much *did not* want to dance with this man. Yet, her mind had gone blank, and she could think of no excuse to decline. She watched Lythmore's brow arch in amusement at her confusion.

"Of course," she announced bravely. "I would be delighted to dance with you, monsieur." Placing her hand in his, she allowed him to lead her out to the dance floor.

Arianne took her place in the formation of the quadrille and concentrated on her steps. She tried very hard to ignore the feeling of being entirely disconnected from her feet. After a few measures, she and her partner came face to face as part of the dance.

"I see you have recovered from your infirmity," Lythmore observed.

"Merely the vapors, your grace, and that was several days ago," she corrected as they moved apart.

"I'm glad it was only a minor ailment," he said, stepping toward her once more. "May I take you walking on Sunday?"

Arianne stumbled at the unexpected invitation but was steadied by the strong hand of her partner. The dance forced them apart again, and she breathed a sigh of relief for the short reprieve while she tried to think of an answer. Coming together, she smiled at him as coolly as she could.

"I do not think that would be appropriate, your grace," she said. "You are a gentleman, a duke, and I am merely a modiste. I should not even be here this evening."

He stopped in the middle of the dance. Arianne was forced to stop also. "You are wrong, Madame de Vouvret," he told her. Taking her by the arm, he led her from the dance floor, out of the room, and into a secluded nook provided for the gentlemen's ease.

Arianne looked about her in shock. "Your grace, this is most inappropriate."

"What is inappropriate, Madame de Vouvret, is your thinking that you should not be here this evening. You are more a lady than many of the titled ladies here."

Although she blushed with pleasure at the compliment, Arianne shook her head in denial. "I am no lady, monsieur. If you truly knew me, you would not say such outrageous things."

"I do know you," he argued. "I have watched you and have heard about you from Mrs. Turner after she returned from your salon. You are kind, gracious, graceful, and beautiful. Arianne."

"No." She shook her head more forcefully. "No, no, a thousand times, monsieur. You know nothing about me." Alarm swept through her. She could not allow this man into her life. His connection to Shipley Hall was too close, much too close.

"I would like to change that," he said with a smile. "Which is why I asked you to go walking on Sunday."

"And then what, your grace?" she demanded. "The theater? A ride in the country? A private dinner in your rooms? An invitation to travel to London with you? A suggestion to close down my business here in Bath because you will keep me?"

"Stop!" he growled.

His mouth, that wonderful mouth that could smile with such dazzling warmth, became a hard, angry line. The sudden change in his manner was frightening, and she fell back a step. Disconcerted, Arianne realized this man was not all elegance and beauty. Beneath that warm exterior ran a streak of cold steel.

He drew a breath as his expression softened. "I'm sorry I frightened you. I want nothing more from you than your company on Sunday, Madame de Vouvret. I wish to become better acquainted with you—as a friend. Is that such a great sin?"

His choice of that last word awoke her serpent of guilt. Arianne lowered her eyes. "Not a great sin, your grace." She sighed. No one had sinned as greatly as she had.

"Then, you will accompany me on Sunday on a stroll through Crescent Fields?" As she began to shake her head in the negative, he told her, "Mrs. Turner will accompany us. Will that suit? Before she could answer, he said, "I will be by to collect you after divine service."

"But, your grace, you know nothing about me." Somehow, she had to persuade him—and herself—that they could not meet on Sunday.

He smiled, and it was full of dazzling warmth once more. "I intend to change that, Madame de Vouvret. I intend to discover everything there is to know about you."

Befuddled, Arianne merely stared.

"I'll take your silence as acceptance," he said.

She took a breath to tell him no.

"Wonderful," he murmured before she could utter the word. "I am very much looking forward to our stroll."

Taking her hand, he turned it over and kissed her palm. The feel of his lips did strange things to her hand, her wrist, her arm. In fact, they did strange things to her head. She was unable to think clearly. All thought fled from her. When he raised his eyes and looked at her, she felt that void open before her and the sands shift perilously on its edge. Afraid she would fall once again, she withdrew her fingers from his grasp.

"We really should return to the dance floor," she suggested breathlessly. "There will be gossip." She stepped back from him and saved herself from slipping into emptiness. "I have a business and a reputation to uphold, your grace. The ladies would not come to me if they suspected I was not discreet." As soon as the words were out of her mouth, she realized what a lie they were. She was anything but discreet, for she would be going on a walk with him on Sunday. Worse than that indiscretion, all the gossip she heard went encoded into her dress designs and directly to Pinard. Ashamed at the wrong she was committing, she could not meet his eyes. "Please, your grace, we must return where there are others present."

His glance was apologetic as he offered his arm. "We shall say that you were feeling a bit faint and needed a breath of air."

She smiled gratefully as she accepted his escort back to Miss Barbara and the others. Relieved that she had not made a fool of herself with this man, her step was confident. Yet, her knees almost buckled beneath her at his whispered words before he left her.

"Until Sunday, Arianne, when I shall learn everything about you."

Frozen, she watched him turn and walk away. She wanted to call out to him, to tell him no, that she would not, could not walk with him on Sunday. She could not afford to allow him to learn anything about her. She must protect her father and little Luc. She must keep her secret. She must hide her sin.

But he was gone, lost in the crowd, and it was too late to tell him anything. She sank to her chair and tried to smile at the questioning look from Miss Barbara. Upon her report that she had been invited to go walking in Crescent Fields on Sunday with the duke and Mrs. Turner, the baroness excused herself abruptly.

Arianne watched her go. Was the lady scandalized that a duke was socializing with a mere dressmaker? Would she spread the gossip that Arianne was involved in a dalliance with Lythmore? Or perhaps she was jealous and wished Lythmore's attentions focused on her. All of the options worried Arianne, for she could not afford to have the baroness whispering innuendoes about her. But her attention was drawn back to her companions because Mrs. Weathersby's brows had risen up in astonishment, and Miss Barbara was nearly swooning in her excitement. Arianne offered to fetch some lemonade in the hope that she would bump into Lythmore and be able to decline his invitation. Yet, the fates were not with her. He was gone, and upon returning to her acquaintances, Miss Barbara was much recovered, and Arianne was forced to drink the lemonade herself.

Jules, Marquis de Pagière stood watching the crowd at the Upper Assembly Rooms, and his mouth twisted in distaste. He disliked this place with its forced gaiety and crush of people. He much preferred to socialize in the gaming hells, the routs, the theater, and in the privacy of his own house, but circumstances prescribed that he be present on this evening. All he wanted was to complete his task and then be gone. His task was not an unpleasant one, but the surroundings did not conform to his idea of congeniality.

Standing inconspicuously apart from the crowd, he saw the Duke of Lythmore move toward the exit. The man was alone. Jules smiled to himself at that. He had seen the duke dancing with the delightful Madame de Vouvret earlier, and that had annoyed him. What dear Arianne saw in the fellow was a mystery, but he could not account for the whims of the female mind, especially one as naïve as that of Madame de Vouvret. Ah, well, time would change that, he was sure.

The orchestra stopped playing in order to take a short intermission. Moving through the milling people, Jules made his way across the dance floor to where Madame de Vouvret was sitting with her acquaintances. Jules repressed a shudder at the thought of having to deal with Mrs. Weathersby and Miss Barbara. When he reached the other side of the dance floor, he ignored the two other women and focused on the delightful Arianne.

"Madame de Vouvret." He greeted her with a bow, then gave a perfunctory nod to the duo.

Arianne glanced up at him, and her lips parted with surprise. He admired the creamy fullness of her breast as it rose and fell with her breath. Her naïveté made his blood race.

"Monsieur le Marquis, this is a surprise," she murmured.

He held out his hand to her. "Would you do me the honor of accompanying me to the punch bowl?"

She shook her head. "I do not think—" she began.

"Madame, please, I will be devastated if you refuse." He pressed his hand to his breast in an attitude of exquisite disappointment.

Her lashes fluttered as she lowered her eyes. He saw the exact moment she changed her mind. Glancing up at him again, smiling coolly, she placed her hand in his.

"How can I refuse such a pretty plea?" she said smoothly. Rising from her chair, she fell into step beside him. When they were out of earshot from her acquaintances, she hissed, "What is the meaning of this charade, Jules? What are you doing here? You never come to such places."

"Are you not pleased to see me, dear Arianne? Perhaps I have reformed and am trying to enter respectable society." He raised a challenging brow and pulled her hand into the crook of his arm.

"That will happen when men learn to fly," she snapped.

De Pagière chuckled. "That might be sooner than you think, *ma petite*. But you are right, I have not reformed. You are still the only woman who haunts my dreams. Take pity on me. Become my paramour."

Arianne pulled her hand from his arm. "If you are going to start that foolishness, I will return to my friends."

Before she could move away, the marquis grabbed her hand. "Don't make a scene, madame. Pinard would not be pleased to hear that you and I argued in public."

Her face paled, and she returned her hand to his arm. "What does Pinard have to do with your presence here this evening?"

"I very much like the feel of your hand on my arm, Arianne." He bent closer as he murmured his words.

Arianne turned her head away, although she left her hand where it was.

Jules chuckled. "Someday, Arianne, someday."

"About Pinard, Jules. What does he want?" she prompted.

Jules smiled as he delivered his message. "It seems Monsieur Pinard would like me to act as your messenger until Courcy returns from France."

"That is impossible. I refuse." She raised her chin and glanced away.

"You can't refuse. Isn't that delicious?" He smiled, relishing her defiance. "You will have to pretend to be my mistress and deliver your dress designs to me at night."

She scowled. "This is an absurd idea. I cannot do that. I have a reputation to uphold."

"A wonderful, lily-white reputation that I would be delighted to sully." Jules could barely keep his glee in check.

The sharpness of her nails dug into his arm as she subtly demonstrated her anger. "If I lose my reputation and my business, then I won't have access to the information Pinard wants. He will become angry, and I do not think you want him angry."

Chuckling, Jules pried her hand from his arm and raised it to his lips. "Pinard need never know. I will never tell, and you will not let on because…well, your reputation and all that." He gave an airy wave of his hand. "So. You will deliver your designs in person to me, *ma petite*. Send a note beforehand to inform me when you will be calling. I will wait in agony until I hear from you." Bowing, he turned on his heel and melted into the crowd.

After collecting his hat and walking stick, he stood outside the door of the Upper Assembly Rooms and breathed the night air. The blood pumped through his veins with white heat. He wanted Arianne de Vouvret with a need that clouded his brain, but first, she had to be schooled, trained, disciplined, tempered. She was not ready yet. He was a patient man, and he would wait. But this gift to him from Pinard would be an introduction for her into his way of life. His lids lowered sensuously as he contemplated the pleasures he would show her. But that was for later. Now, he must slake the need that threatened to explode within him. Moving off into the shadows of the night, he knew just the place to go.

Sunday morning dawned oppressive and overcast. Arianne hoped that rain might fall before the time came for the Duke of Lythmore to call for her. However, her hopes were dashed when the clouds broke, and the sun appeared. She changed her outfit three times. This dress was too alluring. That one too stiff and formal. The one she finally chose was a white lawn walking dress with an under-skirt of pale yellow. Her wide-brimmed straw bonnet, which lay on a table beside the door, had white silk flowers about the crown and pale green silk ribbons that tied beneath her chin. Her parasol was blue moiré silk.

Gazing at her reflection in the long looking glass that hung in her fitting room, she decided she looked presentable with just the proper amount of modesty. Yet, she wished fervently that she had declined Lythmore's invitation. Of course, she might have sent a note around to him but had never seemed to find the right moment to do so. Now, after putting off writing the note for so long, it was too late. He would be arriving at her door at any moment.

She heard the knock announcing his arrival, and her maid let-ting him in. Her heart fluttered up into her throat. How could she have allowed herself to be persuaded into walking with this man?

Her maid came to the fitting room and announced the duke. Arianne wanted to send him away. He was too dangerous for her peace of mind. She could say she was suddenly indisposed. But his cousin was a customer. If she insulted the duke, she could lose his cousin's business. So instead of avoiding him, she said, "Please tell his grace I shall be with him presently."

Sinking down onto a chair, she tried to come to terms with what she had just done. She was committed now. There was no turning back. Despite her fear, despite the secret she must hide, she had to greet the man and go walking with him as if she had not a care in the world. The thought sent her stomach into wild somersaults. Telling herself to remain calm, she stood and walked out to meet the Duke of Lythmore.

As she entered the front room, he turned and smiled. She was undone. The sight of him, his smile, the warm glance of his blue eyes, made the floor beneath her feet disappear. She floated across the void to greet him.

"You are looking lovely, Madame de Vouvret," he greeted her.

Unable to find her voice, Arianne simply smiled and bowed her head in acknowledgment. She turned to the glass hanging on the wall beside her and settled her bonnet on her head. By the time she had finished, she had gathered her wits and was able to speak.

She glanced about. "Where is Mrs. Turner?"

He gestured to the street outside the window. "Mrs. Turner is waiting in the carriage."

Relieved that she would not be alone with him, she said, "You are very kind to invite me to go walking with you, your grace."

"Kindness has nothing to do with my invitation, Madame de Vouvret." His smile disarmed her. "I am guilty of being shamelessly selfish."

"Selfish, your grace?" She glanced at him quizzically as he held the door open for her.

"Of course," he said warmly. "I want to be seen with one of the most beautiful women in Bath."

Arianne could not stop the blush of pleasure that colored her cheeks at his outrageous compliment. It had been so long since anyone had said such things to her. Hearing them pleased her, yet she could not afford to let a glib tongue beguile her.

As they walked to his landau, she said. "I do believe the heat has addled your wits, your grace," she jested. "There are certainly many other women, including Mrs. Turner or Baroness Souffant, much more beautiful than I am."

"If I am addled, then I never wish to be set straight. You dazzle me. Arianne." He spoke her name in an intimate murmur.

The heat rose in her cheeks. She felt the same about him. But she could not let him know that. Not now. Not ever. Little Luc and Papa were too dear to risk on a brief affair with a man who might turn against her if he ever discovered her secret. No, she would enjoy his company for this little while, and then tell him she must never see him again.

"You believe I am being foolish and insincere," he observed.

Arianne smiled. "I believe, your grace, that you have always been granted your every desire."

A shadow of deep sadness passed across his face. "Not every desire, madame. There are some wishes that not even a magic genie could grant me."

Disturbed that her flippant words had caused him distress, Arianne placed her hand on his arm. "I'm sorry if I upset you."

His smile returned, chasing away the clouds. "It does not matter. Come, it is a beautiful day," he said, as he helped her into the carriage. "I have two beautiful women with me whom I will show off to everyone we meet. Mrs. Turner and I want to learn everything about you."

His last words caused her stomach to flutter. After she greeted Mrs. Turner, she bravely quipped, "Isn't a woman allowed any secrets, monsieur? A woman's mystery is part of her allure."

"I definitely agree with that sentiment," Mrs. Turner said with a grin.

"Then I will unravel as much of the mystery as you wish to reveal. Is that a bargain?" He raised a teasing brow.

His light spirit was infectious, and Arianne chuckled. "Yes, a bargain."

He told his driver they were ready, and they set off, soon turning into the street running before the Royal Crescent and stopped. Lythmore handed Arianne down onto the road, then Mrs. Turner. They crossed into Crescent Fields and began their stroll. They had not gone far when Mrs. Turner stumbled and let out a cry. Both Arianne and Lythmore halted, expressing their concern.

"Oh, dear," Mrs. Turner said. "I've twisted my ankle."

Arianne saw the perfect excuse to escape from their stroll and Lythmore's presence. "Then, we must return to the carriage and take you home."

As Lythmore agreed and helped to steady her, Mrs. Turner sent Arianne a surreptitious wink. Then, glancing down the path, she said, "Oh, there's Tandy." She waved at a gentleman who approached from the opposite direction. "Tandy!" she called.

The man who stopped before them was quite broad-shouldered. Ginger-colored hair showed beneath his top hat, and a neatly trimmed beard—unfashionable, but striking—of the same color followed his jaw. "My dear lady!" he exclaimed. "What a delightful surprise!"

Mrs. Turner's eyes twinkled as she introduced him. "May I present Theodore Ramsey, second son of the Laird of Ardrey. He is visiting here from his drafty castle in the Scottish Highlands. I met him at Duffield's bookstore just after we arrived in Bath." She hobbled precariously and emitted a tiny groan.

"Mrs. Turner!" he exclaimed with concern. "What has happened to you?"

"Oh! My ankle! I twisted it, and now I have ruined our stroll with Lythmore and Madame de Vouvret." Delicate tears balanced on her lashes.

"That is quite the fix," he said. "Perhaps I could be of service? My landau is just there on the street beyond. I could drive you home and allow your friends to continue their stroll."

"Why, that is quite generous of you." Mrs. Turner glanced at the street with a forlorn expression. "But I don't think I can walk that far."

"If I may...?" Without waiting for a response, he swept her up into his arms, made a short bow in Arianne's and Lythmore's direction, and strode off with her.

Confounded by the sudden turn of events, Arianne stared after them and wondered suspiciously if Mrs. Turner had pretended to twist her ankle. She was alone with Lythmore, a circumstance she had tried to prevent. Now that Mrs. Turner had gone, walking alone with Lythmore had the flavor of impropriety. She should ask him to take her home. But that flash of deep sadness that crossed his face at her teasing made her want to learn more about him. Despite his charm and apparent carefree nature, she sensed he kept a part of himself hidden.

He smiled at her. She had a choice, either excuse herself from this outing and retain her dignity and her reputation, or give in to her desire to be with this man and discover his hidden depths. Throwing caution to the devil, she smiled back and fell into step beside him. Butterflies of excitement danced in her middle.

Already, many people sauntered the paths or sat on blankets beneath the trees or among the flowers. The day was warm and would get warmer as the sun rose higher. An enterprising young man sold lemonade from a cask strapped to his back, and Lythmore bought her a refreshing cup.

Apprehension gnawed at her as she walked with the duke. Had she made the right choice? To her surprise, no one spurned her, and, in fact, several of her customers nodded graciously to her as they passed. A few men stopped to chat briefly with Lythmore, and they tipped their hats when he introduced her. Only a few matrons raised their eyebrows and their quizzing glasses with a sniff of disapproval. Lythmore whispered they reminded him of fat old pigeons with ragged feathers. Arianne hid a chuckle behind a gloved hand.

Despite her misgivings and despite her need to shut off a part of her, she was having a wonderful time. Because of what Pinard forced her to do, she kept apart from others. She had no true friends and few acquaintances. Only because she was asked by the ladies who came to her afternoon salon to accompany them to the theater or a concert to fill out their party did she have any social life at all. She did not mind being the last-minute addition to an evening's entertainment, for the invitations helped to balance all the lonely nights when she was on her own.

Yet, on this lovely Sunday, the invitation had been only to her. Cameron, Duke of Lythmore, made her feel young and alive, something she had not felt in a very long time. He made her feel wanted. She regretted her resolve to break off all contact with him at the end of their outing. But she had no choice.

They strolled behind a clump of bushes and trees skirted by a flounce of daisies. Shielded from the other strollers, Lythmore took her hand and drew her to him. Arianne, surprised by the suddenness of his movement, gazed up at him.

"Your grace—" she protested.

He tipped his head. "I thought you had agreed to use my name."

She swallowed. "Lythmore."

"Cameron," he corrected gently.

She swallowed again. "Cameron," she said, barely above a whisper.

"I want to kiss you, Arianne." His gaze was dark and intense, his voice low and husky.

Her eyes widened in surprise at his blunt statement, but a frisson of delicious anticipation rippled through her at the thought of his mouth touching hers. "This is not proper, your grace—Cameron." Her words were correct, but her tone held no conviction.

He smiled at her lack of firmness. She should have been insulted at his smug conceit, but she was not. How could she be insulted when all she wanted was to have him kiss her? To kiss him back?

In the cool shade, his deep blue eyes blazed with hot intensity. She was mesmerized by the heat in them. They tugged her a step closer to him. Tentatively, she touched the corner of his mouth with her fingertips. Those chiseled lips quirked up just the tiniest bit. Her gaze flew to his eyes. They seemed to bore into her soul. Heat, then chill, washed over her.

"Arianne." His murmur slid along her nerve endings, caused the hairs at the back of her neck to tingle, caused the blood to pulse through her veins. Swiftly, he removed his hat, and just as swiftly, his arm encircled her waist and pulled her against him. Her heart pounded in her chest. Her breath turned shallow. Was she breathing at all? His hard male body seemed to invite her soft female form to flow around him. Her curves fit exactly with his angles. Inches, fractions of inches, separated their lips. He touched his fingers—oh, so lightly—to her jaw, his thumb to her bottom lip. "Do you want me to kiss you, Arianne?"

A shiver ran through her at his whisper. Her answer was to raise her mouth to his.

Like lightning, the touch of his lips against hers sent a shaft of pure pleasure through her body. And as thunder follows lightning, her body trembled and quaked in the aftershock of such joy. She did not want this to stop. As on the day in Sydney Gardens, when he had carried her in his arms, she wanted to taste, lick, devour his mouth. Forgetting where they were, forgetting their surroundings and the possibility of discovery, she parted her lips to him and invited him to partake while she indulged herself in a wanton exploration of the taste of him. A duel, a mad mating of lips and tongues, made the heat rise and ignite sparks between them.

Arianne shivered, hot and cold and hot, as if in the clutches of some terrible fever. Pressing against him, she felt his ardor in the tight rippling of his muscles, the hard length of him nestled hungrily in the hollow of her hip. Her breasts, crushed against his chest, ached and tingled for his touch. Almost, almost, she reached for the ties of her chemise, to loosen them and offer her nipples to be suckled by him. Almost. And then the sound of voices and laughter from the other side of the trees and bushes crashed her back to reality.

Embarrassment, shame at what she had nearly done, at what she had already done, made her break away from him with a small, tortured whimper. For a moment, wide-eyed and disbelieving at how she had acted, she stared at him. Then, turning her back, she drew deep, calming breaths. She dabbed at her lips with her handkerchief and put her trembling fingers to her hot cheeks. *What have I done?*

Silence came from him. How could she have revealed such a secret part of herself? She heard him draw several ragged breaths.

Then, softly, he said, "Arianne?"

Unable to face him, she merely shook her head. Appalled at her own behavior, she could not answer.

"Arianne, are you all right?" he asked.

Still not able to speak, she nodded.

"Arianne, forgive me, I am sorry for…that. It was quite unseemly of me." He sounded very contrite.

She nearly laughed at the irony of his statement, for she was the one who had acted in an unseemly manner. She had acted wantonly, wildly, wickedly. She had already decided that she would not, could not, see him again. She should not have allowed herself to forget who she was, what she was, and what she had to do. She should not have kissed him. She should not have accepted his invitation to walk with him on this lovely Sunday. She should have stayed away from him.

Forcing a smile to her lips, she turned to face him. "You must think me terribly indecent, your grace. I apologize if I shocked you with my behavior."

"I do not think you in the least bit wanton. You must still call me Cameron." He smiled, took her hand, and raised it to his lips. She noticed a slight tremble in his fingers. "It must be very hard being a widow and living alone."

His understanding and gentleness brought tears to her eyes. "I miss my husband very much, your gr—Cameron. But that is no excuse for—" Shame made words fail her again, and she averted her face. She wanted to hide in a deep, dark hole.

"We will not speak of it again." He smiled crookedly, and his voice dropped into a conspiratorial whisper. "But I must confess, I enjoyed it very much."

Arianne was forced into a laugh at his admission, despite the blush it brought to her cheeks.

Bending down, Cameron picked one of the flowers beside them and held it out to her. "A daisy for the fairest flower of them all."

Arianne stared at the flower. Ian had given her such flowers. Ian, who no longer walked this earth, whom she remembered with a terrible twist of guilt. She nearly turned away, but she could not do that to Cameron, who had picked it for her with sweet compliments.

With a shaky hand, Arianne took hold of the stem. "*Une marguerite*," she whispered, as memories, some pleasant, some horrible, crowded her mind. Ian used to call her his Marguerite.

"What did you say?" Cameron's words snapped. All gentleness had left his face. In its place was an intensity that made his eyes appear like two burning flames and his mouth a slash of dark anger.

Astonished at his sudden change in attitude, she repeated, "*Une marguerite*." She was startled out of her own murky thoughts. "It is the French name for such a flower."

"Ah, of course!" Cameron exclaimed as if some new truth about man's existence had suddenly been revealed to him. "*Une marguerite*. Marguerite," he muttered. "Why didn't I see that before?"

"See what?" His manner frightened her.

"Nothing." He smiled at her, but the expression was forced. His eyes were not truly looking at her, but at something else only he could see. "I have just solved a bit of a mystery," he murmured. He held out his arm, becoming the proper gentleman again, cool and polite. "Come, the sun is getting high, and it's getting too warm to be walking. I should return you to your home."

Arianne was relieved by his sudden decision to end their walk, and she was troubled by his questioning. What did he know of the significance of the simple flower called a marguerite? Again, she wondered if his connection to Shipley Hall was more than coincidence. No, coincidence was all it was. He could not know anything about her part in the tragedy that had occurred in that house. Forcing herself to put thoughts of that awful past out of her mind, she pasted a smile on her lips.

Although Cameron was as solicitous and courteous and charming as when they had started out that morning, he seemed distracted. Telling herself she should be relieved that he was not as attentive as he had been before, a part of her missed his warmth and the focus of his eyes on her alone. As they rode in the landau to her establishment on Milsom Street, they chatted about inconsequential things. Arianne made sure to fill any short stretches of silence, for she could not allow herself to think on the kiss they had shared, nor the significance of the daisy. If she dwelled on it, she would squirm in embarrassment and guilt. Lythmore smiled and responded in all the proper places, but his responses were cool. Yet, when they reached her door, his ardor returned full force. Taking her hand, he raised it to his lips. His eyes held her easily, solidly above the void that opened at her feet.

"Until we meet again, Arianne," he murmured.

"I do not think…" Suspended in mid-air above nothingness, she could not find the words to finish her thought.

"We *shall* meet again, you know." His smile dazzled and held marvelous secrets. "I have discovered wonderful things about you, Arianne de Vouvret."

His words made her tingle. The memory of their kiss made her burn. "I do not think…," she began again.

Turning over her hand, he kissed her palm. "Don't think," he advised. "Just feel and move with your feelings." He smiled, let go of her hand, and tipped his hat. "*A bientôt*, Madame de Vouvret. Until we meet again." Turning, he sauntered away.

Arianne watched him for a moment, then opened her door and entered her salon. Her mind was dazed with what had occurred. Her feet did not seem to touch the ground as she floated up the stairs to her rooms above. As she removed her hat before the looking glass, she could not remember the steps she had taken to get from her door to where she stood at that moment.

Focusing finally at the face that stared back at her, a cry escaped her lips at what she had done. She had allowed herself to be swayed into feeling by a dazzling smile, a hypnotic pair of eyes. She could not let that happen again — ever. She could not let her emotions and personal needs cloud what she must do. She had to keep Luc and Papa safe. The only way to do that was to remain aloof and keep her feelings locked up deep within her. Nothing, no one, would unlock that door, no woman, no man. *No man.* Not even the Duke of Lythmore.

Her gaze fell on the flower he had plucked and so gallantly presented to her. A daisy — *une marguerite.* One in her past had called her that. *"Tu es ma marguerite,"* he had said many times. *You are my daisy.* At that time, she had laughed gaily, enjoying the admiration of such a handsome man, even knowing she would betray him. But never, never had she believed the end would be so tragic, so terrible, so evil. Never had she believed the man would die.

That serpent of guilt writhed within her so strongly that she had to lean on the tiny table before her for support. She could not go on like this. If only she could run away and hide in some faraway city, but she could not. Little Luc and Papa needed her. She could not leave them to Pinard. Somehow, she had to find a way out of that madman's clutches. But she could see none.

Frustrated, angry, trapped, she snatched up the daisy, crushed it, and flung it from her. She wished the flower were Pinard. Striding to where it landed, she stomped on it and mashed it beneath her toe. Again and again, she brought her foot down on the poor, bruised daisy until it was only a stringy pulp.

With her anger expended, she gazed down at what she had done. Cameron, who had nothing to do with what had occurred two years ago, had given this flower to her. Cameron, who had made her feel young and alive, whom she had kissed with such abandon. Cameron, who made her heart flutter and the earth disappear from beneath her feet. Cameron, whom she would never kiss again, for she could not allow any complication into her life.

One petal had escaped her wrath, and she plucked it from the floor with gentle fingers. As if she carried a fragile bubble, she took the petal to a shelf that contained a few books. Pulling down a copy of Jane Austen's *Pride and Prejudice*, she placed the petal lovingly between the book's pages. Miss Austen would understand her feelings, she decided, and would safely keep this simple token of a lost opportunity.

Feeling calmer, she replaced the book on the shelf and called her maid to fetch something to clean the mess she had made.

Cameron returned to his house in the Royal Crescent. Although outwardly, he was smiling and pleasant, inwardly, his thoughts seethed and roiled. The woman for whom he searched was not named Marguerite at all. The name had been only a pet name that his brother had given to her. How was he going to find this woman and destroy her as she had destroyed his brother?

Ian had never described the woman. He had only mentioned her name once or twice, and then had gone on to extol her virtues, never her physical appearance. She was modest and kind. She was alluring, but not a flirt. She was intelligent and talented. Who could she be? He had met the Baroness Souffant, and he remembered that the Viscount Ayles's wife, whom he had met at the theater several nights ago, was a French emigrée. But perhaps the woman had not been French at all. Perhaps her accent had been a sham, a ruse to lure his brother into her trap.

His thoughts wandered back to Arianne de Vouvret, Arianne with the changeable eyes and lush mouth. The sweet memory of their kiss made his lips curve in a smile. She took his breath away and made his blood sing with the intensity of her passion, a passion she held so tightly within her that when she let it loose, it exploded like a huge fireworks display. He longed to be the one to see that passion completely explode.

Yet, he sensed that she would not unleash it easily. Today, he had surprised her into letting down her guard, but that would not always happen. In the future, she would be more cautious, more controlled, more reluctant to be relaxed with him. Something made her wary and reserved. Something about close relationships frightened her. Perhaps the death of her husband caused her constraint. Or perhaps it was something else.

He thought back to their first meeting and her sudden faintness when he had introduced himself. He remembered that morning when he had accompanied Sally to her establishment and the messenger had arrived — that strange messenger with the haughty attitude. He recalled Sally's explanation of the bit of parchment with its wash of colors and snatch of letters across the bottom. These were all odd occurrences. If he coupled those with the fact of Arianne's French accent and her explanation of the French name for a daisy, did he end up with a correct total? Was Arianne the woman he sought?

He shied away from the idea. Coincidence. That was all it was. Everything had a perfectly logical explanation that had nothing to do with the mystery woman. Arianne's swoon could have been a result of the heat and long hours. The messenger was merely a churlish fellow who should be dismissed. The bit of parchment was nothing more than a dress design being smuggled across the Channel. Arianne just happened to be French, and of course, she would know the name of a daisy in her own language.

He would continue to investigate her as well as the other French emigrées in the city. Any one of them could be the woman he sought. His brother's Marguerite might not be Arianne at all.

Having put off his suspicions about the woman with whom he had shared a kiss with such abandon, he whistled as he entered his townhouse and loped up the stairs. When he reached the floor where the bedchambers were, he was met with mass confusion. Dresses, shoes, petticoats, and piles of various other pieces of clothing and accessories were scattered over every bit of furniture. Two maids hustled back and forth between the drawing room and Sally's bedchamber. He heard Sally giving orders, admonishing, and exclaiming in exasperation. When one of the maids noticed him, she stopped short, causing the other maid to barrel into her. After disentangling themselves, they both bobbed a curtsey and scuttled to the bedchamber to announce his arrival. Sally appeared immediately, walking with no hint of a twisted ankle.

"Darling," she greeted him a bit breathlessly. "I did not expect you to arrive back so soon. Please forgive the confusion." She waved her hand gracefully about her.

"So you are moving out," Cameron observed.

Sally pursed her lips, and her large, expressive eyes darkened. Without another word, she walked to him, took his arm, and guided him to a sofa. Pushing aside the billowing mass of silks and satins, she pulled him down beside her.

"You know," she said as she took his hand between both of hers, "that I have a great fondness for you." She shook her head. "No, my feeling for you is stronger than that, but we have both moved on." As Cameron opened his mouth, she placed her fingers against his lips. "Shush, my darling, and let me finish. We will always be friends, you and I, because of what we shared when we were so very young. But I am not so young anymore. I must see to my future. I wish to settle down, find a husband, perhaps have children. I am moving to my own suite of rooms."

Taken aback by Sally's sudden decision to depart, he argued, "But you are supposed to be my widowed cousin under my protection."

"I have hired a woman who will be my companion," she said. "Everything will be quite proper. You may say, if you are asked, that I wished to set up my own household here in Bath."

Skepticism created a line between his brows. "I see."

Sally dimpled. "No, you do not see at all. Mr. Ramsey—Tandy—has asked if he might call on me. And the Marquis de Pagière has been most attentive while you have been mooning over Madame de Vouvret."

"I have not, as you say, been 'mooning' over Madame de Vouvret," he contradicted with some heat. "I know nothing about this Ramsey fellow. Let me look into his family and resources for you. And I did ask you to be careful regarding that Frenchman."

Sally tinkled a laugh. "I have been very careful, darling. I have taken rooms in Cavendish Crescent."

"I do not like it," Cameron grumbled.

A mischievous smile curled Sally's lips. "I do believe you are jealous, your grace, Duke of Lythmore."

Was he? No, but he had always regarded Sally with a great deal of fondness and had looked upon her lovers as passing fancies. Perhaps he did think of her as a favorite cousin, with more truth to their ruse in Bath than he realized. Cameron shook his head. "I am not in the least bit jealous. I wish you all the happiness you can find. I just don't trust de Pagière."

"Ah." Sally nodded knowingly. "I shall be very careful, and I will still help you in any way I can."

Cameron's eyes narrowed in speculation. "You know, this move may be rather fortunate. You would be able to give me details about the connections and movements of the marquis."

Sally's brows rose. "Do you think he had something to do with Ian's death?"

"I don't know, but I feel the answer to the mystery is here in Bath. Somehow, I'll find the people responsible and bring them to justice." Resolutely, his mouth thinned into a line.

"I hope you do find them, darling." Sally patted his hand. "I wish I could have helped more. Attending Madame de Vouvret's salon has not given me one tiny bit of information."

Mention of Arianne's name brought back the delightful memory of their stroll through Crescent Fields. And it brought back his suspicions that he had tried to push from his mind. If she were the mystery woman he sought, then he wanted to know now, before he entwined himself any deeper with her. An idea popped into his head.

"There is something else you can do for me," he said. "I would like you to keep attending Madame de Vouvret's salon, but instead of just listening for bits of information, I would like you to let Madame de Vouvret in on a little secret."

And he told her exactly what he wanted her to say.

CHAPTER 5

"…For sweetest things turn sourest by their deeds; Lilies that fester smell far worse than weeds."

Arianne tried not to squirm as Mrs. Sally Turner finished reciting Shakespeare's *Sonnet 94*. Applause rippled through her salon while Sally dropped into a deep curtsey. Cameron's cousin had offered to do a recitation for Arianne's guests at her weekly salon. Now, after listening to the last poem, she wished she had not been so gracious, for the words of the sonnet seemed to be directed at her and her dark secret. Telling that serpent of guilt to be quiet, she moved forward to congratulate and thank the woman as the other guests began to chat and mingle.

Sally dimpled at Arianne's compliment. "You have been very kind to me and made me feel quite welcome, madame. Please, call me Sally."

Arianne smiled politely at the offer of friendship, but the twinges of guilt brought on by Sally's recitation kept her from returning the favor. This woman was the cousin of the man who had purchased Shipley Hall. The man who made the earth disappear beneath her feet. The man who thought she was merely a simple, innocent modiste. She tried to tell herself that she had no business pining after a man — and that man in particular — when she must keep her wits about her. Instead, she only succeeded in falling deeper into the pit of regret.

Sally threaded her arm through Arianne's. "May we go somewhere private and talk?" Sally asked quietly.

Arianne checked to see that her guests were well supplied with refreshments and engaged in enjoying each other's company. Satisfied that she could slip away for a few moments, she led Sally into the fitting room. A sofa and chairs with a low table before them were grouped against one wall for the comfort of her patrons. Arianne sat on one of the chairs. Sally stopped before the triple looking glass and turned this way and that as she admired her reflection.

"You have a magic touch with a needle, Arianne. May I call you Arianne? I feel so close to you even though we have known each other only a short time."

Calling each other by their given names meant they were friends. Arianne liked Sally and wanted to be friends with her, but she could not afford that luxury. She could not allow anyone to get close enough to be considered a friend, so she remained silent.

Without waiting for Arianne's response, Sally went on, "This dress is so flattering, not like some others I have acquired in London. They look lovely in the design, but when I put them on, I look like a frumpy sausage. I do wish you would bring your shop to London." She met Arianne's gaze in the mirror.

Arianne shook her head. "I couldn't do that. I have people here who depend on me. The move to London would be much too dangerous." As soon as she said the last word, she knew she had blundered. Why had that word popped out of her mouth?

"Dangerous?" Sally queried. "What an odd thing to say."

Arianne floundered with an explanation. "London is so busy, and the thieves and cutthroats are everywhere. Besides, I like Bath, and the quiet months of the winter when I can sketch new dress designs." She willed Sally to believe her explanation and not pursue the matter further. She could not move to London. Pinard would not allow it.

"Well, I believe you would have many more customers if you made the move." Sally sat in the chair beside Arianne. "The reason I wished to speak with you is…well…I want to ask you about the Marquis de Pagière."

Relieved that Sally had changed the subject, Arianne lied, "I do not know him very well."

Sally's brows rose in surprise. "But he is your countryman, isn't he? And I have heard you have dressed several of his mistresses."

"Yes, that is so." Arianne wished she had not dressed his mistresses. He always bought extravagantly, but paid very slowly in dribbling amounts, and sometimes not at all, especially when Pinard was not pleased with him.

"What kind of a man is he?" Sally demanded. "Is he kind? Generous?" She leaned close and whispered, "How does he treat his women?"

Arianne was taken aback at Sally's forthright questions and curious about why the woman would be asking about de Pagière. Was Sally considering a liaison with the Frenchman? That was definitely not a good idea. The man was depraved. But Arianne did not want to tell that to Sally, for it would reveal she knew more about him than was proper.

She answered vaguely, "I really couldn't say what kind of man he is."

"But surely you must know something of him," Sally pressed.

Arianne shrugged helplessly.

With a tiny frown, Sally scrutinized her a moment, then she smiled. "I understand. You are wondering why I am asking you such things." She rose and stood before the mirror again. "I feel as though I can confide in you, and you will be discreet. I am re-entering the world after my period of mourning. I find I am very attracted to de Pagière. Is he married?" Sally waved her hand in dismissal. "It does not matter. His wife need never know."

Arianne's heart stuttered at this announcement. Mrs. Turner was not looking for a husband. She was looking for an affair. Arianne wondered if she should do the same. No. Reality came crashing back. She could never do that. Her reputation would be ruined. And there was Pinard. She had to protect Luc and Papa. Her secret still caused that serpent of guilt to writhe within her.

"Are you certain you know so little about de Pagière?" Sally was asking. "You must know more about him than I do."

Arianne wanted to lie and tell Sally that the Frenchman was rich, rich, rich, that he was the kindest man on the face of the earth, that he would be the most wonderful protector for her in the world. But she could not. Her conscience wouldn't allow it. She nearly laughed aloud at that, for she had been forced to silence her conscience for two years over what she had done.

"Isn't your cousin, Lythmore, making inquiries about him?" she asked, trying to avoid an answer.

Sally turned to face her. "Well, of course he is." Her voice dropped to a conspiratorial level. "But, you know, women share things that a man just wouldn't discover." She pirouetted back to face the glass and poked a curl back into its perfect place. "I thought since we have decided to become friends, you might be willing to share your opinion."

Watching Sally study her reflection in the glass, resentment flared in Arianne's chest. The woman moved through the world without a thought, while Arianne was bound to a hateful man in France who pulled her strings like a puppet master. Yet, even in her resentment, even in her need to keep her secret hidden, she could not bring herself to lie to the woman. Sally had decided they were friends, and Arianne had not had a friend in a very long time. Besides, she liked Sally and did not wish to see her caught up in de Pagière's net.

"De Pagière," she finally said, "is not as wealthy as he appears."

Sally stopped her preening and turned to look at her. "No?" Thoughtfully, she cocked her head. "Of course, you would know, wouldn't you, because of his debts to you. How then does he live so extravagantly?"

Arianne shrugged again. "I couldn't say." She knew the woman did not believe her, but she would not tell her more. Before Sally could question her further, she stood. "I really must return to my guests. They will wonder what has become of me."

"Of course." Sally linked her arm through Arianne's again as they strolled back across the fitting room. "You have been most helpful, you know. A girl can't be too careful when she is choosing the men in her life. I find de Pagière a charming man, but perhaps I should look elsewhere. I have been sternly cautioned by Mr. West on that account."

"Mr. West?" Arianne queried weakly. The name brought a cold fear that clutched at her insides.

"Oh, forgive me." Sally tinkled a laugh as they emerged back into the salon with the chattering women. "It is my cousin, Lythmore. When I was quite young, I used to tease him by calling him that. West is his family name, but of course, since he gained his title, he has not used it."

82

"Oh, of course," Arianne murmured.

She had to get away, be alone before she made a fool of herself. Forcing her frozen lips into a smile, she excused herself with a mumbled explanation about seeing to the refreshments and fled the room. Stumbling into her office, she closed the door behind her and leaned against it. Her stomach rolled and pitched as if she were standing on the deck of a ship. Nauseated, she moved to a chair and sat down heavily. *It could not be.* Cameron, Duke of Lythmore, was the brother of —. No, she could not even think it. The thought was too monstrous.

Yet, the thought stayed with her. It niggled and nagged and brought that serpent of guilt out of hiding once more. The fact that Cameron and Ian West were brothers explained many things — the fact that Cameron had bought Shipley Hall, the odd sense of familiarity she had when she'd first met him, and his sudden interest in the daisy called *une marguerite*. Cameron was Ian's brother, and he knew of her involvement in Ian's death. That was why he had come to Bath — to seek her out, destroy her.

He knew.

Icy cold, in sharp contrast to the heat of the day, made her shiver and rub her arms. Panicky, she stood and began to pace the small room. He knew, and she had to find a way to protect herself and Luc and Papa. Back and forth, back and forth she paced while her thoughts flew in a hundred directions at once. What to do? What to do?

Her glance fell on her open appointment book and brought back the memory of their first meeting. Had he known then, she wondered, when he had handed her his letter of introduction? Or had he known at Sydney Gardens, when he had lifted her to the seat of his curricle and driven her home? Or had he known last Sunday, when they had walked in Crescent Fields?

No. He did not know. He could not know. His ardor had been too obvious, too real. He could not hide his feelings that well, she was sure. If he knew, he would hate her, despise her. He would not be able to kiss her with such passion. His desire, his ardor had been real, she was sure.

She was sure.

Her panic slowly subsided. She drew in a few deep breaths and regained her composure. She had to be very careful now that she knew Cameron was Ian's brother. One small mistake on her part could destroy her, could ruin Luc's life, could bring Pinard's evil down on Papa's head. She could not risk that. She would not be able to see Cameron West, Duke of Lythmore, again.

With her decision made, she quelled her pang of deep disappointment at the loss. She had no right to expect she should be able to feel or to love like other women, for she had to protect those who were so dear to her. Her spine straightened, and her chin went up. Taking another deep breath, smoothing down her skirt, she opened the door to her office and rejoined her guests with a smile fixed on her lips.

Cameron stood outside the door to the Pump Room as his eyes became accustomed to the bright sun. He congratulated himself on what had just occurred inside during a game of Whist. Although he had lost a goodly sum, he had been invited to invest in a mining venture for diamonds in India. A similar venture, which had lost a substantial amount, had been offered to his brother, Ian, just before he had died. Cameron had covered the debt but had been unable to discover the names of the other investors, or who had launched the venture. Now, since he had been offered a nearly identical opportunity, all he had to do was wait and watch to see what would happen. If the venture suspiciously lost capital, then he would know that the persons involved had also been involved with his brother's destruction.

A pony cart and a flash of yellow and white caught his attention. His blood pumped faster at the sight of Arianne. His delight at seeing her obscured his suspicions. As he stepped out into the street, she stopped beside him.

"Madame de Vouvret, what a pleasant surprise." He tipped his hat politely.

"Your grace." Her smile was tremulous, and her face seemed unusually pale. "You really must forgive me if I do not stay and chat. I am in a great hurry."

"Perhaps I can be of some assistance?" he asked. "I could drive your cart for you."

"No!" Her eyes flashed alarm at his suggestion. She bit her lip, glanced away down the road, then back at him. "No, thank you," she said more calmly. "That is very kind of you, but I must decline your offer."

Her distress touched him. Her fright made him suspicious. Despite that, Cameron wanted to comfort her. "Arianne, is something wrong? Can I help you in some way?" If she allowed him to help, he might discover why she seemed so distraught.

She shook her head. "There is nothing wrong. Why should there be?" She laughed, but the laughter had a ragged edge. "Please, I must be going."

Cameron refused to let her go. "Arianne, I want to see you again."

His announcement appeared to upset her even more, as if she would urge her pony into a gallop. "No, I can't. I mustn't."

Disappointment stabbed through him. He wanted to enjoy her company again. And he needed to discover if she was the woman he sought. "Don't tell me no, Arianne. Say yes. Do it without thinking. Just feel." He took her hand and caressed the bare skin just above her glove with his thumb. Her tiny gasp was all the answer he needed. Smiling up at her, he allowed her fingers to slip away. "Until we meet again, Arianne."

Her lips trembled with her smile, and he thought he caught the shimmer of tears in her eyes as she snapped the reins and drove away.

Cameron watched her disappear down the road and wondered at her haste and her obvious distress. Once again, his suspicions reared up. He wanted to follow her, but he had walked to the Pump Room, so he had no horse or carriage. Her pony cart was already turning out of sight. Where was she going in such a hurry? Why was she so distressed? Despite the questions, he wished he could wipe the uneasiness from her eyes. He wanted to stroke away the tiny lines from between her brows, the tenseness from her shoulders. He wanted to do much more than hold her hand. The feel of her skin beneath his thumb and the thought of her smile brought back to mind their delightful walk in Crescent Fields. The memory of the kiss they had shared and the hint of her wild, unbridled passion made the blood pulse through his veins. Like some hot-blooded youth, he stared after her long after she had gone.

Then he remembered the daisy. *Une marguerite.* He tried to bring back the memory of how she had reacted when he gave her the flower, but all he could see was her distress over their kiss. He had no reason to suspect her more than any of the other French women in the city.

As he walked to his townhouse, his mind soared on a flight of fancy as he contemplated the elusive and lovely Arianne. He would enjoy finally breaking down all her barriers, unlocking all her secrets, and having her reveal herself completely to him. His fantasy on the first day he had gone to her establishment with Sally rose up in his mind. He envisioned Arianne with her hair tumbled about her shoulders, in the moonlight, in only her chemise. He saw her eyes, changeable and glowing with desire.

Foolish. Absurd. His fantasy ended as he caught himself standing on the step before his building, with his hand on the door latch, and not knowing how long he had been there. He chided himself on his brainless wanderings. He could not allow himself to be distracted from his purpose in Bath, not even by an alluring, mysterious woman. When he opened the door, he was met by Sally. Obviously, she had not yet made the move to her own lodgings.

"Oh, Cameron, darling, I did just as you told me," she announced. "I asked Madame de Vouvret about the Marquis de Pagière, but you know, she would not tell me much at all, only that the man is not as wealthy as he appears. But the strangest thing happened when I called you Mr. West. The oddest expression came over her. Why, she actually turned green, as if she were about to be ill!"

Cameron was brought up short by this last bit of news. Did the mention of his family name trigger her discomfort? Had the bit of information that Sally dropped been that terrifying?

Suspicion rose up like a dark bird of prey. If Sally's information frightened Arianne and caused her to race out of the city, then perhaps she was the mystery woman who had been involved with Ian. Regret tightened his chest. Excuses popped in his head. Perhaps her haste had been caused by something entirely different, like a suddenly sick friend.

Frustrated, he only half-listened to the rest of Sally's report of Arianne's afternoon salon. What was wrong with him? He had never been so undecided about someone he suspected. Somehow, he had to discover exactly where Arianne had gone in such a hurry so late in the day. If he could learn that, he might be able to decide if Arianne were innocent or a conniving Jezebel.

That night, One-Armed Lewis sat amid the pile of scraps deep in the shadows of the fancy dressmaker's shop. Afraid to move, afraid almost to breathe, he tried to make himself as invisible as possible as he peeked across a tumble of black crepe. The gent still stood in the shadows across the way. But this wasn't the same one as the other night. One-Armed Lewis willed him to leave so he could go about his own business of gleaning the best of the pieces of cloth from the scrap heap. He fingered the black crepe. Probably not much worth the taking. Some rich cove must have hopped off so all his women would have to be dressed like crows. Those high-toppers had some strange habits. When he went to his reward, he wanted all of Mrs. Wiggit's girls to throw a great blow-out and wear their best frills, like some of the scraps he sold them.

Bored with the black crepe, he turned his attention to the bloke again. He had been standing there since just after midnight, just after One-Armed Lewis had come around to look for scraps. Lewis had to hide in the refuse and hadn't had a chance to rummage through it. He was without a bit of cloth to show for the night. Frustrated, he peeked at the gent again. Only folks who had something to hide skulked about in the dark and shadows. Dressed like the other bloke, he was, in dark cape and hat, even though it was a clear night, not like the other night when the damp made a body's bones ache. But this bloke kept deeper in the shadows while he waited. The fancy dressmaker sure had some peculiar friends. They all wanted to hide until she showed up, then jump out at her.

One-Armed Lewis peered through the dark. There was just enough moonlight to catch the angle of the gent's face, the slant of his arm, the breadth of his shoulder. This one was better dressed than the other, but he looked just as dangerous, maybe even more deadly. Lewis narrowed his eyes. Something about this one made Lewis think he might be interested in knowing about the other bloke who had waited for the dressmaker. He wondered how much this one might be willing to pay for the information. From the looks of him, he could afford a pretty penny or two.

Greed made Lewis brave. Slowly, he slipped down to the back of the pile. He tried not to disturb anything so the gent wouldn't see him. Gaining his feet, he sidled about in the shadows until he reached the darkest spot where he could cross to where the gent stood. His heart pounded, and his mouth was dry. His knees shook beneath him. The thought of easy coin urged him on, and he scuttled into the open. Just as he gained the gent's side, his throat was gripped in a paralyzing hold, and his back was slammed against the brick wall. He heard the unmistakable hiss of a dagger eased from its sheath. The point of a very sharp knife pricked his neck. Lewis looked up into the dark eyes of the Devil himself. Blue sparks seemed to come from those eyes. Lewis thought he was surely about to die and enter hell.

"Who are you? What do you want?" the bloke demanded.

Lewis tried to answer, but all that came out was an unintelligible, strangled noise. The gent loosened his grip enough so Lewis could talk.

"Help," Lewis rasped.

"There's no help for you here," the gent told him coldly.

Lewis shook his head as much as he dared with the knife at his throat. "I can help."

"Help me part with my coin? With your friends hiding in the shadows? I think not, good fellow," the gent said smoothly.

"Help you. With the lady." Black spots erupted across Lewis's vision.

"How can you help me?" The question held an undertone of dark humor.

"Information."

The gent stared at him with those devil eyes for a long moment. Lewis wondered if he should start praying and asking forgiveness for his sins before he was sent to his eternal reward. Finally, the gent dropped his hand from about Lewis's throat and stepped back, but he still held the dagger within a whisper of Lewis's neck. Lewis sucked in a deep breath and blinked away those black spots.

"What information do you have?" the gent asked. "Anything concerning the lady who lives here?" He jerked his head toward the dressmaker's rooms.

"Won't be comin' back tonight." Lewis coughed and gulped air into his lungs.

"Where did she go?" The question snapped out.

Lewis shrugged, very carefully, because of that sharp dagger so close to his neck.

"Then how do you know she won't be back tonight?" Suspicion underscored every word.

"Went north, took the Camden Road. When she goes out o' th' city as late as she did on that road, she never comes back afore mornin'." Lewis squinted up at the gent. "Good information, right, guv?"

"How do I know you're telling the truth?" the gent asked coolly.

"I'm One-Armed Lewis! Ask anybody wot knows! Ain't nobody better at gettin' good information."

"What were you doing here, One-Armed Lewis?" The gent's question sounded more deadly because of his smooth tone.

Lewis squirmed a bit, but not too much because of that sharp knife. He decided he had better tell the truth. "Lookin' for scraps. Sells 'em to Mrs. Wiggit's girls, I do. A bloke has to make a livin', don't he?"

"So, you're here often?"

"Well, some." Lewis did not want to give away all his secrets.

"And you see who comes and goes?"

"Maybe." Lewis risked a shrug.

The gent finally lowered the knife. "How would you like to do some work for me, Lewis?"

Lewis wasn't sure he liked the sound of that. He had never done an honest day's work in his life. "Depends."

The gent reached into his pocket and flipped something up into the air. Lewis saw the gleam of a coin and snatched it out of the air. It was a half-crown.

"Wot you want me t'do?" Lewis was impressed by the gent's generosity.

"Watch this place. If anyone comes to visit the lady at night, or if the lady goes out at night, I want to know. Every time you bring me information, I'll pay you. Do we have a deal?"

Lewis considered for a moment, then nodded. This gent would be interested to learn of the other bloke that came at night. He wondered how much this gent would pay for that information. It was easy money, and he could think of many ways to spend it. Why he might even have enough to afford one of Mrs. Wiggit's girls. "Where can I find you?"

"Go to the sign of the Boar and Stag and ask for Mr. West. The barkeep will tell you what to do."

"Right enough, gov. A deal it is." He stuck out his hand.

The gent shook it firmly. "I'll expect to hear from you, Lewis. Don't disappoint me."

"The sign of the Boar and Stag," Lewis repeated to reassure the bloke. "Ask for Mr. West."

When the gent gave a nod, sheathed his knife, and finally walked away, Lewis gave a great sigh of relief. He was sure he had been about to meet his Maker. Instead, he had made some gelt. Glancing first in the direction the gent had gone to make sure he was no longer in sight, Lewis held up the coin in the slant of moonlight that seeped between the buildings. The coin seemed real, but he would look closer in the daylight. For now, he pocketed it and turned his attention to the scrap pile. The black crepe spilled over everything. Lewis decided there was no point in looking for any more scraps. He had his coin, and in a day or two, he could go to the sign of the Boar and Stag and ask for Mr. West. Then he could sell the gent the information about the other bloke who had waited in the shadows for the fancy dressmaker.

Two nights after her salon, when Mrs. Sally Turner had revealed Lythmore's family name, Arianne stood just inside her door and pulled the hood of her cloak over her head. The knowledge that Ian West was Cameron's brother sat in the back of her mind like a looming gargoyle, but she could not let it dissuade her from what she had to do.

Blowing out the single candle on a small table beside her, she eased open the door. She did not expect to see anyone, for it was the dead of night, in the hour after midnight, but she had to be sure. No one could see her performing this deed, for her reputation would be ruined if she were seen. The alley appeared deserted. Clutching the dress design close to her beneath her cloak, she slipped out the door.

She had only taken a few steps when a sound made her freeze. Goosebumps puckered on her arms, and the hairs on the back of her neck rose up. There it was again. It came from her right, from somewhere near the refuse pile. The sound was odd, raspy, husky, drawn out. She was sure she had never heard anything like it before.

The sound came a third time. Holding her breath, she tiptoed closer to the pile of discarded scraps of cloth. She heard the sound a fourth time and discovered its source. One-Armed Lewis was asleep, snoring in the middle of the pile. Annoyed that he should take such liberties and scare her half to death besides, she reached out to nudge him awake and order him to be off. Her hand stayed before she touched him. If she woke him, he would see her leave to perform her errand. Not even Lewis should see that.

Quietly, she stepped away. Careful not to make any noise, she hurried down the alley toward the street. She frequently checked over her shoulder to make sure she was not followed.

Lewis did not follow her, but her heart raced with dread at being seen as she slipped in and out of the shadows. Stopping occasionally in a dark doorway, she watched to see if anyone followed. Not only was she fearful of possible discovery by one of her acquaintances, but the threat of violence from cutthroats looking for mischief was very real.

She was angry at de Pagière for forcing her to bring the dress design to him at such a hideous time. They had exchanged notes three times before he demanded she come on this night at this hour. This was not the proper hour for a well-respected modiste to be out on the streets. Besides, she was tired. She had arrived back from her visit with Luc very early that morning and had been awake and working ever since. All she wanted was to complete her task and go home to bed.

A couple approached from the opposite direction. The woman hung on the man's arm, and they walked so closely together that they appeared like a fat, two-headed monster. Arianne heard the coarse laughter of the woman. This was no respectable couple out for a stroll. Even so, she pulled her hood closer about her face and ducked her head so she would not be recognized. As she passed, the man tipped his hat and murmured a greeting. Arianne did not acknowledge him. She hurried on.

Around a corner, down another street, across a road, up a hill. Finally, she stood before the door to de Pagière's townhouse. A light burned in the front room. Checking to make sure no one observed her, she lifted the knocker and let it fall. The noise seemed unusually loud in the still night. A moment passed, then the door opened. She was surprised to see the Marquis de Pagière himself standing in the doorway and not his butler.

"Ah, *bon soir*, Madame de Vouvret," he greeted. "How very pleasant of you to visit this evening."

"Let me in, Jules," she snapped. "I don't wish to be seen standing in the street outside your door."

Chuckling, the marquis stepped back and waved her into the house. "You are much too concerned with what others think of you, my dear Arianne. Please, come into my drawing room and refresh yourself with a bit of wine." Without waiting for her to answer, he closed the door and led her deeper into the house to an open doorway where light spilled out. As Arianne followed him across the threshold, he said, "Monsieur le Duc de Lythmore and I were just discussing that very notion of reputations and how they can so easily be ruined."

Arianne halted abruptly as she saw Lythmore rise from a chair. She wanted to run, hide, disappear. What must he think of her, coming to the house of the marquis, alone and at such an hour? His expression gave nothing away, except he did not smile that wonderful, dazzling smile. Instead, his brows rose quizzically, and his eyes were cool. Somehow, she found her voice.

"Your grace." She bobbed a curtsey. "What a surprise to find you here."

"No more of a surprise than seeing you arrive at the door of the marquis at such an hour," he said.

"I invited Lythmore for a late supper," de Pagière explained. He moved behind Arianne and placed his hands on her shoulders. "May I take your cloak, madame?"

She saw Cameron's eyes narrow at the marquis' familiar gesture. Stepping away from the Frenchman, she said, "I won't be staying, thank you, Monsieur le Marquis. I only came to…" To do what? Dismay froze her. Should she give the dress design to the marquis and pretend that it was nothing more than what it appeared? Surely Cameron would think it very odd for her to be delivering such an item *to a man* at such a late hour. But she could think of no logical reason for her to be knocking at the door of a man's house in the middle of the night, except for the most obvious one—that she was arriving for a secret rendezvous.

Cameron placed his glass of brandy on the table beside him. "I must be leaving, de Pagière. I would not wish to interfere with any business you wish to discuss with Madame de Vouvret." His emphasis on the word "business" made clear what he thought that might be.

"We have no business to discuss," Arianne said, then realized how suggestive her words sounded. "I mean, we—de Pagière and I—" Lost in her quagmire of explanation, she turned to the marquis for help.

De Pagière merely smiled pleasantly. When he said nothing, and the silence coming from Cameron was so heavy she felt its weight on her shoulders, she decided to rely on the truth, the part she could tell. Holding out the rolled parchment bearing the dress design, she said, "I came to deliver this."

"Ah, yes, the dress design," de Pagière chuckled. "And here I thought you were coming to sweeten my night, dear Madame de Vouvret."

"Dress design?" Cameron's tone dripped disbelief.

The marquis unrolled the parchment and held it up for Cameron to see. "*Voilà*. For my new paramour. Delightful, *n'est-ce pas?*"

"This is a very strange hour to be delivering dress designs," Cameron observed.

She decided the only way to convince him was to act insulted. "Your grace, I am a very busy woman. The only time I could discreetly deliver this design to monsieur le marquis was at this hour. I was out of the city last night and did not return until quite early this morning."

"I hope your evening was spent pleasantly, madame." De Pagière's tone was mild, but his gaze brimmed with curiosity.

She realized she had made a grave mistake in speaking of her trip to visit Luc in front of the marquis. He obviously thought she was meeting a secret lover.

"A visit to a sick friend, wasn't it, madame? I do recall how troubled you were when I saw you yesterday." Cameron offered an easy explanation.

"*Oui*, yes, that was it." Arianne flashed him a grateful smile. Pulling her cloak close about her, she nodded to both men. "I must be leaving, gentlemen. Monsieur le Marquis, please let me know if you wish any changes in the design."

"Allow me to accompany you to your home, madame." Cameron stepped forward.

"No, no, monsieur. Do not trouble yourself." The last thing Arianne wanted was his company. She had too many secrets she must hide from him.

"It is no trouble." He took another few steps forward. "You should not be out alone at this hour."

"Please, your grace, I prefer to walk by myself. The night is pleasant, and I do not live far." With another smile, she fled from the room.

The marquis followed and caught up with her at the door. "Why not stay, Arianne, and let us enjoy your company?"

Arianne turned on him in anger. "You cad, Jules. Why did you invite him when you knew I would be delivering the design?"

"Because I wanted him to know that you are not the virtuous, innocent modiste that he thinks you are." His words snaked out with smooth malice.

"You are a swine, Jules," she hissed.

He laughed and took her hand. "I have been called worse things, but none by so lovely a woman as you, dear Arianne." He raised her hand to his lips.

Snatching her hand from his grasp, she pulled open the door and fled into the night. She heard his satisfied chuckle as she hurried away down the street.

CHAPTER 6

Arianne met the duke again two days later. She had accompanied Sir Roderick and Lady Crump, Mrs. Weathersby, and Miss Barbara to a performance of the new opera, *The Barber of Seville*, composed by Gioachino Rossini. Everyone who was anyone was at the Theater Royal this evening. She should have realized she would meet the Duke of Lythmore. She had been stupid to think she would never see him in the crush of the crowd. But her mind had not been functioning properly for the past several days, ever since she had learned that the owner of Shipley Hall was the brother of the man she had helped destroy.

The surprise of seeing him at de Pagière's townhouse had rattled her even more. Even if he did not know for certain that she was involved in his brother's death, then surely his opinion of her had dropped a hundredfold when she showed up on de Pagière's threshold at such an hour. What had Pinard been thinking when he ordered the marquis to replace Courcy as her messenger? Pinard obviously wanted to show his control over her, for he knew the sort of man de Pagière was — debauched, depraved, and perverted. And what had de Pagière been trying to accomplish by having Cameron at his house when she arrived with the dress design? That had been reckless. What if Lythmore already suspected her? Surely, the odd circumstances would make him more suspicious.

Fear had been her constant companion since her salon last Tuesday. Dread had followed her since she had delivered the dress design. Sleepless nights had become the norm.

She had been able to contain her panic enough to get through life as if nothing disturbing had happened. On the outside, she appeared her usual cool, contained self. She smiled serenely at all her clients. She suggested this chambray gauze over that watered silk. She urged her seamstresses to make their fingers fly for a distraught customer, lately arrived from America, who had lost her complete wardrobe overboard in a storm.

On the inside, however, panic gripped her with a steely claw. That was why, on last Tuesday afternoon, as soon as the guests at her afternoon salon had departed, she had flown out of Bath to be with Luc. She had needed to see his dear face, to hear his sweet laughter, to believe that he, at least, did not hold her accountable for her past sins. As she had driven out of the city, seeing Lythmore standing before the Pump Room had nearly given her heart failure. His smile had been warm, reaching out to her and caressing her chilled heart. She had no memory of how she had acted. He did not seem offended, so she must have observed the rules of etiquette. She did not remember much of that wild ride out of the city to the Inglis's cottage except the feeling that the dogs of hell were after her. Only when she tightly hugged Luc had her panic subsided enough for her to think more normally. Seeing the duke again in de Pagière's drawing room had unnerved her even more. Only by burying herself in her work could she keep the demons of terror at bay. Now, in the lobby of the theater, with Miss Barbara at her side, Cameron, Duke of Lythmore, stood before her again, and that anxiety rose up in her so strongly she could barely breathe.

"Madame de Vouvret, Miss Barbara," he greeted them with a bow. "Are you enjoying the opera?"

"Oh, yes," Miss Barbara exclaimed. "The story is so delightful, and the music has the most wonderful melodies. Why, some of the other composers will fairly put one to sleep with their tranquil measures, but Mr. Rossini certainly knows how to stir the soul."

"I daresay he does." Cameron nodded, then turned to Arianne with his dazzling smile. "And you, Madame de Vouvret, does he stir your soul, also?"

Although merely a polite question, the undercurrent of meaning in his words was unmistakable to Arianne. Swallowing down her panic, telling her traitorous, fluttering heart to behave, she forced her lips into a smile. "I find all music stirring, your grace."

His answering smile conveyed more than just friendliness, as if he knew the conflicting emotions running rampant through her. As he was about to say something else, they were interrupted.

"There you are!" Mrs. Weathersby puffed up to them. She simpered a greeting to Lythmore, then took her daughter by the arm. "Come along, Barbara, there is someone you absolutely must meet before intermission is over." She excused them and hurried the young woman away.

Arianne looked after them with longing. The last thing she wanted was to be left alone in the company of the man before her. She had exposed too much of herself on that walk they had shared in Crescent Fields. She had allowed him to peek into the hidden corners of her soul. He no doubt considered her late-night visit to de Pagiére a foiled lovers' tryst. And she had learned he was brother to the man she had helped destroy. What if he discovered her dark secret? Her panic rose up from her belly.

"May I get you a glass of champagne, Madame de Vouvret?" Cameron's question brought her a tiny flicker of relief.

"Oh, yes, that would be delightful." She hardly ever drank champagne, but she thought she would be able to disappear while Lythmore went to fetch it. He stepped into the crowd. She waited, nodding and smiling at acquaintances, for the perfect moment to slip away.

Abruptly, he appeared before her again. "What luck! I found a waiter." He held out a glass of the pale, bubbly liquid. "Your champagne, Madame de Vouvret."

Arianne took the glass with trembling fingers and sipped. The champagne tasted like water, but the bubbles popped reassuringly in her mouth. Somehow, they made her disquiet subside a bit. She took a larger swallow.

"Carefully, madame," Lythmore said. "Champagne seems like an innocent drink as the bubbles pop on your tongue, but when you have had your fill, you find yourself in a quagmire of inebriation. It's a bit like a person keeping secrets who gets tangled in lies."

Arianne covered her apprehension by asking coyly, "Is that a warning, your grace? Or perhaps you find yourself mired in secrets."

He smiled with good humor. "Everyone has secrets. I will divulge a secret if you will answer a question."

The champagne was making her incautious, perhaps even fool-hardy. She took another sip. "Why not, your grace? I am merely a modiste. I certainly could have nothing to hide." The lie fell easily from her lips.

His smile turned predatory. "Where were you going in such a rush when I saw you outside the Pump Room?"

Arianne searched frantically for an answer. Her little charade of being carefree and without mysteries had turned against her. She could not answer truthfully and reveal her son's existence. She didn't know if this man might use Luc as an instrument of his revenge if he ever discovered what she had done to Ian, his brother. Certainly, Pinard would have no qualms about doing so. Perhaps Lythmore might even pass along his knowledge of Luc's existence to Pinard in a twisted sort of retribution. No, she could not answer the truth. Never that.

"I was going for an afternoon ride." She took another sip of champagne.

Cameron's smile held knives. "You are lying, Arianne."

She choked and drew the attention of several people standing nearby. Fighting for her breath, she tried to come up with some other plausible answer. Cameron guided her to a quiet corner. After she regained her composure, she remembered what he had said at de Pagière's when they had been discussing that same excursion.

"I was going to visit a sick friend. You guessed as much at the home of the marquis," she said blithely.

His brow lowered. "I was saving your reputation, Madame de Vouvret, something that you seemed unconcerned with that night. But there was no sick friend you were going to visit, was there?"

Arianne covered her fear with annoyance. "I said I would answer your question, your grace, and I did. What you deem to be true is your own affair."

His mouth flattened. "You won't reveal any of your secrets to me, will you, Arianne?"

"Why should I?" she demanded. "What you consider my secrets are none of your concern." She glanced away as she attempted to keep her temper. Drawing a breath, she looked back at him. "I have told you where I was going, now it is your turn to reveal a secret. Are you here in Bath to take the waters? Do you have some hidden malady that no one knows about?" She took another sip from her glass.

"No, I have no malady. I came to Bath to look over my new property at Shipley Hall." He smiled then, a secret smile, a knowing smile, that same dazzling smile that had first muddled her brain. "I am staying because I find the society invigorating and very attractive." His eyes, those very dark blue eyes, looked directly into hers as if they could see down to her soul. "May I see you again?"

The question startled her, even though she knew it would come. Her answer the last time he had asked had not been decisive enough, and she knew how charmingly persistent he could be. She had dreaded his request at the same time she wanted to see him again. But she had prepared her answer. Her desires had nothing to do with her need for keeping her secrets safe. "I am sorry, your grace. I do not think that would be wise."

"Why is that, Madame de Vouvret?" A single brow shot up. "You did not seem to find my company offensive when we walked in Crescent Fields."

"I do not find your company offensive, your grace," she said coolly. "I merely believe that it is not appropriate for a modiste to socialize with a duke. Surely you can understand my feelings in this."

His brows drew together. "No, I do not understand your feelings at all, madame, especially when you betrayed your feelings for me with your kiss."

The heat rushed to Arianne's cheeks. "Your grace, please! A gentleman does not mention such things in public."

"I will mention them in public all I wish, especially to a woman who arrives alone, in the small hours of the night, at another gentleman's door." His tone challenged.

"You know why I was at de Pagière's." Arianne's temper began to rise.

"Delivering the dress design was a convenient excuse," he stated flatly.

"What are you accusing me of?" Her fear that he might discover her true errand made her heart pound.

"I am accusing you of having poor judgment," he said. "I have heard stories of the marquis and what goes on behind his doors."

She narrowed her eyes to cover her relief. "Then I wonder what you were doing at his house at such an hour, your grace. Were you perhaps engaging in some debauchery?"

"Gentlemen often engage in debauchery," he said coolly. "Ladies do not."

She scowled. "Perhaps not *ladies*, but I am not a lady. I am merely a modiste."

He shook his head. "No, you are more a lady than many of those who claim the title." He smiled. "Perhaps we are both guilty of poor judgment." His tone softened as he took her hand. "Arianne, I find myself quite attracted to you, as I believe you are attracted to me. I want to see you again. If you are concerned about gossip, we can be very discreet."

"No, your grace, I—"

"Lythmore!" The Marquis de Pagière stopped beside them. "I am delighted to see you again." The marquis bowed. "Madame de Vouvret, a pleasure as always." As he straightened, his glance fell on Arianne's hand, still in Cameron's clasp. "I am disturbing you. Forgive me." He cast an inquisitive look at Arianne.

She pulled her fingers from Cameron's hand. "Not at all, Monsieur le Marquis. His grace was merely speaking of gossip and how it can spread so quickly."

"Ah, I see." De Pagière's words were bland, but his gaze was sharp with speculation.

Before the marquis could comment further, a group of theatergoers surrounded them. Arianne knew some of the ladies as customers, and some of the gentlemen also, but they were there to invite Cameron to an after-supper gaming hell. Under cover of their chatter, while they had Cameron occupied, the marquis guided Arianne away.

"Have you reported your acquaintance with Lythmore to Pinard?" he demanded.

Of course she had not. She could not bring herself to give Pinard a chance to destroy another man. Fear grabbed at her. She could not afford to make Pinard angry, but she could not show that she was afraid before this man. He would surely note her weakness and use it for his own gain. Shrugging, she said casually, "I did not think it was important. I don't believe it's necessary to tell Pinard all that I do."

"*Au contraire, ma petite,*" he said mildly. "You must tell Pinard everything. He will not be pleased you have left that out of your last reports. His displeasure could cost your dear papa's life."

Arianne's fear made her snappish. "Do you always do as Pinard orders, de Pagière? Do you jump and beg when he speaks, like an obedient lapdog?"

The marquis shrugged philosophically. "*Hélas, ma petite,* some of us do not mind the task set us, for the reward is worth the toil."

"I find no reward in being forced to commit horrible atrocities." She frowned and glanced away.

"You must put aside your inhibitions, madame." He lightly touched the hand at her side.

She put another half-step between them. "My inhibitions, as you call them, keep me sane. I do not indulge in debauchery as you do, Monsieur le Marquis."

The Frenchman smiled benignly. "My debauchery gives me, as well as my bed partners, a great deal of pleasure, madame. Perhaps I could give you a few lessons in this delightful amusement."

She huffed an angry breath. "Is that what you hoped for when you had me deliver the dress design at such an ungodly hour?"

"My dear Arianne," he said smoothly. "You mistake my intention. I would never have supplied such lessons on your first visit. I do not rush into such things. No, they must be orchestrated and planned. The pain of anticipation is part of the pleasure. Someday, perhaps, I can teach you of such pleasure."

Arianne shivered. "I think not de Pagière. My pleasure will come from a man I love, or not at all."

"Foolish woman," he murmured.

Cameron's acquaintances drifted away, and he rejoined them. He glanced accusingly at Arianne. "Discussing dress designs?" he asked with sharp sarcasm.

Arianne's temper flared at his insinuation that her conversation with the marquis was more than casual. He obviously thought the reason for her late-night visit to the marquis had been amorous. Her fingers itched to slap both men, one for his jealousy, the other for his dominance.

Instead, she smiled sweetly at Lythmore. "We were discussing deep secrets, your grace. I am afraid they are just too dark and disturbing to reveal," she said, ironically using the truth to pretend she lied. At that moment, an usher came through the lobby, banging a small gong to announce that the next act of the opera was about to begin. "If you gentlemen will excuse me" she murmured and slipped away before either of them could offer to escort her back to her seat.

She was done with both men for the evening. The marquis, with his reminder of Pinard's vigilance, and Lythmore, with his insistence to learn everything about her, frayed her nerves. And now that she knew the connection between Cameron and Ian West, she wanted to curl into a tiny ball and disappear forever. All she wanted was to be left alone, to be able to live out her life quietly, taking care of her son and her father. All she wanted…

What she wanted did not matter. Her desires were of no consequence. What was important was keeping her father alive and the existence of her son hidden. So far, she had succeeded, but how long before the Duke of Lythmore discovered all her secrets?

Slipping into her seat next to Miss Barbara, she forced a smile at the young lady. She was relieved when the musicians began to play so she would not have to engage in idle chatter. Her head buzzed from her quandary and from the champagne she had consumed. Despite the fact that the opera was engaging, she found no solace in it. All she could concentrate on was the fact that she was caught in Pinard's evil web with no way of escape. Lythmore—Cameron—thought she was de Pagière's plaything. If he only knew that was the last thing she would ever become. The music soared around her, but all she wanted to concentrate on was the feel of Cameron's fingers as he held her hand, and the way his smile dazzled her beyond thought. But she could not dwell on those things. She had to stay away from him. She had to keep her secrets.

Later that evening, Arianne wearily unlocked her door and pushed it open. All she wanted was to undress and climb into bed. Meeting both Cameron and de Pagière had exhausted her. When an arm came out of the dark and reached around her to hold the door open, a cry of alarm escaped her lips.

"Quiet!" Edouard hissed. "Do you wish to wake up the whole city?"

With her hand at her throat, Arianne swallowed down her fear. "Don't sneak up on me like that if you don't want me to scream in fright." She took a breath to calm herself and allow her heart to return to its normal rhythm. "What are you doing here? I thought you were still in France."

"Inside, Madame de Vouvret," he commanded.

Arianne turned and obediently led him up the stairs and into her sitting room. Her maid dozed by the fire. Arianne shook her awake and sent her to fetch some tea. As the girl hurried off, she sent Edouard Courcy an accusatory glance.

"You have jeopardized us, Edouard," Arianne said. "I told you not to come here except when my shop is open for business. And now my maid is wondering about a man visiting me so late at night. Why are you here?"

Edouard took a turn about the room before he answered. "Pinard was not pleased to discover you withheld information from him."

She bluffed bravely, "What information? I have sent everything I have heard."

"Everything?" he asked. "What of everything you have seen? What of everyone?"

Arianne glanced away. She had not included news of the arrival of the Duke of Lythmore in any of her messages.

"You know Pinard punishes disobedience," Courcy stated.

Fear for her father's safety clutched at her. "He has not—that is, has he—?"

"Frightened, my little pet?" Edouard smirked. "You should be, you know. Monsieur Pinard has been very good to you."

"He has been no such thing," Arianne flared. "He is a monster, as you are, Edouard."

Edouard chuckled. "Not a monster, surely. You must come up with a more original description, Arianne."

Her fingers crushed the skirt of her gown, but that was the only outward sign of her hatred. "Is my father all right?"

"When I saw him, he was as peevish as ever." He removed his hat and tossed it on a table.

With relief, Arianne sank into a chair. She had been selfish when she had omitted the news of the arrival of Lythmore in Bath. Wanting to defy Pinard, she had thought only of her own satisfaction and not the danger in which she had placed her father. Now she realized how foolish she had been. Even so, the fact that Pinard had been the least bit upset was gratifying.

"You have escaped punishment this time, Arianne," Edouard noted. "Don't be so foolish again."

Arianne watched him wander aimlessly about the room as he touched a knick-knack here, straightened a candle there. His relaxed manner was at odds with the chill warning he had just issued. She sensed that he had more to say to her, but she knew from past experience that he would tell her what it was in his own time. Her nerves wound tighter and tighter as the moments ticked by. Finally, she could stand it no longer.

Jumping from her chair, she strode up to him. "Leave off your trifling, Edouard. What else do you wish to say?"

He turned to her with a cold smile. "My, my, you are the impatient one. So eager to do Monsieur Pinard's bidding."

"What does he want me to do?" She knew that whatever he would say next would not be pleasant.

"Pinard was so pleased with the way you handled the Ian West affair, that he would like you to help him in another small matter of a similar nature."

"No." Arianne turned away, hiding her disgust. "I can't do anything like that again. It was too foul."

"You will, you know," Edouard purred arrogantly. "Your obedience is inevitable."

A chill shivered down her spine at his tone. "I can't." She swung back to face him. "Please, Edouard, intercede for me. Tell him I will botch the whole thing. Tell him I am not up to the task. Tell him I will do anything else he asks."

"Anything, sweet Arianne?" Edouard reached out and ran his finger across the skin exposed by the deep décolletage of her gown.

Forcing down her distaste, she did not knock away his hand. "Anything."

He laughed in lecherous delight and dropped his hand. "Well, we shall have to look into that later, won't we?" He backed away a few steps as if not trusting himself to stand too close to his prize. "Monsieur Pinard was most adamant about this latest request. I don't think he will accept anything less than your complete compliance — unless, of course, you are willing to sacrifice your dear papa's life."

Arianne knew she was beaten. She could not risk her father's life over her own scruples. Keeping her father alive had to be her first priority. Nothing else mattered — except Luc. Whatever Pinard forced her to do, she hoped the Almighty would understand that she had no choice.

"What does he want me to do?" Her words were flatly resigned.

He shrugged with casual indifference. "It should not be difficult, nor a hardship for a lovely woman such as yourself. Monsieur Pinard would merely like you to become romantically involved with a certain gentleman. When this gentleman has succumbed sufficiently to your charms, then Pinard will tell you how to proceed."

Arianne could taste the bile rise up in her throat. What Edouard described was the exact course of events that had occurred with Ian West. Then, she had been too naïve to understand to what lengths Pinard would go. Now, she knew exactly what he would do, and the knowledge nauseated her.

Twice, she opened her mouth to speak, and no words came out. Finally, on the third try, she was able to ask, "What gentleman?"

"Why, the Duke of Lythmore, of course."

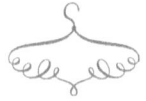

CHAPTER 7

Arianne urged the pony pulling her cart into a canter.

Why, the Duke of Lythmore, of course. The words of Edouard Courcy echoed in her brain over and over and over.

She could see the pony roll its eyes back at her as if in reproach. The poor animal hardly ever moved quicker than a trot.

Why, the Duke of Lythmore, of course. Of course. As if it were the most natural thing in the world.

A twinge of guilt at causing the animal some discomfort nagged her, but she did not slow the pace. She was impatient to see Luc.

Why, the Duke of Lythmore, of course. Lythmore… Cameron. Oh, Cameron!

All night, after Edouard had left, after she had fallen exhausted into bed, she had tossed and turned, worrying about her dilemma until she could no longer think. She could not commit another atrocity like the one she had committed with Ian. She could not do that to Ian's brother. She could not do that to Cameron. Not to Cameron. Yet, if she did not, then her father's life would be taken. What to do?

She did not see the passing scenery, the trees in their summer foliage, the hedgerows alive with the chirping of birds, the cultivated fields, the pastures dotted with wildflowers. All she could see was the horrific picture of Ian West, dead, dangling like a broken puppet above the entrance of Shipley Hall. Her nausea, a constant companion since the night before, threatened to overwhelm her. The pony stumbled and brought her attention back to the present. Slowing the pony to a walk, she drove the cart to the side of the road and onto the edge of a field.

She drew several deep breaths as she tried to get her emotions under control. Glancing at the tranquil scene, she realized she could not visit Luc in her present state. That would do neither of them any good. She was too distraught to pretend to be carefree with him, and Luc would sense something was wrong. Certainly, George and Bess Inglis would be able to see through any façade. They would question her out of concern, and she could not bear lying to them. She had too much deceit in her life already.

She became aware that her gaze rested on several towers that were visible above the treetops. They were part of an estate a mile or two away. It was the home of the old woman known to her only as the Countess. The mansion was secluded, surrounded by heavy woods and a very high stone wall. The gates would be closed and locked, guarded by an old gatekeeper who spent his days sitting in the sun and feeding the birds and small animals who lived in the woods. No one ever came to visit, and the Countess rarely if ever ventured forth. Arianne had been there only once, several months after she had arrived in England. Inside that fortress, attended only by the old woman, she had given birth to Luc.

The Countess had been the contact in England whom Pinard had used to help Arianne get settled and set up her dress-making business. With cold proficiency, the Countess had performed the task and then announced that she had emerged from her home only because Arianne was a woman in need of assistance and for no other reason. Even though Arianne's pregnancy hardly showed, when she had been only a few days in England, the Countess had guessed her condition and made her confess to it. In the last few months of her pregnancy, when Arianne could no longer hide her condition, the Countess had whisked her away to her estate and kept her in seclusion until after Luc's birth. Somehow, the woman had convinced Courcy that Arianne was ill and bed-ridden to keep him from asking too many questions. After Luc was born, the woman had found George and Bess Inglis to care for Luc and arranged for a wet nurse. When Arianne's strength had returned enough for her to go back to Bath, the Countess informed her that she never wanted to hear from her again. That was Arianne's payment for the silence of the Countess concerning the existence of Luc.

Arianne worried her bottom lip as she tried to decide if she should attempt to see the woman. She wondered if that would negate their agreement. Despite the cold and abrupt manner of the Countess, she had been the only person who had shown any compassion for Arianne, and she had displayed an intense hatred of Pinard. Right now, Arianne could use a little compassion. Deciding to take the risk, she turned the pony cart back onto the road and headed for the fork that ran past the estate.

She arrived at the gate after a short ride. The old man who guarded it sat before his small house and dozed in the sun. A dog as ancient as its owner lay at his feet and opened its eyes upon her appearance.

"Good day to you!" she called.

The dog struggled to its feet and waddled to the gate. It stuck its snout through the bars and growled a half-hearted warning. The old man peered at her with sleepy eyes.

"Who's that?" He took up an archaic rifle and pointed it in her direction.

"I wish to see the Countess." Arianne watched the rifle tremble in rhythm with the old man's tremors. She hoped the weapon would not discharge by accident.

"No one can see the Countess." Although the man's tone was wheezy, his words were definite.

"I wish to speak to her about Pinard." Arianne used the name as a password. Although it had never been spoken between her and the Countess, she felt it was their connection, like a secret talisman.

The old man squinted at her. "Pinard, eh? Well, now that's a name I haven't heard in some time." He stepped down from his porch and hobbled over to the gate. "You been here before, mistress?"

"Once, several years ago."

"Thought as much." He nodded. "You look familiar. Well, I s'pose you can enter, mistress, and go on up to the house, but don't be surprised if they turn you away up there. The Countess don't see no one these days."

He unlocked the gates and swung them wide to allow Arianne to enter. The dog barked a greeting and wagged its tail. With apprehension, Arianne urged the pony through the gate and up the winding drive to the house.

"Good luck to you, mistress." The old gatekeeper waved.

The drive was long—longer than the lane leading to the gate. The Countess held an impressive amount of land. Arianne's courage wavered as she drew nearer, and she wondered if she had made a mistake coming here. After a very long time, she finally arrived before the front entrance. A stone portico, which at one time held the workings of a portcullis, sheltered the front door. Inside, she knew that the cavernous entry hall had been the open bailey of the castle centuries before. The Countess came from a very old, very wealthy family.

No servant rushed out to secure the pony while she stepped down from the cart. In fact, the mansion seemed deserted. But that, Arianne remembered, was always the case. She would not be inside very long anyway, so she was not too concerned about unhitching the pony from the cart. Tying the reins about a nearby post, she walked boldly up to the massive, carved wooden door. Before she could change her mind, she lifted the heavy brass knocker in the shape of a gargoyle head and let it drop. She heard it echo inside.

There was silence for a moment, then the approaching bark of two very watchful and protective dogs. They were wolfhounds, huge and hairy, with fangs that could rip a man to shreds in minutes. The Countess had named them Romeo and Juliet. Arianne always wondered at the whimsical nature of that impulse. She could see nothing romantic about them.

The dogs snarled and barked on the other side of the door then were silenced by a single command. The door creaked open, and the very proper butler stood in the opening.

Arianne smiled brightly. "Cranston, isn't it? How wonderful to see you. I was in the area, and I thought I would pay a visit to thank the Countess for the gifts she sent for my son. I have not seen her in so long." As she spoke, she edged forward, trying to force the butler to move out of the way. He did not budge.

"The Countess," he said, peering down his nose, "is not at home."

"Oh, come now, Cranston. Of course, she is. Where is she? Out in her garden?" Arianne waited for a reply, but all she received was stony silence. "Cranston, the Countess never goes out. Of course, she is here. I really must speak to her." Cranston began to close the door in her face. "Cranston, please, I won't take up much of her time." The door was almost completely closed. "Cranston, I have come about Pinard." The movement of the door stopped suddenly, then was swung wide.

"Come in, madam." Cranston stepped back and allowed her entry as if he had never denied her entrance.

Arianne stepped into the foyer and halted immediately. Romeo and Juliet sat on their haunches with their teeth bared and a warning rumble in their throats.

"Romeo, Juliet, have you forgotten me?" She put out her hand so they could sniff her fingers. The dogs' ears pricked up, and they stretched their necks forward to catch her scent. Their tails started to thump against the slate floor, and they whined to be allowed to get up and greet her. Arianne walked forward and scratched them behind their ears. She was rewarded with their tongues laving all over her hands. "Good boy, good girl," she crooned. "So you haven't forgotten me after all, have you?"

Her reunion with the two dogs was interrupted by Cranston's suggestion that sounded more like an order. "If you will follow me, madam?"

Arianne gave the dogs one last scratch, then followed the butler. He did not leave her in one of the many salons or drawing rooms to wait to be announced, but instead led her directly out to the formal garden at the side of the house. The dogs trotted behind.

Bright sunshine blinded her for a moment after the dark interior of the house. As her eyes adjusted to the light, she could see the tall, regal figure of the Countess directing the gardeners with her cane. Arianne doubted the woman really needed the instrument to help her walk, but merely used it to tyrannize people. Dressed all in black, taller than most women, the Countess intimidated just with her presence. Arianne drew a breath, swallowed, straightened her spine, and followed Cranston to the edge of the garden. Cranston approached the woman alone.

The Countess turned as he drew near. Arianne was close enough to hear their conversation.

"What is it, Cranston? Can't you see I'm busy?" The Countess's glance traveled past the butler and landed on Arianne. A cold veil seemed to drop across her eyes. "You allowed this person into my house? When I expressly stated I never wanted to set eyes on her again?" She pierced her butler with her gaze.

Arianne could see even the indomitable Cranston pale slightly at the Countess's displeasure. "She wished to speak with you concerning..." He glanced about to make sure none of the gardeners were within hearing. "...Pinard."

The Countess's mouth thinned, and the knuckles holding her cane turned white. "Very well. She may stay." She gave a dismissive nod. As Cranston bowed and turned to leave, she said, "We will discuss this later, Cranston."

The butler halted in mid-step. "As you wish, my lady." Then he retreated with dignified speed.

"Do not go far, Cranston. Our visitor will not be staying long." She watched him disappear into the house, then she imperiously beckoned Arianne to join her on the garden path. The dogs, who had remained behind, whined to get the attention of their mistress. "Go. Hunt." At the command, they bounded off in search of rabbits or squirrels or other small animals that chewed on the tender plants and flowers in the garden.

Arianne was alone with the Countess. She wished the dogs had been allowed to stay.

The Countess turned her cold gray eyes on her. "Well? What is it about Pinard that you wanted to say? Make it brief, girl, I am in the middle of transplanting some fuschia plants."

Arianne could think of nothing else except the bald truth. "He wants me to do it again."

"Do what?" The words snapped out.

Arianne swallowed. "He—he wants me to destroy another man."

"Well, what would you like me to do? Tell Pinard he is a naughty boy?" She raised a haughty brow.

Arianne flushed at the woman's sarcasm. "No, of course not. I thought you might be able to tell me something about him so that I could find a way to get out of his clutches."

Her gaze turned as sharp as a blade. "What makes you think I could tell you anything about him?"

Arianne shrugged. "I don't know. I just thought...I mean before it seemed..." She took a steadying breath. "I felt as though you had known him for a long time."

The Countess stared at her a moment with a strange expression on her face, then she laughed the most humorless laugh Arianne had ever heard. "Oh, yes, I have known him for a very long time."

"Then you can help me?" Arianne hated how pathetically hopeful she sounded.

The Countess rapped her cane on the path so hard that it stuck into the ground. "Do not be presumptuous, girl. What I *can* do and what I *will* do are two entirely different things."

Arianne resorted to begging. "Please, Countess, please help me. If you won't help me, help my son. You sent the gifts. Some small part of you must care."

The Countess turned and walked away several steps, then stopped. After a moment, she motioned for Arianne to join her. "Who is this man you are to destroy?"

Arianne told her.

"The brother of the man who died two years ago?"

"How did you know?" Arianne gasped.

The Countess slanted her a sardonic look. "Do you think because I choose to remain within my walls that I know nothing about what goes on beyond them?" Arianne began to shake her head in answer, but the Countess ordered, "Walk with me."

They strolled out of the formal garden in silence and onto the lawn that stretched away to the woods beyond. At the bottom of a gentle slope, a folly resembling a tiny Greek temple had been built beside a man-made lake. They entered the open shelter, and the Countess seated herself on a stone bench that hugged the wall. She motioned for Arianne to sit across from her.

"This man you are to destroy, this Duke of Lythmore," The Countess began, "do you love him?"

"No, of course not. I hardly know him." Arianne was sure she did not lie.

The gaze of The Countess narrowed. "Then why should it matter to you what happens to him?"

She was appalled at the nonchalance of the question. "I have a conscience, and what Pinard is forcing me to do is wrong."

The Countess's mouth quirked down. "He does not think so."

"Countess, don't *you* think what he is doing is wrong?" Arianne's brow wrinkled in confusion.

"Oh, I gave up thinking about Pinard and his deeds long ago. I could not bear it." Her tone was brittle, and the absent wave of her hand was jerky.

Arianne had a sudden insight. "He has hurt you a great deal, *n'est-ce pas?*"

"I am beyond hurt. His deeds do not affect me any longer. He no longer has any hold over me." The lady's words held very dark emotion.

Remaining silent, Arianne wondered how Pinard could have entwined this strong, imperious woman in his evil web-spinning.

The Countess looked straight into her eyes. "He is my son."

Arianne's mouth dropped open, and she gasped.

A cold smile curved the Countess's lips. "Now you understand why I helped you and why I wanted nothing further to do with you. When he contacted me, I believed he had reformed, that his motives were charitable." She gave a disillusioned bark of laughter. "I later learned how wrong I was. He is cruel, like his father, only worse. He threatened—" Her words halted, then she shook her head as if rejecting her words. "I refuse to get involved in his need for revenge. I have no control over him, and I will not allow him any control over me." She stood. "I have told you more than I ever intended. You will leave here now and say nothing about this to anyone."

"But Countess—"

"No more."

"But why does he want to destroy the Duke of Lythmore? Why did he want to destroy Ian West?" Arianne pressed.

"You must ask Lythmore that question." The Countess began to walk away.

"Please."

Swinging about, The Countess banged her cane on the marble floor of the temple. The sharp report echoed inside the curved roof. "Enough! Do not try my patience any further, young woman." She turned and left the temple.

Arianne trailed her across the lawn and into the garden. Cranston was waiting for them. The Countess returned to her supervision of the gardeners as if Arianne were not there, as if she had never revealed her shocking secret. With little ceremony, the butler escorted Arianne back through the house to the front door. She knew it would be useless to try to get him to talk about what she had just learned. Taciturn and unresponsive, he closed the door behind her with finality.

After climbing up into her pony cart, she started the animal back down the long drive. She had not learned what she had wanted — the reason for Pinard's evil revenge — but she had gained the vital factor in the connection between Pinard and the Countess. Although she was no closer to solving her dilemma, she felt the shocking bit of information might be useful at some point.

Calmer, she waved to the gatekeeper as she passed through. At least now she could have an enjoyable visit with Luc. With a bit more thought, she might be able to arrive at a solution to her problem. She turned the pony into the road leading to the Inglis's cottage.

The horseman hid in the foliage at the fork in the road and watched her drive past in her pony cart. He could have been any gentleman out for a ride in the country, except for the fact that he remained hidden from view. He had often seen her driving out in her pony cart but had not suspected anything more than a ride in the country. Foolish of him, now that he thought about it. Yet, her confession in the small hours of the morning, when she had revealed that she had been out of the city all night — something had clicked into place. He had to see for himself where she went, whom she saw. This secret of hers was just too delicious not to investigate.

He knew the estate where she had just been, the abode of that old crone known only as the Countess. Odd that the two women were acquainted. But that had not been her primary destination. She had stopped farther down the lane, turned her pony cart around, and driven to the estate as if she had been on an important mission.

Emerging from the foliage, he followed her, unnoticed, all the way to the small, neat cottage. Curious about who lived there, he stationed himself where he could observe, yet remain unseen. When the door opened, surprise lifted his brows a fraction. Then his eyes narrowed in speculation. A pleased smile appeared on his lips when he saw the little boy emerge and run into his mother's arms. Turning his horse about, he rode back down the road, back toward the city. After a few minutes, he laughed out loud. What he had just discovered was a priceless piece of information, something he could use later to coerce. Arianne de Vouvret had a son!

In the public room of the Boar and Stag, Cameron sat at a table in the corner with his back to the wall. From this vantage point, he could see everyone who came and went through the entrance. After only a few moments, the uneven silhouette of One-Armed Lewis appeared in the doorway. Cameron raised his tankard to signal the serving girl to bring another pint and caught the attention of Lewis. The serving girl and Lewis arrived at the same time.

"Rum for my friend here," Cameron told the girl. Since he had tipped her generously when he had first sat down, the rum appeared immediately. He turned to Lewis. "What have you learned?"

Lewis took a swallow and smacked his lips noisily. Wiping the back of his hand across his mouth, he grinned. "I like a man wot shares a drink. Knew a bloke once never drank a drop. Dried up, pinched old man, he was. Died of thirst." Lewis guffawed.

Cameron smiled mildly, but the expression did not reach his eyes. As Lewis began to lift his tankard, Cameron covered it and pushed it back to the table. "Your information, Lewis, please."

One-Armed Lewis let go of the tankard with reluctance and heaved a sigh. Cameron had not been pleased that Lewis had slept through Arianne's visit to de Pagière and had let the little scoundrel know it. Since Lewis was acutely aware of his place in society, he wanted to please those who were higher up in the food chain if he could benefit, and Cameron had let him know he would be well rewarded.

Lewis's head bobbed. "Right, guv, right. Well, that fancy dressmaker lady had 'nother visitor last night. Same bloke as afore."

"Same man? Are you saying this man has been there other times?" Cameron's brows rose in surprise.

Lewis's head bobbed again. "Right y'are, guv. Goes in, stays a bit, then leaves. This time, though, he looked mighty pleased when he left."

Cameron felt an odd, sinking sensation in the pit of his stomach. Did Arianne have a lover? Jealousy twisted in his chest. "How long did he stay?" He fought to keep his voice even and cool.

"Not long. A body can't do nothin' but sit an' wait, 'cause surer than piss runnin' downhill, he'll be out again in no time." Lewis winked. "Not even Mrs. Wiggit's girls are that fast." He glanced at his tankard and Cameron's hand still covering it. "You gonna let me take another drop o' rum, guv?"

Cameron realized his fingers had tightened so hard around the soft pewter that he had begun to turn the circle into an oval. Releasing his grip, he motioned for Lewis to take a drink. That sinking feeling went away. Although he was relieved Arianne didn't have a lover, anger surged through him. Whatever Arianne was doing, he did not like it.

"What did this other man look like?" he demanded.

Lewis put down his mug and licked his lips. "Can't say, guv. It was dark, ya know. But he weren't as big as yourself. A mite shorter, too." He snickered. "He don't use no fancy tailor, neither." A sly look came into his eyes. "You want to know what I saw this mornin', guv?"

Controlling his anger, Cameron leaned back in his chair. "What did you see this morning, Lewis?"

"How's about another drop o' rum, guv?" Lewis asked slyly.

Cameron signaled to the serving girl. After she had brought the rum, he prodded, "Well? What did you see?"

"It'll cost ya, guv." Lewis's eyes turned crafty.

Flipping a coin onto the table, Cameron covered it with his hand before Lewis could snatch it up. "After you tell me."

Lewis eyed the coin shining between Cameron's fingers. Clearing his throat, he said, "That fancy dressmaker rode out o' the city again like her skirts was afire. Took the north road, she did."

Reluctantly, Cameron removed his hand from the coin. He did not wish to hear that Arianne had received a stealthy, nighttime visitor, nor that she had hurried out of the city. She was obviously involved in something that she wished to keep secret. That sinking feeling came back. He had the suspicion he knew what that secret was. He did not like it. Not one bit. But he had to be sure. It was time to put the rest of his plan into action. It was time to lay his own trap.

Tossing another coin on the table, he stood. "Enjoy your rum, Lewis. If you see anything else of interest, be sure to contact me." The assurances of One-Armed Lewis receded from Cameron's hearing as he strode across the public room and out the door of the tavern.

CHAPTER 8

Arianne bid goodbye to the last of her guests at her Tuesday afternoon salon and headed to her office. She had nothing of import to tell Pinard. No marriages, no deaths, no new scandals. Only the old fact that Lythmore had purchased Shipley Hall and was spending lavishly on refurbishing it. That Mrs. Sally Turner had rejected the advances of the Marquis de Pagière and returned to London with—it was rumored—a certain Mr. Ramsey who was visiting from Scotland. And that Cameron, Duke of Lythmore, had been seen dancing at the latest ball with nearly every available young woman—and some who were not so available. He was obviously in the market for a wife—or a mistress.

Pinard would be ecstatic at the news—if she told him. His latest order to become romantically involved with Lythmore tore her apart. Her greatest desire was to be with Cameron, but knowing that she would be the instrument of his destruction tortured her. She could not help Pinard destroy another man, especially not Cameron. She had already lost a slice of her soul. If she followed Pinard's orders, she would lose the rest. Cameron would know that she had been involved in his brother's death. Somehow, he would know. The hate and disgust he would feel when he discovered the truth made her blood run cold. She could barely live with herself now, but if he learned the truth… She did not want to contemplate that.

She was relieved at the news of his socializing, for she would not have to rebuff his invitations to stroll, or dance, or go for a ride in his curricle. He had obviously given up on her and was looking elsewhere for female companionship. She could tell Pinard he would have to look for another accomplice in his evil scheme. Yet, disappointment and loss created an ache in her chest. And jealousy that some other woman would receive Cameron's affections twisted that pain.

With a sigh, she straightened a rose in a flower arrangement on a side table. She was being foolish. Lythmore wanted her only as a diversion, but she would be no man's plaything. She would discourage any future interactions between them. Now that Mrs. Turner was no longer in Bath, he would have no reason to visit her shop. Their paths might never cross again. If she did not see him, then she could not do Pinard's bidding. Lythmore was safe from the monster for now. That bit of comfort calmed her.

As she escaped to her office, the tinkling of the bell over the door to her shop announced a visitor. She paid no attention. Her apprentice would take care of the customer.

She heard the murmur of voices and then Marie, her apprentice saying, "I'm sorry, monsieur, but Madame de Vouvret cannot see you now." And then, "Monsieur, please, you cannot go in there!"

Arianne did not turn around to see who was being so persistent. She did not want to see. And then a voice — his voice — called to her, "Madame de Vouvret!"

She halted. She should not turn around. She should not receive him. She should ignore him, shut herself in her office, and lock the door. She did none of those things. Instead, she turned to the sound of his voice. Cameron was striding toward her. When their eyes met, he stopped. Something calculating, something dangerous flashed in his gaze and was gone. She thought perhaps she had imagined it. And then he smiled. Her heart stuttered.

"Madame de Vouvret." He bowed his greeting.

Her heart resumed at a quicker, fluttery pace. That annoying void opened again beneath her. Floating, falling, she was held by the safety in his eyes. Time slowed to a standstill. The action around her seemed to become frozen into a tableau. Unable to voice any words, she could only stare, transfixed by the sight of him. Her whole body felt drawn to him, like a magnet's tug.

No. She could not. Pinard. His orders. His evil. Not to this man. Never to this man.

Cameron.

No. She could not allow herself to become entangled with him. Too dangerous. On many, many levels.

At the edge of Arianne's awareness, Marie was babbling. She finally heard what the girl said.

"Madame de Vouvret, I am so sorry." Marie shifted from foot to foot. "He pushed right past me. I could not stop him. I am so sorry. I know you said you did not wish to be disturbed, but there was nothing I could do. I am so sorry."

Without taking her gaze from Cameron's face, with a wave of her hand, Arianne eased the young woman's distress. "It's all right, Marie. I will take care of the gentleman."

Taking a breath, Arianne grabbed her composure with both hands, smiled, and landed finally on solid ground. "Please come into my office, your grace." On the outside, she hoped she appeared coolly professional. On the inside, she wanted nothing more than to wrap her arms about him and drag his lips down to hers so that she could taste, lick, suck, devour him. After their last meeting, she thought she might never see him again. Within the last few minutes, she had decided she would *never* see him again. Having him here, now, made her insides quiver. More than that, his presence made her itch to press herself against him. As she led him into her office, she told herself how absurd she was being. The strain of dealing with Pinard's newest demand had to be unhinging her mind. Yet, sensing Cameron behind her warmed her back and sent heat spiraling to pool in her cheeks and between her thighs. She tried to ignore her arousal as she stood beside her desk and waited for him to close the door behind him. The click of the latch closed them in. Anticipation made her wet her lips.

"How may I help you, your grace?" Her voice turned husky with the effort she expended to remain calm. Even to her, it sounded intimate and inviting.

He tossed his hat on a chair, smiled, and took two steps toward her. "You may help me first by not being so formal and by calling me Cameron. I thought we had gotten past that. Your servants and employees cannot hear you now."

"F-Forgive me. Cameron." Saying his name felt much too intimate for her peace of mind. She was unnerved with him so near in an enclosed, private space. Her self-possession slipped away. "Why are you here?" she blurted.

He raised a mocking brow. "Why, to settle my bill, of course."

"Of course." Disappointment slithered through her at his mundane explanation. Then she remembered. "But I have not yet sent you any bill."

"Really? Then I am mistaken. Perhaps I have confused you with my tailor." He affected an innocent air, but the mischievous glint in his eyes revealed the lie. He tipped his head. "But you do not in any way resemble my tailor."

At his teasing and his grin, Arianne laughed. She could not help herself.

"Arianne, your laughter is delightful. You should indulge in it more often. Your eyes light up like the sun on water." He moved closer. His voice dipped to a lower pitch. "I love to hear you laugh. Why do you do it so seldom?" He traced his fingers down her cheek.

The sensation of his touch felt magical. Arianne remained perfectly still so she would not disturb him. She held her breath until his fingers reached her jaw, toyed there a moment, then dropped away. Swallowing, she regained her equanimity.

She told him with a shrug, "There is little I have to laugh about."

"I should like to change that." His answer sang along her nerve endings.

"No." Her denial came out strangled as she fought against his attraction.

"Why do you resist me, Arianne?" He stepped closer, so close that she could feel his warm breath come and go against her cheek.

She knew she should move away to a safer distance, but she could not. She wanted to be close to him, closer, in fact. That warmth between her thighs throbbed and pulsed with need. Staring up into his eyes the color of the midnight sky, she dredged up some small spark of sanity as she whispered, "I can't."

"I can change your mind," he whispered.

With that declaration, his arms went about her and pulled her against him. Her whimper of protest was silenced by his lips. That sound was her only resistance, for as soon as their mouths came together, she molded herself to him. Giving herself up to the dark whirlpool of desire, she parted her lips and invited him to drown with her in the waters of passion. Hands roved and clutched as tongues dueled and mouths tasted. Clothes became a barrier to their rising need.

She fumbled with the buttons on his waistcoat, then his shirt. His talented fingers unbuttoned the tiny closures down the front of her bodice. She felt air on bare skin where propriety demanded there should be none. She didn't care. His touched intoxicated, made her mindless, broke down all her barriers.

His lips trailed down her neck to suck on the pulse at the base of her throat. Arianne's breath stalled. Deftly, his fingers pushed the unbuttoned bodice of her dress and her loosened chemise from her shoulder, down her arm. As if unveiling a work of art, he pulled the material away from one breast. His hand caressed as his eyes worshipped it.

"Beautiful," he murmured.

Arianne smiled at the simple word, happy she pleased him.

Then he took the bud between his lips and sucked. At the first pull of his mouth, pleasure streaked through her. A moan of delight purred in her throat. Clutching his shoulder with one hand, she snaked the other beneath his gaping shirt and found his flat male nipple. Like a tiny pebble, it hardened beneath her fingertips. His own moan vibrated into her breast.

Her need, her pleasure, his touch, his fire made her forget everything—who she was, where she was, what she had to do. She had no thought, no awareness of anything except his mouth, his hands, his body. She wanted him like she had wanted nothing else, no one, ever before. The throbbing between her thighs became a dark, primeval hum calling to her. Her body knew what she wanted, what she needed. Her brain, with its confusion of proprieties, scruples, guilt, machinations, and logic had been silenced. This man, with the touch of a god and the smile of a devil, was her whole focus. This man, who could make her heart stop and the earth disappear beneath her feet, was her whole world.

She leaned on the desk behind her to brace herself. She hit the oil lamp, and it toppled, crashing to the floor and spilling the unlit oil. As the crystal shattered, so did that gossamer veil of desire. She froze and stared up at him. *What am I doing?*

"No," she whispered. "No." She edged out from between his body and her desk.

"Arianne, what is it?" Like a drowning man, he reached out to her.

"I can't." Her words strangled in her throat, and she took two steps back from him.

"Why?" He took a step forward.

"I just…can't." She pulled her bodice back onto her shoulder and took another step away.

He followed. "I don't understand."

"I can't explain." She focused on rearranging her clothing.

She felt him watching her. His gaze tugged at her, but she resolutely kept her attention on those tiny buttons. His silence made her fingers tremble.

Finally, he drew a deep breath. "I see," he said stiffly. "There is someone else."

"No. Yes." Apprehensively, she bit her bottom lip and hoped he would not press her further.

His eyes narrowed. "Which is it, Arianne? Yes or no? Or is there some other reason why you kiss me with such passion and then suddenly become cold as ice?"

She couldn't answer, so she only shook her head.

"Is it money you want? Is that what it is? Well, then let me indulge you." He reached into his breast pocket and pulled out a large wad of banknotes. Tossing it onto her desk, he snarled, "Is that enough to satisfy you?"

"No!" She pushed the money back to him.

With the speed of a whip, his hand shot out and pinned her wrist against the wood. "Don't insult my intelligence. I know when I have been played for the fool. Does de Pagière pay you more?"

Arianne could not believe how the situation had so quickly degenerated into something obscene and indecent. Hurt by his accusation, trapped by her predicament, tears welled up in her eyes. She turned away so he would not see. The last thing she needed was to have him think she was using her feminine wiles on him.

Forcing her voice to remain level, she said, "Please take your money. I don't want it. Ever." She swallowed, trying to regain her composure, and gathered up some semblance of anger. "I am insulted at your offer of that." She waved her hand in the general direction of the banknotes. "I am not that sort of woman, your grace. I am a modiste, well-respected by my clientele. I have a reputation to uphold." She nearly winced at the irony of her words. If anyone discovered what she had done, she would have no reputation. She would be shunned completely.

Slowly, he removed his hand from her wrist. Instead of straightening up, he leaned forward, and, taking her chin, he turned her to face him. "You're crying." Amazement lightened his tone.

"No. You are mistaken." Turning her back to him, she focused on buttoning her bodice. She felt his fingers on her shoulder. Oh, she wanted his touch, his arms about her more than anything. She wanted so much to have Cameron's trust and affection, but because of Pinard, she would only have his disgust and hatred. Better he should think her a chilly-hearted tease. Busying herself with her fastenings, she tried to ignore him.

"Perhaps I jumped to the wrong conclusion," he said. "Perhaps you have a perfectly good reason for your actions."

Arianne had a fleeting moment of vacillation. What if she confessed it all? What if she told him she was the Jezebel who had enticed his brother, then cruelly rejected him? What if she admitted to being present at his brother's death? No, she could never do that. But then, how should she proceed from this tangle? Should she hold on to her anger and pride and drive him away? If she did that, he would be safe, but she would bear the brunt of Pinard's fury. Or should she forgive his insult and thus lure him into Pinard's web? She wanted to forgive him, to have him smile at her, to have the opportunity to kiss him with abandon. Yet, by doing so, she would be sending him to his death. Her guilt writhed. Her desire for him nearly choked her. She balanced on the knife's edge of indecision. Surely, there must be some way she could allow Cameron into her life and still foil Pinard's plans. At the least, she did not want this man as her enemy, for she felt he would be a deadly, dangerous foe. Determined to find such a solution, she turned to face him.

"Perhaps, your grace, you should not kiss a lady when she is trying to conduct her business," she reprimanded.

Skepticism narrowed his eyes. Then his lips curled in a polite smile, and he bowed. "I stand corrected, Madame de Vouvret. I apologize for my grave error. Will you ever forgive me?"

"Perhaps." Warm, silky skin peeked from the gap of his unbuttoned shirt. She could not resist touching her finger to that stretch of temptation. The muscles beneath shivered at her touch. "I think, your grace, you might try dressing with a bit more decorum when you come to pay your bills."

Grasping her fingers, he raised them to his lips. "You drive me mad, Arianne."

Disengaging her hand, ignoring his passionate words and tempting touch, she coolly turned to the bellpull beside her desk. "I will ring for tea. Or perhaps you would care for some sherry?"

"Sherry," he told her with a nod and then hurried to fasten his shirtfront and tie his neckcloth before the maid appeared.

When the maid had come and gone, they both sat. Feeling safer with the desk between them, she tried to calm her flustered state by fussing with the designs on her desk. "I understand you are renovating Shipley Hall," she said, trying for a neutral topic.

"I had no idea that was common knowledge," he observed.

"News concerning the most eligible bachelor in Bath travels very fast." She toyed with a quill. "When do you plan to occupy it?"

He shrugged. "I have no idea. Whenever the renovations are complete."

"That could take weeks, maybe months. Will you stay in Bath that long?" While her question sounded only like an innocent query, Arianne found herself wanting very much to hear the answer.

His gaze teased. "Would you like me to stay?"

A tell-tale blush heated her cheeks.

He grinned. "Perhaps I'll move in tomorrow."

She smiled. "Are you being coy, your grace?"

"I am being truthful, Madame de Vouvret. If I had a very good reason to take up residence, then I would do so. I have no wife, no children. Therefore I have no reason to hurry the process along." He tipped his head thoughtfully. "You could give me a reason, Arianne."

She was saved a reply by the return of the maid with their sherry. After the girl had gone, Arianne pushed the wad of banknotes across the desk to him.

"You must put this away. It is a very large sum."

He picked it up and turned it over thoughtfully. Then he tossed it back onto the desk. "Take it as settlement for my bill."

"Oh, no, it is far too much." She pushed it back toward him.

"Then I will use it to commission a gown," he declared.

Arianne's heart dropped to her stomach. What lucky woman would be the recipient of such a gift? "A gown?" she asked, trying to keep her tone level. "Will the lady make an appointment for a fitting?"

He grinned. "The gown is to be a surprise. Something simple but elegant."

"An afternoon dress, then." She scribbled a note.

"Hmm. Something a bit more formal," he said thoughtfully.

"A dinner dress," she suggested.

"If you think that is best," he agreed.

"May I ask this woman's height? Her proportions?"

"She is of your height, and your proportions."

Arianne made some notes. "And her coloring?"

"She has eyes as changeable as the sea and hair like copper. I want the gown to be blue, the color of a spring sky, shot with gold." He gazed at her. "Would that be a pleasant color for her?"

Arianne nodded while she wrote. "Oh, yes, of course. That shade of blue has always looked well on me." As she said the words, her fingers froze. She suddenly realized that Cameron had described her. Not raising her head, she croaked, "Who is this gown for?"

"Arianne, haven't you guessed?"

Her stomach plummeted. "Oh, no, I couldn't." She shook her head vehemently.

"Why not? It's only a gift." A line appeared between his brows.

"It is much too extravagant." She shook her head again. "And such an intimate gift."

He leaned forward and whispered, "I wish to be intimate with you, Arianne."

She swallowed in a dry throat. "No, I—" Wanting exactly what he wanted, she found it difficult to find her willpower. "Please, don't ask me."

Sitting back in his chair, he announced, "I will wear you down, you know. You will tell me why you refuse my advances. I will have you in the end, Arianne."

Her temper flared at his arrogant declaration. She had made a mistake allowing that one kiss and forgiving him, but she wouldn't make another. And now, she had a way to end his pursuit of her. She jumped from her seat. "You know nothing about me, your grace. Nothing. *Rien*. And I will tell you nothing. *Sacré bleu*! I will not fall into your bed because you have declared it. Neither will I take your expensive gifts. Do you think because I do not take your money, I will accept extravagant presents instead?" She picked up the wad of banknotes and threw them at him. "Take your wealth and get out."

Cameron stood also and ignored the scattered money. His gaze drilled into her. "I want you to make that gown. I want it to be the most lovely thing you have ever created. If you refuse, then I will let it be known that you ruined Sally's gowns by using cheap materials and shoddy workmanship."

Arianne gasped in horror. "You wouldn't! That would ruin my business!"

He leaned over the desk and stated, "Exactly."

Furious, angry, unable to think beyond her burning, roiling emotions, she slapped him across the face. "Bastard! *Cochon*!"

He straightened, rubbed his cheek, and gave her a rueful smile. "I should have realized a woman who kisses with such passion would have a magnificent temper." He picked up his hat and sauntered to the door. With his hand on the knob, he turned back to her. "How long to complete the gown?"

Arianne could not look at him. Was he no better than Pinard with his threats and bribes and blackmail? With stiff lips, she said, "Three days."

"Then we shall meet again in three days' time." He bowed and placed his hat on his head. "Good day, Madame de Vouvret." He stepped through the doorway and closed the door softly behind him.

Arianne slumped into her chair. Now that the first flood of emotions had drained away, she felt depleted and weak. Yet, her anger was a congealed lump deep inside her. She had hoped that Cameron might be her salvation from her purgatory. That had been a meaningless dream. Realizing she had pinned her hopes to the one man who could never be her lifeline, her frustration grew and fed her anger. Snatching a piece of foolscap from the pile on her desk, she picked up her charcoal and with slashing strokes, laid down the lines, shadings, and curlicues that would create a dress design and transpose her information into a message for her father's jailer. She would let Pinard know that the Duke of Lythmore had purchased Shipley Hall and was refurbishing it extravagantly. She would let Pinard know that the Duke of Lythmore had danced with every available young woman and some who were not so available at the last ball. She would let Pinard know that the Duke of Lythmore was in the market for a mistress — or a wife. She would let Pinard know…

Arianne's hand froze as she started to write the code words for Cameron — green satin — across the bottom of the page. What was she doing? Because of her anger and hurt, she was sending another man to his destruction and death. But not just any man. A man who made her heart stop with his smile and the earth disappear beneath her feet. A man whose touch made her forget who she was and whose kisses made her mindless.

She stared down at the design she had just drawn. It was elegant in its stark simplicity, unlike anything she had ever designed before. On a separate sheet of foolscap, she wrote *green satin*. Beneath it, she wrote *black lace*, her own code words. Then she circled the four words together. She looked back at the sketch. She began to form an idea that might save Cameron from Pinard's clutches. The idea was so simple and so obvious, she could not believe she had not thought of it before.

At the bottom of the sketch, she finished writing the code words for Cameron and then added her own code words to it. She would make this dress. She would make it of green satin and trim it in black lace — very unfashionable colors. This would be the gown that Cameron had commissioned, the one he had blackmailed her into creating. And she would wear it for him. He would not know that the mating of green satin and black lace held more meaning than her defiance of his wishes. All he would see was that she had complied with his demand in an outrageous manner. But he would not care, because she would give him something else besides.

She would become his mistress.

All along, she had been trying to stay away from him in order to keep him safe. She thought that by keeping her distance, she would cool his ardor. In fact, just the opposite had occurred. And then she had received her orders from Pinard — destroy him. Her revulsion of that command made her want to distance herself even further. But she realized now that she had been running in the wrong direction. What she had to do was remain close to Cameron in order to protect him. Her anger and hurt at Cameron's arrogance had to be put aside. His life was more precious than her own wounded sensibilities or her reputation. By becoming his mistress, by staying near him, she could warn him of the menace from Pinard's other pawns. And she knew there would be deadly peril from them, for they were all desperate people in their own way and for their own reasons. And she could warn him when Pinard chose to strike.

The noose around Cameron was beginning to tighten. If she could help deflect its stranglehold, then maybe, he could slip free. And if she were very lucky and very clever, perhaps, she, too, would be able to escape with the lives of her father and her son.

CHAPTER 9

The next day, Arianne walked down Milsom Street to the shoemaker's shop situated at the other end from her own establishment. It was morning and not the fashionable hour for ladies to be out and about in the shops, so she met few people. Several coffeehouses were located on this street, and they were moderately busy serving the men who gathered at their tables to discuss a friendly business deal or the latest outrage of the Prince Regent.

She was alone this morning, for the errand was a personal one, one she did not wish either Marie or her maid to know about — at least not yet. She was hurrying to the shoemaker's to order a pair of green satin slippers to go with the gown she was making at Cameron's command. Having decided to become his mistress, she determined she would look the part for their first night together. She would be his strumpet, his seducer, his lover.

As she passed one of the coffeehouses, the door opened, and two gentlemen emerged just in front of her. Arianne almost bumped into them.

"Madame de Vouvret!" the Marquis de Pagière exclaimed. "What a delightful surprise!"

Caught in the middle of her personal errand, Arianne felt the heat rush to her cheeks. She glanced at the second gentleman who stood slightly behind de Pagière and felt her mouth go dry. Cameron gave her an insolent, lop-sided smile.

"Oh, forgive me. I did not see you." Her apology sounded breathless to her own ears.

"Are you alone, madame?" De Pagière's polite question seemed to have a strange undercurrent.

"Yes, I am just going down the street to the shoemaker's." Arianne did not wish to stand and chat with either gentleman. She began to edge around them.

Cameron cut off her escape. "Perhaps you would allow me to escort you."

De Pagière slanted him an annoyed glance. "Perhaps we could both escort you."

Arianne looked from one to the other. Her gaze was chilly. "Thank you, that won't be necessary. I am only going to the end of the street, you see."

"It is no problem," de Pagière said.

"We were going in that direction anyway," Cameron added.

She saw no way to avoid the company of the two men. Falling into step between them, pretending nothing was amiss between her and Cameron, she observed, "I had not realized that you gentlemen spent so much time together. How pleasant for you both."

"A business arrangement always brings men together," Cameron said.

Arianne nearly halted as dread swept through her. A business arrangement? Between Cameron and de Pagière? She felt Pinard's shadow hovering about them as surely as if he had been there in person. This was another strand of the evil web he was spinning about Cameron. He would have de Pagière lure Cameron into a false investment scheme and steal all his wealth. After Cameron became infatuated with her, Pinard would have her cruelly break off the relationship, and then de Pagière would inform him that the investments were lost. Both his woman and his money would be gone. And if Pinard repeated his cruel scheme exactly, somehow, Cameron would be dishonored. He would end up a broken man, in the same position as his brother.

No! She couldn't let that happen. She wanted to break into a run, to hurry to the shoemaker's and urge him to have her shoes completed by the end of the morning, to rush back to her shop and make her fingers fly with her needle and thread to complete her gown. Three days, the time she had told Cameron it would take to finish her gown, was too long. She had to become his mistress sooner than that, to protect him, to protect herself and her sanity.

Forcing herself to remain calm, to keep her feet moving at a sedate, steady pace, to act as if everything were normal, she glanced at Cameron. "I understood you were in Bath for recreational purposes, your grace, not for opportunities of investment. Surely, Monsieur le Marquis can provide you with better sport than a business arrangement."

"I have tried, madame, believe me, I have tried," de Pagière professed. "I thought I had convinced Lythmore to sample some of my entertainments on that evening when you so kindly delivered the dress design, but, *hélas*…" He shrugged philosophically.

"Perhaps his grace prefers to choose his entertainments himself." Arianne raised an inquisitive brow.

"I most certainly do, madame." Cameron's warm smile held unnamed promises.

Arianne's heart fluttered at the heat in his eyes and the underlying meaning of his statement. For once, she could allow herself to bask in his glow and not shove her feelings into a tiny, locked box. Although her decision to become his mistress was made only for his protection, it was so aligned with what she actually desired, that, for a while at least, she could pretend to herself that she was doing exactly what she wanted with no Pinard directing her every move. But because of how they had parted at their last meeting, she glanced away as if uninterested.

"A shame," de Pagière said with a forlorn shake of his head. "You are missing out on a pleasurable experience." He turned to Arianne. "I will be paying a visit to your shop later, madame. I have some business to discuss with you."

Arianne saw the tick of the muscle in Cameron's jaw. Jealousy, perhaps? Despite the tension between the two men, she was amused. "I am always willing to discuss business with you, Monsieur le Marquis." She smiled at him, but apprehension cut through her at the predatory expression in his eyes. Forcing her tone to lightness, she quipped, "Dresses for another new mistress, or perhaps you wish to smuggle a gift to your wife in her lonely chateau in Burgundy?"

De Pagière chuckled. "You are the only woman I allow to say such outrageous things, madame."

"Your other women do not have the intelligence to say such outrageous things. Except, perhaps, for one," Arianne answered.

"Ah, you are referring, of course, to Mrs. Sally Turner," he said with a sad shake of his head. "*Hélas,* Mrs. Turner has left Bath and returned my gifts. I am devastated."

She exchanged a quick glance with Cameron and saw her relief mirrored in his eyes. At least Sally was out of the perverted clutches of the marquis. But she pretended ignorance at the news. "I was unaware of that. I am so sorry."

"How kind of you to say so." The smile of the marquis conveyed more than his appreciation of her understanding, much more.

Arianne tried to control her shudder of revulsion. Now that the marquis had no lover to occupy him, he would start again with his persistent, subtle pursuit of her. The game he played was dangerous, for Pinard would never allow the two of them to have an alliance, not that she would ever want one, but the marquis enjoyed living dangerously. His way of life was the reason he had become one of Pinard's pawns.

They reached the cobbler's shop, much to Arianne's relief, and she extended her hand to the two men. "Thank you for your company, gentlemen. I feel honored to have had two such handsome men escort me down the street."

The marquis bent over her hand first. "Until later, madame." His reference to their impending meeting was made with more warmth than was proper. Arianne pulled away as soon as she could and shot him an aloof smile.

"I look forward with pleasure to our next encounter," Cameron said as he brushed his lips across her fingers. His smile was wolfish. Arianne felt the heat surge through her and pool between her thighs. With an effort, she raised a cool brow and gave a tiny sniff. She could not let him know what she was planning—not yet.

Turning from the two men, she entered the shop. The relief she felt at escaping from their overwhelming presence was enough to make her knees weak. The cobbler, seeing her distress, ordered one of his apprentices to fetch the lady a chair and a cool drink. As Arianne sipped the refreshing lemon-flavored water, she tried not to dwell on the reason the marquis wanted to visit that afternoon, nor the throbbing rush she had felt at the touch of Cameron's lips on her fingers.

Relax, stay calm, she told herself. *One step at a time.* But that was difficult when fear clutched at her, and desire flowed through her veins.

Cameron left the marquis and rode out to Shipley Hall. The large manor was not far outside the city. He had bought the property without ever having seen it as soon as he had learned it was for sale. He certainly did not need it, for he had his principal residence, Lythmore Manor, in Surrey, along with several other properties scattered about the country, and his townhouse in London. For some reason, he had the feeling that Shipley Hall would lead him to the answer to his brother's death. He had not been able to bring himself to visit before now. This had been the last place where his brother had been alive. Before, it had been too painful to see. But now that he was on the quest to find his brother's destroyer, he felt the property might be a magnet to draw that person closer.

As he dismounted and tied his horse to the hitching post near the front door, his thoughts wandered to Arianne. Guilt twinged at him, for he had hurt her when he had threatened her, forcing her to accept his gift of the dress. But he sensed that her cool retreat and pretended insult after their kiss had more behind it than protecting her reputation. He thought he had seen a flash of fear, not of him, but of something deeper, darker. His suspicion that she had been involved in his brother's death rose up again. He didn't like that possibility. The idea of Arianne as a cold-blooded seducer, a murderer, didn't match the woman who had kissed him so passionately, desperately, the day before. The woman who so bravely ran a successful business. The woman who lured him with her cool exterior. He sensed she hid deeper, more complex sensibilities than she let on. He intended to discover what she was hiding, so he wove his own web. And until he had her firmly caught in it, he would enjoy the chase.

A tiny smile caught a corner of his mouth. Arianne. Of the changeable eyes and coppery hair. She fascinated him, beguiled him, puzzled him, enticed him. He wanted her. Now. In his house. In his bed.

Standing before Shipley Hall, he gazed up at its front façade, an expanse of gray stone punctuated by many mullioned windows. Inside, workmen painted, plastered, papered, and washed. He had told the foreman that most of the work had to be completed in three days and had bribed the man with an outrageous sum to get him to comply. In three days, he would bring Arianne here, and he would finally unleash that passion she held so tightly controlled. In three days, he would see his fantasy brought to life. In three days, he would see her standing naked in the moonlight with her hair tumbled in abandon about her shoulders.

But between now and then, he had to act the rake on the prowl for a new mistress. He had to find the woman who had played the Circe and lured his brother into destruction and death. This house, with its extravagant trappings, was part of the bait. Walking up the few steps and through the front door, Cameron felt a surge of anticipation. He sensed that he was very close to discovering his unseen prey.

As he gazed about the entry hall in satisfaction at the workmen's efforts, he allowed himself a moment of smugness. Already, he had received two nibbles about mysterious but supposedly secure investments, similar to what his brother had described to him. Both could be legitimate. Either one could be a fake, meant to entice him into investing a large sum. The woman — that Circe who had first lured his brother — was the key. Somehow, she would let him know which investment was the one he sought. By doing so, she would reveal herself and point to the man who was the other corner of this deadly triangle. And perhaps, the puppet master who pulled their strings.

Cameron walked up the wide, main staircase with its sweeping banisters and into the drawing room. Workmen were painting the ceiling and woodwork. One clumsy fellow dropped his bucket just as Cameron passed. The paint spilled across the drop cloth and spattered all over his pantaloons and boots.

"Gaw!" the workman exclaimed. "Forgive me, sor, forgive me." He knelt down and tried to rub the paint off Cameron's clothes. All he managed was to smear it about.

"Here, stop that," Cameron ordered tersely. "You're only making it worse." Annoyed, he tried to shake the fellow off.

The workman gave another few swipes at Cameron's boots. "'Ere now, I'll get it off ye, sor, surely I will. Please don't tell the foreman, sor. 'E'll send me packin', fer sure."

"Serves you right for being so clumsy," Cameron muttered. At the man's wail of protest, he sighed. "No, no, I won't mention it. Just leave off that groveling."

The fellow stood up then and met Cameron's eyes. "Oh, thank ye, sor. I got me a wife and six little 'uns t'feed."

"Six little ones, is it?" Cameron repeated with a narrowed gaze. "Well, we certainly wouldn't want to deprive them, would we?"

"Oh, no, sor!" The fellow shook his head and bobbed obsequiously at the same time.

"Well, come with me. There is a spot that needs painting where you won't hurt anything if you spill again." Cameron turned and led the fellow out of the room. He was having great difficulty keeping a straight face, for he had recognized his friend, Adrian, Duke of Dunbary.

When they were in the dining room and out of earshot of anyone else, Cameron finally allowed himself to laugh. "You had me completely fooled! When you sent word that you had information for me, I expected another jaunt through dark alleys and back gardens."

"Gaw, sor, a body can't be too careful these days. A bloke has t' work where 'e can get it." Adrian grinned and winked at his friend.

"You could have been a bit more careful," Cameron mused as he examined his ruined clothes. "I just paid my tailor and bootmaker for these."

"With what you're spending on this house, I think your finances can stand the strain." Adrian let his gaze wander appreciatively about the room.

"Speaking of finances, what did you discover about those investment opportunities?" Cameron asked.

"Nothing."

"Nothing?" Cameron's brows flew up in amazement. "But I thought—"

Adrian held up his hand to stop him. "That's what so interesting. Both of them are so secret that no one has heard anything about them."

"Or they just don't exist," Cameron mumbled.

"That's a very good possibility." The Duke of Dunbary paused, then said, "I did discover something else. The small trading company that your brother invested in had a silent partner. In France."

Cameron's eyes narrowed. "Ian's death seems to have several connections to France." Although he tried to quash the idea, he thought of Arianne and her delightful French accent. But to be fair, he also was reminded of the Marquis de Pagière and the Baroness Souffant and the French wife of that Viscount Something-or-other.

"I understand that there are several people in Bath who have connections to France," Dunbary observed quietly.

"Yes."

"I understand you have made their acquaintance." Adrian sent him a speculative gaze.

Cameron gave a snort of laughter. "I'm glad you're on my side. You don't miss much, do you?"

His friend shrugged. "It's my job. You used to be just as good."

Cameron stiffened. "I don't need to be reminded of that." He was very aware he had lost his edge after his brother's death.

"Don't be insulted, Cam." Adrian sighed. "I'm concerned. So is Wyndham. What's happening here is too close to what happened to Ian. Someone destroyed him, and someone is out to destroy you."

Cameron frowned fiercely. "And I intend to find out who that is."

Dunbary shook his head. "Wyndham believes this person is more than what you think. More than a spymaster. I agree. There is an evil mind behind this."

"Stop worrying like an old woman." Cameron waved away his friend's concern. "I know what to expect, so I'm prepared. Ian didn't know what was happening to him, so he was vulnerable. I won't be duped by attractive investment opportunities or a seductive smile."

"Hmph. I've seen you duped more than once by a seductive smile." Adrian's lips twisted wryly.

Cameron took a playful swipe at his friend.

"Oh, no, sor, surely you wouldn't beat me!" The Duke of Dunbary ducked his head and covered it with his hands.

"You are a worthless fellow, and I should beat you black and blue." Cameron fell in with the act.

"Just try it," Adrian muttered.

Cameron grinned at his friend's challenge. They had met many times in the boxing ring and were an even match, each of them winning as many times as the other. He jerked his chin in the direction of a corner of the room. "That part of the ceiling needs another coat of paint, and when you finish that, you may report back to your foreman."

"Cheeky brat," Adrian muttered.

"If you do a good job, you'll get a bonus to help feed those six little ones," Cameron said with a grin.

His friend sighed with regret. "I should have dumped the paint on your head."

"My greetings to your beautiful wife," Cameron murmured as he sauntered out of the room.

Adrian would silently disappear out of the house as soon as there was no one around. While Cameron returned to survey the work being done, his thoughts churned over what he had just learned. Although he had no hard evidence that there was some mastermind residing in France, everything pointed to that. But who could it be?

And who were the puppet master's puppets? Rathbone, who invited him to invest in an expedition for diamonds? De Pagière, who hinted at an excellent opportunity to invest in some mining project in the jungles of Mexico? Sir Lindsey Wooten, who cheated at cards and talked of horseflesh and racing? The Baroness Souffant, with her coy smiles? The French Viscountess who had barely made an impression? Or Arianne, with the changeable eyes and lush lips, who had not asked him to invest in anything? Who kissed with abandon and then closed herself away from him like an ice princess?

He found himself in his own bedroom and staring at the spot where the huge bed would be. He had told the foreman he wanted this room to be completed first. His blood began to race in his veins. Was it Arianne who would finally betray him? Three days. In three days, he would know. In three days, he would see her in the gown he had commissioned her to make. In three days, he would bring her here, to this house, to this room. In three days, he would unlock her passion and watch her lose herself in desire. In three days, he would have a lover or an enemy.

In three days.

"The Marquis de Pagière to see you, madame," the maid announced to Arianne.

She stood from behind her desk and smoothed her skirt. The uneasiness that had assailed her that morning when the marquis had asked to see her had remained with her throughout the day. She had no new information, so no new dress design to deliver to Pinard. The purpose of de Pagière's visit was for more than ordering a new gown for some female companion, but she could not settle on any plausible explanation, no matter how hard she tried. She felt a small sense of relief that he was finally here, and she would discover the reason for this meeting.

Walking out into her salon, her uneasiness turned to anger. He was there, speaking with Marie. Handsome, suave, charming, with just a hint of sin about him, he held Marie's fingers in his hand and smiled down at her. Poor, innocent Marie did not have a chance against the onslaught of that overwhelming personality. The girl gazed up at him as if he held her in a trance. Within a very few moments, she would agree to anything he asked of her.

"Marie!" Arianne snapped. "Lady Pettigrew's gown must be hemmed. Please see to it."

Marie jumped and snatched back her hand as if she had been bitten. With a guilty murmur, she hurried to the workroom. Arianne waited until she was out of hearing, then turned on the marquis.

"I would ask that you not seduce the girls in my employ," she said. "They are here to sew and learn the dressmaker's trade. They are not here for your pleasure."

The marquis put a hand to his breast. "Arianne, you wound me deeply. I was merely telling the lovely Marie that she had exquisite eyes."

Arianne's mouth flattened. "The eyes of my apprentice are for her to see her work, not for your enjoyment. I do not want you toying with my employees. Do I make myself clear, Jules?"

He smiled and bowed. "Your every wish is my command."

Arianne made a small sound of impatience at his mockery. She knew that he would continue his seduction of Marie at the very next chance he had. He did as he wished, when he wished. He was amoral. As she turned to lead him into her fitting room, she decided to keep the girl busy elsewhere whenever the man was scheduled to visit.

Arianne had chosen the fitting room for this meeting for its privacy and its spaciousness. She had not wanted to meet with him in her office because the room was too tiny. Despite the desk that would be between them, she would be forced to sit too close to the marquis. Besides, it was in her office that she had kissed Cameron with such abandon. She did not want to sully that memory with whatever indecent notions Jules had in mind.

The fitting room had a sofa and chairs with a low table before them for the comfort of her patrons. Against the opposite wall stood three angled mirrors. Arianne sat in the only chair that was not visible in the mirrors. She did not want de Pagière to see any more of her than she wished. The marquis relaxed on the sofa as Arianne poured his favorite Madeira wine.

Holding the glass up to the light, he admired its color before he saluted her with it and took a sip. "Ah, Arianne, you always know how to please. Your mother taught you well in the womanly graces."

Arianne said nothing, not wanting to encourage him. Nor did she wish to bring her mother into the conversation.

He leveled his gaze on her. "You know, I do wish you would reconsider becoming my mistress," he went on. "I could take you away from all of this toil." He waved his glass about, indicating her surroundings.

The thought of becoming his mistress sent chills down her spine. She covered her revulsion with a short laugh. "Jules, you can barely keep the creditors from your door. How could you possibly afford someone like me as your mistress?"

"Perhaps you are right," he allowed with a smile. "I shall have to practice some patience. But when we have completed this latest chore for Pinard, I shall have the wealth that a woman like you deserves."

Arianne sighed, holding onto her patience. "No, Jules, I will never become your mistress."

"We shall see." As he took a sip from his glass, he smiled secretively. He placed the glass on the table before him and leaned forward. "Our meeting this morning was rather fortunate. I had just been discussing the merits of investing in a mining project in Mexico with our dear Duke of Lythmore. He seemed quite interested. I believe it's time for you to begin discussing this venture at your next salon. Having the ladies speak of it to their husbands will make the scheme more believable. Perhaps we can persuade some of them to invest and make a bit of a profit. And of course you must discuss this with Monsieur le Duc."

Arianne held back her sigh of relief. De Pagière's visit was not about blackmailing her into becoming his mistress. Although she was sickened by what she would be forced to do, she felt she had some bit of control over the outcome, for she could warn Cameron. He would not have to fall unwittingly into Pinard's web. Yet, when she had met the marquis that morning, she sensed that there was some other, darker reason behind his call. Her relief upon realizing she had seen demons where there were none made her calmly accept her orders.

"Of course," she murmured. "Whatever you say."

The marquis raised a brow. "My dear Arianne, am I hearing you correctly? Do you agree to this with no argument, no protests? Have you finally become as wicked as the rest of us?"

She had blundered with her meek acquiescence. Always before, she had argued and begged not to have to follow Pinard's orders. In order to keep de Pagière from realizing what she intended, that she planned to save Cameron from Pinard's clutches, she had to keep that moral attitude. Summoning her anger, she bit out, "I have no choice but to agree. What good is there in fighting the inevitable?"

Applauding quietly, de Pagière sat back. "Bravo, madame. You play your role of the injured innocent so well."

"It is not a role I play," she snapped. "I hate this deception."

De Pagière's lips curled in a sly smile. "You hate the deception forced upon you, yet you deceive the very man who holds your life in his hands."

His words turned Arianne's insides cold. "What do you mean?" But of course, she knew he meant Pinard.

He picked up his glass once more. Holding it up to the light, he swirled the liquid about. "It is amazing, is it not, how one must crush and destroy the grape in order to create such a magnificent drink?" He gazed directly at Arianne. "Some people are like grapes, you know. They must be crushed and destroyed in order to create something new and magnificent."

She scowled. "What are you talking about, Jules?"

"Why you, of course, my dear Arianne." He smiled a knowing, sinister smile. "I know your little secret, the one you keep hidden away in the countryside, the one that Pinard does not know. I have seen him. Such a sweet child."

Arianne went completely still. What would he do with the information? Fear kept her silent. She had to keep Luc safe at all costs.

"What? No protests that he is not your child?" His smile held a perverted gentleness. "He has your eyes, Arianne. He will grow into a beautiful young man."

Horrified at where his thoughts were going, Arianne could barely draw a breath. She would kill to protect Luc from the man before her.

"But that will not be for many years yet," he said. "You do wish to keep his existence a secret, do you not?"

Arianne's head jerked in a nod.

He carefully placed his glass on the table before him. "Well, I certainly see no reason why I should tell Pinard something he has no need to know. Perhaps we can work out some arrangement."

"What do you want from me?" Her words were too anxious, but she could not help that. She would do anything, even make a bargain with the Devil, to keep Luc safe.

He steepled his fingers thoughtfully. "Become my mistress?" he mused. "No, not yet. Like the crushed grape, you must be allowed to ripen and ferment." He stood and sauntered to some gowns hanging beside the mirrors, waiting to be delivered to their owners. "I have always admired your designs, Arianne. I have found a friend I wish you to dress, but with the utmost discretion. If you do this, then we shall keep our little secret between the two of us. Are you agreed?"

Arianne felt like a deflated sack of air. If all he wanted were a few gowns from her without having to pay, then she would gladly make him a wardrobe. "Of course. When will you bring your friend for a fitting?"

De Pagière turned back to her. "I think some evening, and through the back door if that is convenient. You see, he is very young and very shy."

Arianne swallowed. She knew the marquis was fond of men as well as women, but he had always been discreet about his tastes. And his lovers had been grown men, old enough to know their own desires.

"How young?" she managed to ask.

He gave a careless shrug. "I did not inquire. But he is a dear boy, and he has confessed a fondness for ladies' garments. I cannot deny him."

Arianne blinked, glanced away, and caught a glimpse of her very pale face in the mirror. If any of her customers learned about this arrangement, they would be horrified and stop coming to her for their frocks and gowns. Her business would be ruined. Taking a deep breath, she told herself to remain calm, to keep her composure. She could do this. She could keep the secret. Anything to keep Luc safe.

Then she realized she now knew something about de Pagère that would ostracize him from society. More than that, it could get him arrested and hanged, away from her and innocent youths he had designs on. She was not as powerless as she first thought.

"I refuse," she declared. "I won't be a party to your perversions. A whisper here and there and your filthy secrets will become the gossip of the year. I dress the wives of many important men. What do you think those men will do when they hear what you truly are?"

His eyes snapped to angry slits. Then after a moment, he turned back to the gowns, as if her threat were of no consequence. "Exposing me, dear Arianne, could be just as dangerous for you, for you have secrets as well. How do you think Lythmore will react upon learning what you have done? And your dear father, held in Pinard's grip, might very well find that grip tightening around his neck. Your business, of course, would fail, but if you are in prison, that would not matter. As for your son…" He finished with a casual shrug. Pulling a frock from the ones before him, he swung back toward her and held it up. "This is lovely. Perhaps something like this for my friend."

Arianne drew a shaky breath. She was trapped, for she had no way of knowing what connections de Pagière had that would allow him to release that information about her, and he could do it all in the blink of an eye, even before she made good on her threat to expose him and have him thrown in prison. No doubt, he could destroy her from behind prison walls if he wanted. But she vowed somehow, someday, she would seek her revenge.

"You must send word before you come," she said, surprised that her voice sounded so steady. "I will take care of the fittings personally."

"You are a very intelligent woman, Arianne." He smiled indulgently. "I have always admired that in you."

Arianne bowed her head. Her fingers twisted tightly in her lap. She couldn't bear the sight of him any longer.

"Well, I shall leave you." De Pagière's manner was brisk, now that he had performed his errand. "Your hospitality, as always, is gracious. Until we meet again, dear Arianne."

He bowed and left the fitting room. The door did not close entirely behind him, and she heard her maid seeing him to the door. Fortunately, he was so pleased by what had just transpired that he did not take the time for another attempt at seducing her maid.

Arianne sat where she was, feeling dirty and used. She could see no way to extricate herself from the tangle she was in. De Pagière was a predator. If she wanted to keep Luc safe, she had to perform the marquis's little chore. There was nothing else she could do. Pouring herself a glass of Madeira wine, she took a large swallow as she tried to wash the bad taste out of her mouth. It was only one more secret she would have to keep. Only one more task, a fitting for gowns like all the hundreds of others she had done. No one would have to know.

She would think instead of Cameron, and the night she would spend with him as his mistress.

Leaning back in her chair, she forced herself to push de Pagière's blackmail into that dark corner where she hid her other secrets.

Instead, she pictured Cameron in her mind, his dazzling smile, his midnight eyes. She fantasized about what becoming Cameron's lover would be like. By doing so, she would be able to save him from Pinard. A smile finally touched her lips. But when she rose to attend to her duties, she was very careful to avoid looking at herself in the triple mirrors.

CHAPTER 10

Two days after his visit to Arianne, Cameron stood in the foyer of Shipley Hall. "Hello?" he called.

There was no answer. He glanced around at the pile of paint pots in a corner, a rolled-up drop cloth, a ladder on its side leaning against the wall. The foreman of the refurbishing crew, Headley, had sent him a note asking to meet him about some problem with a ceiling cornice. Cameron gave an impatient sigh. He really didn't care about the cornice, even though it had apparently been part of Sir Christopher Wren's original design for the manor. The least the foreman could do was be on time.

The empty house was gathering shadows as night approached. Twilight was turning the world into deep purples and thick blues. He wished he had remembered to bring a lantern. A sound so soft he could have imagined it tickled the edge of his awareness.

"Hello?" he called again. "Headley, is that you?"

He climbed the stairs to the next floor. Before him, the salon was hunching in on itself in the deepening twilight. The skeleton of a ladder stood in the middle of the floor, and paint pots huddled about it as if coming home to roost for the night. He looked to the right and left, but only dark emptiness greeted him.

Glancing up to the gallery at the top of the staircase to the floor above, he thought he saw a faint glow. He muttered to himself about the churlish behavior of the labor force these days as he began to climb the stairs. The glow seemed to come from his left, from the open door of the suite he planned to occupy. His annoyance began to turn to anger as he anticipated some problem with finishing that part of the house first. He wanted it completed by the following evening. The deadline he had given Arianne would have approached by then.

"Now see here, Headley," he began as he strode into the room. His words broke apart and disappeared like bubbles. His feet seemed weighted to the floor, and his jaw hung slack.

"*Bon soir*, Monsieur le Duc. I'm glad you came." Arianne's lips curved in a sultry smile.

Cameron stared. She stood near the back of the room, which was lit by clusters of candles about its perimeter. Several layers of gauzy material draped the windows and drifted on the evening breeze. Next to her on the floor lay a feather mattress covered in linen and lace with pillows of every size imaginable strewn about. A decanter of wine and two glasses, and a plate of cheese and fruit were placed on the floor, conveniently within reach of the mattress. All this registered on the fringe of his consciousness, even though he did not take his gaze from the woman before him.

She was magnificent. The dress she wore was the style of the day, but rather than being a straight column of stiff or fluffy layers, it caressed her curves. The insipid, virginal white or pastel that were all the rage had been exchanged for a deep, sensuous green. With no decoration, the dress was so simple it was nearly stark. Only a bit of black lace peeped above the daring décolletage of the neckline. She took two steps toward him, and he was able to see the outline of her hip and the roundness of her thigh as she moved. He realized she wore next to nothing beneath that slither of green.

"I made the gown, you see," she said, as she swept the skirt wide then let it slide back into place. "But I changed the color you requested. I hope you are not too disappointed."

Cameron's body leaped into arousal so quickly that he could barely focus his thoughts enough to answer. "No," he croaked. "It's…" He couldn't finish his sentence.

Her smile deepened. "I am glad you like it. Would you care for some wine?" She made a graceful gesture to the decanter and glasses.

"Yes, please." He focused on the wine flowing into the glasses while he tried to keep his desire from galloping away with his self-control.

As he accepted the glass she held out to him, he noticed his hand trembled. Her fingers brushed his, and he nearly dropped the fragile crystal. Closing his eyes, taking a swallow of the wine, he willed himself to remember that he was a gentleman, that whatever else Arianne was, she was a lady. But she did not look like a lady, standing there in that green satin invitation to sin.

He wanted very much to accept that invitation.

Arianne sipped her wine to help calm her nerves. She had never done anything like this before. Jean-Paul had courted her with gentle persuasion, and then they had wed. Their love-making had been tender and open-hearted. This man standing before her might have a tender and open-hearted side to him, but she sensed his passions ran deep. The desire in his eyes drew her in. Excitement made her pulse race. She had to remind herself she was doing this to save him. When this was over, when, somehow, she had convinced him to leave, he would be safe, and she would disappear.

She watched over the rim of her glass as Cameron emptied half of his in one gulp. So far, her plan had worked. She had caught him off-guard. The exquisite tailoring of his pantaloons did nothing to hide his arousal. Pleased, she allowed herself a smile while she tried to ignore the throb between her thighs.

Bending down, she placed her glass carefully on the floor beside the decanter. The neckline of her gown gaped open just the tiniest bit and allowed a peek of the black lace and silk chemise beneath. Straightening again, she took another step closer to him.

"I thought about your gift, and I decided I was much too serious," she said. "I guess that is what happens when one runs a business. I am not accustomed to accepting gifts from…people."

"From *people*?" he queried.

Embarrassment made her lower her eyes. "From men," she corrected. "The last man who gave me a gift that I accepted was my husband."

"Then I am flattered that you decided to accept mine." His tone was dry, his threat of ruining her hanging between them.

She laughed softly. "What I am trying to say, your grace, is that in the end, I would have accepted your gift despite your delicate nudge."

He chuckled at her irony. "You put that very nicely." His glance slid away, and he said, "I apologize for intimidating you."

Arianne caught her breath at his humble apology. Words nearly failed her, but she was able to murmur, "You are forgiven."

A corner of his mouth deepened. "*Merci.*" He placed his empty glass on the floor, took a step closer, and touched her cheek. "My gift looks magnificent on you."

His touch made her heart jump. She forced air into her lungs. "There is more."

"More?" His question broke in the middle.

"Mmm. More." Her lips parted as his fingers stroked her jaw, and she nearly succumbed to the lure of his touch. Then, remembering her intent, she spun away from him with a light laugh. She lifted her skirt and held out one green, satin-clad foot. "See?" she said with a grin. "I could not wear a gown like this without matching slippers." Pulling her skirt just a bit higher, she showed off her ankle. "And stockings. Quite expensive silk stockings."

His lashes swept down as he considered her display of foot and ankle. Then he met her gaze with a lop-sided grin. "Very nice."

She dropped her hem into place. "And there is one other thing." Taking a step closer to him, she touched the bit of black lace peeping from her neckline. "But you will have to find that yourself," she whispered.

His gaze dropped to the bit of lace. He lightly traced its edge. She saw the tiniest tremble in his fingers. His touch along her skin made her nipples pucker. A throb of desire deep in her core made her suck in a breath. How could this man have such an effect on her?

He raised his eyes, intense, burning.

"Arianne." His voice was a husky growl.

Her name on his lips in that tone drew her forward until they nearly touched. Those lips fascinated her with their sculpted perfection. She had wanted to mark their outline from the moment he had walked into her shop. She remembered the embarrassing moment when he had lifted her in his arms in Sydney Gardens, and her impulse had overridden her good sense. When she had touched that mouth.

Tonight, her good sense was locked firmly away.

With no hesitation, she touched his top lip and swept her finger from corner to corner along its curve and middle dip. Tender, but with a firm edge. Then she slid it across his bottom lip. Plumper, softer. His tongue flicked out and licked, then he drew her finger into his mouth and sucked.

The pull of his mouth stopped her breath. She felt an answering pull between her thighs. Her gaze flew up to meet his. Hot. Dark. Canny, as if he knew what she craved before she did.

His hand landed on her hip. She felt its warmth through her thin layers of clothing. He released her captive finger but caught her wrist with his free hand. Turning his head just the tiniest bit, he placed a kiss just above where his fingers held her. And then with that beautiful mouth, he rained kisses up the inside of her arm. Her eyes slipped closed as tingles erupted up her arm, down her spine, at the backs of her knees. She wanted to feel that mouth, those lips against hers very badly.

He eased her closer until she brushed against him. His heat enveloped her. His scent—woodsy and rich—filled her nose. She felt herself falling into that void again, but this time, it was a soft, gentle descent, as if cradled in a floating feather. He kissed his way across her shoulder, and then his mouth landed on the sensitive spot beneath her ear, where he sucked. With a sigh, she swayed against him.

His arms wrapped around her. His hands cupped her bottom and pulled her tight to him. His erection pressed hard against her belly. She wriggled closer, slipped her arms around his waist, binding them together.

And then his mouth claimed her lips. Desire ripped through her like a fire out of control. Feeling his arms about her, feeling the strength of him, she knew in her last coherent thought that she was doing the right thing. Somehow, she would save him.

Her need blocked out everything else. She wanted to taste, lick, devour him as she had that first time when he had carried her in Sydney Gardens. She wanted to feel every inch of his body. She wanted to dissolve into him. She wanted to flow around him. She clasped him closer as she parted her lips and invited him to taste.

Their mouths meshed, tongues slipped and licked, lips sucked. Frantic to feel more, she ground against him and whimpered.

Cameron raised his head at the tiny sound. Taking a breath, he fought for control. This woman flooded his senses, made him forget everything except her. Her scent. Her touch. Her taste. He wanted to taste more of her. He wanted her on her back on the mattress, sprawled beneath him, pliant with passion. But not yet.

Gently, he put her from him. "Slowly, Arianne. I want to savor this." Reaching up, he pulled the pins, one by one, from her hair. It tumbled, as heavy as satin, about her shoulders and down her back. A length of it flowed across his hand. It was soft and luxurious, a silken skein. He let it slip from his fingers. He followed the strands, trailing his fingers across her shoulders, then down the bare skin revealed by the deep décolletage of her neckline, to the crevice between her breasts where that bit of black lace peeked. He was wildly curious to see what was attached to that black lace. Yet, the dress defied him. He could see no obvious fasteners that would allow him into the gown or Arianne out of it.

His brow crinkled in bewilderment. "How do I—?"

Her smile interrupted him. "You will have to discover how to unfasten the gown by yourself."

Ingenious lady. He grinned. "Ah, search and discovery. I always enjoy an adventure."

Placing both hands on her shoulders, he ran them down her arms and back up again. Until he figured out the secret of her gown, he would tease and tantalize. The chase was always exhilarating. The vixen might even relent and unfasten the gown herself.

Arianne shivered at his touch and marveled that her arms should be so sensitive. Standing very still, she closed her eyes as he explored. Everywhere he touched, he started tiny fires on her skin. When his hands cupped her neck and she felt his thumb brush against her bottom lip, she opened her eyes. She was lost in the depths of the hunger in his gaze. Slowly, he replaced his thumb with his lips. Nibbling, caressing, his mouth tested, taunted, teased. It both satisfied and aroused her. But she wanted more.

She wanted to show him where the gown was fastened, to rip it from her body and stand before him in the tiny chemise. She wanted to crush herself against him, to feel the length of him, hard and unyielding. But she waited. This night was too precious to rush.

He began his exploration again, tracing the neckline of her gown, down to her breasts. Her nipples puckered against his fingers. She gasped at the pleasure that streaked through her.

He smiled. "Will you show me how to unfasten your gown?" he teased.

Her words were gone, lost in her desire. She shook her head in silent refusal.

Bedeviled by her dress, he slipped his hands down to her waist, then her hips. He cupped her buttocks and dragged her close. Her soft curves through the thin layers of satin and silk were more arousing than he could have imagined. He had never experienced anything so erotic, so enticing, so bewitching. She had him enthralled. Wanting to feel more, he slipped his hands down to her thighs, and he inched his fingers around to where her thighs met, to where she would be throbbing with need, to where he most wanted to be. She pressed against him.

"Arianne," he whispered.

Arianne drew a sharp breath when he teased her there. His hands on her body felt wonderful, magical. His fingers at her breasts sent pulses of pleasure through her. Yet, there, where her womanhood centered, was where she truly wanted him to be. His hand, his fingers, massaged and caressed, tenderly, carefully, through the satin of her gown. Her legs trembled, and her knees felt slushy. Placing her hands on his shoulders for support, she wondered how long before she collapsed onto the floor in a boneless heap. He drove her wild, arousing, igniting, never quite touching where she needed to be touched the most.

"I want you," she managed to whisper.

Her words spurred Cameron to further discovery. He wanted very badly to see what was connected to that bit of black lace. Sliding his hands back up over her hips, up her sides, he discovered a bow beneath her right arm. When he pulled it loose, the front of her dress fell open and revealed another layer underneath. Under her left arm was another bow. He tugged it apart. The final layer of green satin fell away. It revealed a strip of black silk and lace between the two sides of her gown.

He caught his breath. She was beautiful, luscious. A Siren. He needed to see more. Pushing the dress from her shoulders, he allowed it to pool about her feet. He took a step back. The black lace that had peeked from the neckline of her gown was attached to a tiny, black silk chemise that barely grazed the top of her thighs. Green satin and black lace ribbons held up her stockings. She was delectable, delicious. And he was victorious. For there, before him, was his fantasy come to life. Cool, aloof Madame de Vouvret stood before him in nothing but a chemise with her hair tumbled about her shoulders. Her eyes, the color of a turbulent sea, were dark with desire. He had ignited that passion. Only he would satisfy it. His blood pounded through him like thick honey. And just as sweet was the hot need for her that pooled in his groin.

His clothes stifled him. Dragging off his coat, he tugged at his neckcloth. He wanted to be naked, up against her, feeling that slink of black silk slide over his skin.

Arianne felt his gaze on her like a steamy caress. The approval, the passion in his eyes aroused her as much as the touch of his hands on her body. When he pulled off his coat and began to tug on his neck-cloth, she stepped forward and placed her hand over his to stop him.

"Let me do that," she said.

Untying his neckcloth, she slipped it off and let it drop to the floor. She trailed her fingers around the curve of his ear, down to that sensitive spot on his neck. She wanted to kiss and suck there, but she refrained. Now she wanted to undress him, to see the hard body that she had only felt through his clothes.

Dragging her fingers down his chest, she unbuttoned his waist-coat and pushed it from his shoulders. Then, infinitely slowly, she undid his shirt, all the way to the waistband of his pantaloons. Parting his shirt, she ran her hands over the springy, soft mat of hair that covered his chest. She found his flat, hard, nipples and toyed with them. When his breath caught in his throat, she smiled. With one finger, she followed the dark line that arrowed down and disappeared into his pantaloons. His muscles jumped beneath her touch. One by one, she unfastened the buttons of his pantaloons. His manhood sprang free, arrogant and stiff, silk over steel. She licked at one dark nipple, feeling it pebble beneath her tongue. His hand cupped the back of her head, holding her in place. Her hand snaked down and captured his erection. As she wrapped her fingers around its hard length, a low growl came from his throat. The sound sent a hot jolt through her. He grabbed her by the upper arms, pulled her straight, and fastened his mouth on hers.

This kiss was not tentative like the last, but a hungry con-verging. He devoured her, licking, sucking, tasting. She needed to feel every inch of him. Arianne ground herself against him. She loved the mass of him, the strength of him. She loved the length of his arousal pressed into the hollow of her hip. She wanted him inside her.

Breaking apart from him, she stepped back. "I want you," she said again. Her breath, ragged and quick, sounded loud in her ears. His hungry gaze seemed to bore into her most intimate places, heat-ing them. He jerked off his shirt. As he pulled his arms from his sleeves, she pushed his pantaloons off his hips. The rest of his clothes fell to a heap on the floor. She stared, fascinated by his body—his muscles rippling beneath his skin, the sprinkling of hair down his arms and legs, the mat between his thighs, and his glorious, male arousal. He was beautiful.

He took two steps toward her and swept her up into his arms. Where his skin touched her, shivers tingled on her skin. She couldn't keep her hands from him. Touching his cheek, she trailed her fingers to his mouth and indulged in those perfect lips. Tangling her fingers in his hair, she dragged his mouth down to hers and licked, sucked, tasted until they were both breathless.

He laid her on the mattress and knelt over her. "You are so beautiful," he murmured. He ran his hands down her body, from her shoulders to her toes. No part of her was missed.

Arianne lay back, open and inviting, letting him do as he wished. The touch of his hands was intoxicating. When he bent over her and took her nipple into his mouth through the black silk, when he teased it with his teeth, she cried out in pleasure and arched up. His hand slipped up her thigh beneath her chemise and finally, finally, touched her where she was throbbing, pulsing with need. His fingers had barely brushed her when she felt herself convulse into a climax.

She clung to his immobility while her senses flew apart, and a wild, spiraling cry escaped. A moment, infinity, passed while she soared and then languidly gathered herself. Realizing what had happened, a bit chagrined and embarrassed at her wild, wanton response to his touch, she gazed up at him with a wide stare.

"That was…" She had no words to describe what she'd felt.

His gaze was possessive. "You are magnificent." He touched her cheek and knelt between her knees. His fingers trailed down her throat to her breasts, where he toyed once again with her nipples. "I am going to make you mine, Arianne." His smile was superior, arrogant.

Arianne knew he spoke the truth. She wanted to be his. Her body craved him. Her reason for being with him this night was to keep him safe, but she knew in a secret part of her that she wanted him, to be with him like a normal woman, not Pinard's puppet.

When he cupped her breasts, and his thumbs strummed across her nipples, she moaned as pleasure streaked through her. She needed him, opened herself to him as he slid into her. He filled her, completed her. This was what she wanted, needed. His solidity, his mass above her made her feel soft, feminine, a woman. When he moved in her, she clung to him. She thought she had been saving him, but perhaps, he was saving her. Higher, farther, beyond thought, until her cry, his shout mingled in space among the stars.

He collapsed on top of her, and she gathered him close. While they lay quiet, while their senses returned to earth, Arianne had never felt so shattered and so fulfilled. Not even with Jean-Paul. The thought sent a pang of sadness through her. Jean-Paul, with his quiet and gentle ways, still owned a spot in her heart. Had she betrayed him by becoming Cameron's mistress?

A tear fell from the corner of her eye and slipped down her temple to disappear in her hair. Then a sob that she could not quite hold back escaped from her throat. No, she would not cry. She had not cried that night Jean-Paul had been shot — murdered — nor any night since then. She would not cry now, not now, with Cameron lying boneless and sated from their love-making above her. But somehow, the tears fell, and she could not repress her sobs.

Cameron raised his head and looked down at her. "Arianne, what is it? Did I hurt you?"

She shook her head. "No, oh, no, you were *magnifique.*" Her attempt at a smile was unsuccessful.

"What is it then?" He smoothed a lock of hair from her cheek and rolled off her.

"It's only — only — " She could go no further before she dissolved into tears.

He gathered her in his arms and held her while she cried against his chest. As he rubbed her back and spoke soothing words, she clutched at him again, finding solace in his solidity. Even in her distress, she marveled at the way she so easily turned to him and felt comforted by him, by the way she wanted to open herself to him, body and soul. Even as she cried for her loss of Jean-Paul, her husband, her life-mate, she realized she had come to love the man who so quietly, so sensitively, held her. The man whom she was supposed to destroy.

No! That was not supposed to happen. She was not supposed to fall in love with Cameron. He was the brother of Ian West, the man she had helped destroy two years ago. When Cameron discovered the truth, he would despise her. She could not love him, not now, not ever.

But she did.

The knowledge made her clutch him harder.

Cameron held her tightly against him until he felt her tears finally fade away and stop. He had never had a woman dissolve into tears after making love. Disconcerted, he wondered if he had hurt her, despite her denial.

Stroking her back, trying to calm her, he asked again, "Arianne, what is it? What's wrong?"

Wordlessly, she shook her head.

He placed a kiss on her temple. "What did I do wrong?"

"Nothing." Her voice was muffled against his chest. "I have never felt so...so...*incroyable*."

Incredible. Her description made him smile with satisfaction. He had felt the same, soaring, reaching heights of pleasure he had not known existed. Yet, her tears puzzled him. If he had not hurt her, if she had never experienced anything so wonderful before, then why was she...? Inspiration struck.

"Arianne, is it because of your husband?" he asked. "Is that why you're crying?"

"*Oui.*"

"Is it because you haven't—Is it because this is the first—" Not quite sure how to ask the next question, he stopped and drew a breath.

"You are the first man I have been with since my husband," she confessed in a low murmur. "I feel I have betrayed him, you see. I am sorry. I did not mean to ruin your night."

At her confession, something splendid soared inside him. He was the first man she had been with since her husband's death. He felt honored, humbled, alive. "Arianne, you have not ruined my night. You were—are—wonderful. *Magnifique.*" He tucked a strand of hair behind her ear. "Arianne, look at me."

"No, no, my eyes are puffy, and my nose is all red." She demonstrated with a sniff.

He lifted her chin with a finger. "Look at me."

She raised her head. Her eyes were watery, her lashes spikey. She sniffed.

"You are beautiful." He dropped a kiss on her red nose. "I am honored that I am the first man since your husband. You should never forget him, but you are still here, alive, and you cannot crawl into the grave with him."

"But I...he..." She floundered.

"You are young and beautiful," he said earnestly. "You should have children."

Arianne stared up at him. Children. Little Luc.

De Pagière.

Pinard.

No, she would not think of that now. Now, tonight, she was with Cameron as his mistress, with no cares, no worries. She reached up and touched his cheek. "You are a good man, Cameron, Monsieur le Duc."

His smile was ironic. "There are some who might disagree with you."

She touched his lips. "Then, they have not made love with you."

He chuckled. "No, they haven't."

His humor lightened her mood. Grinning, she pushed him onto his back and sprawled above him. "But I have made love with you, and I should like to do it again."

"Again?" His brow crinkled. "I'm not sure..."

"I will help you." She dropped a light kiss beside his mouth.

"Well, I don't know...," he hedged playfully.

"Of course you can." She traced his ear with her tongue.

"It's not that easy for a man..." he teased.

"I will make it very easy." She sucked at the pulse throbbing in his throat.

He sighed as if reluctant. "Well, perhaps..."

She placed her lips against his and squirmed against him. Immediately, she felt his hard response. Raising her head, she smiled down at him. "You are a good man, Cameron, Monsieur le Duc," she said again but meant it in an entirely different way.

He laughed and rolled her onto her back.

She tangled her fingers in his hair and pulled his head down to her so she could taste his mouth again.

There were no words after that, only pleasured sighs and, finally, wild cries of passion. They slept, then, for a while, tangled about each other. And when they awoke, once more, before the dawn came to invade their secret place, they made love again, lingeringly, clinging to each other like a lifeline for their wrecked souls.

Cameron awoke with the sun glaring in his eyes. He snapped them shut, rolled over and reached for Arianne. His hand groped among the tumbled pillows and sheets. He was alone on the mattress. A tug of loneliness pulled at him and created a vague ache. He thought she might be beside him when he awoke.

He enjoyed a satisfying yawn and stretch, then lay sprawled across the mattress as he relived the past night. Arianne had been magnificent. In turns, the seductive temptress and cuddling kitten, she had aroused him until he had been mindless, filled with her touch, her scent, her need. He had never wanted a woman so badly or been so fulfilled.

His plan to seduce her to learn her secrets, to discover if she were the woman he sought, had gone awry. She had given up no secrets last night. She had, in fact, turned the tables on him by surprising him with her acquiescence. As he thought about that, he sat up and gazed about the room. The candles had all spent themselves, and the candlesticks sat amidst pools of hardened wax. The plate of fruit and cheese lay untouched. Their wine glasses still sat where they had left them. They had not needed either food or wine. Only each other.

Across the foot of the bed lay the green satin dress. His eyes narrowed at that. The minx had planned so well that she must have brought other clothes for her morning escape. Atop the dress was a single white flower, a daisy, like the one he had given her after their first kiss. He scooped it up and twirled it between his fingers. The blood surged through his veins and pooled in his groin. Just the thought of her made him want her again.

Rolling from the mattress, he drew on his clothes as he wondered how soon he would be able to see her again. He would have to tread softly, for she was a woman with a mind of her own and reluctant to become his mistress. She had so many secrets she had not yet shared with him. His brain caught on one word. Secrets. He stared down at the flower lying on the mattress where he had tossed it. Had she left it as a reminder of their walk in Crescent Fields? Or as a message of something else?

A daisy. *Une marguerite.* Marguerite.

The name of the woman who had destroyed his brother.

Realization flashed in his brain. Marguerite and Arianne were the same person. She had left the daisy as a confession.

His suspicions had been right all along, but he had ignored them, discarded them because she had rebuffed him, because he had been blinded by her beauty. Because he had let his desire override his common sense. He had been so stupid. She had played him like a maestro played his instrument.

His rage exploded in a blinding red haze. With a roar, he hurled one wine glass, then the other against the wall. Crystal shattered, and the wine dribbled down the freshly painted plaster like blood. Sweeping up the decanter, he sent that after the glasses. His foot slammed against the plate of fruit and cheese and sent it careening across the floor. Ripping the gauzy layers from the windows, he shredded them into tiny pieces. Like a madman, he tore the sheets from the mattress and mauled the pillows until feathers flew like snowflakes in a blizzard. A wild mantra sounded in his brain.

Arianne.

Marguerite.

Arianne.

Marguerite.

Arianne.

She was the Circe who had enticed, then destroyed his brother. She was the Jezebel. She was the mystery woman for whom he had been searching. He had allowed his passion to wipe out his good sense. The pain at learning the truth clawed at him. Marguerite. Arianne.

Oh, Arianne!

Panting, spent finally, he surveyed the damage he had done. He felt exhausted and depleted, old, used up. Used. The only thing to escape his wrath was the dress, the green satin Siren's song, the dress of a whore. Picking it up, he crushed it in his fist. Whose whore was she? Who pulled her strings?

A cold, hard thing congealed inside him. He would discover the answer to his question. He would destroy whoever had destroyed Ian, whoever was out to destroy him, and then...

Then meticulously, exquisitely, with infinite patience, he would destroy Arianne de Vouvret and her puppet master.

CHAPTER 11

"Thank you, Sir Roderick, for seeing me to my door," Arianne told the gentleman as she stepped across her threshold. "I enjoyed myself as always this evening, and you have been most kind."

"Yes, well." He harrumphed. "Always a pleasure, madame, always a pleasure." He squinted past her at the dark interior behind her. "Where's your maid? Insolent of the girl to take herself off to bed and not leave a light burning."

Arianne airily waved her hand. "Oh, I told her not to wait up for me. The lamp has most likely burned out. Good night, monsieur, and thank you again." She closed the door nearly in his face. Leaning against it, she let out a sigh. The evening at the theater with Sir Roderick and Lady Crump, Mrs. Weathersby, and Miss Barbara and the post-theater dinner party at Lord and Lady Houghton's should have been delightful. Instead, she had found the evening tedious, for her thoughts kept straying to Cameron and the previous night. All she wanted was to be in Cameron's arms, surrounded by him, engulfed by him. She would have settled for a glimpse of him at the theater, but he was not in attendance. Nor had she heard from him during the day. She would have thought after the magical night they had spent together that he might have sent a note, something to acknowledge what they had shared. Her disappointment was a crushing, heavy thing. She had to force herself to be gay and charming in the company of her acquaintances.

Dragging her feet, she climbed to her rooms above. She had lied to Sir Roderick. She had not told her maid to go to bed. She was alone in the house, for she had given the girl the night off, as well as the following day. Tomorrow, she would drive out to see Luc. That thought cheered her.

She pushed open the door to her dark sitting room. Annoyed at the inconvenience of having no lamp lit, she jerked the shawl from her shoulders and flung it away. She took an irritated stride into the room. A dark shape materialized before the paler starlight of the window. She halted abruptly.

Startled, then angry at the intrusion, she unleashed her ire. "Edouard, what are you doing here? How did you get in?"

A light flared and illuminated a different face than the one she expected.

"Cameron!" Delighted, she took two rushing steps toward him, to fling herself into his arms. The cold set of his features made her feet falter.

"Who is Edouard?" he asked, his tone wintry. "Your protector? Or just another man you have seduced. Or perhaps you will destroy Edouard, too."

Arianne's joy withered and died. He knew. He knew of her secret, her sin. She had left the daisy for him the night before as a reminder of their first kiss. She should have known he would have made the connection to his brother. Perhaps, she had also left it because deep down, she wanted him to learn of her sin. And now he hated her, despised her, as she knew he would. All she could do now was what she must to protect her father and Luc.

She shook her head forlornly. "No, he is none of those things." Like her happiness, her voice was flat, dead.

"Then who is he?" His question was a chilly demand.

She found shelter in the aloofness she had practiced for so many years. "That, your grace, is none of your business."

"*Who is he?*" His voice shook with his fury.

Daunted by his rage, she pretended composure. "If you must know, he is my messenger, the man who carries designs to certain of my customers for their approval before I begin their gowns."

His eyes narrowed in his disbelief. "If that is all he is, why would he be here in your rooms at such an hour?"

"He has an inflated idea of his importance to me. The man has delusions of becoming my lover." Which was true. She did not lie.

"*Becoming* your lover?" He stalked two steps closer. "I think you lie, Arianne de Vouvret. I think the man is already your lover."

The idea of wanting Edouard Courcy in her bed made her laugh and made her say something very foolish. "Then you must believe I am very indiscriminate in my tastes."

"That is exactly what I believe. Whore." He whipped the word at her.

It felt like a physical assault. Arianne flinched, both from his accusation and her own guilt. Although she had never given herself to any other man like she had to Cameron, not even to Jean-Paul, in a sense, he was right. She had played the coquette because that was what Pinard had ordered her to do. She had tormented Ian West, had made him love her. But what she had given to Cameron the night before had nothing to do with Pinard and everything to do with her love for the man before her, the man who now hated her.

He picked up a bundle from the chair beside him. Throwing it at her, he ordered, "Put it on. I don't want to forget what I'm dealing with."

The bundle landed against her chest, and reflexively, she caught it. Even before she glanced down at it, she knew what it was—the green satin dress and the black silk and lace chemise. She wanted to ask him not to force her to wear the dress, for she had made it for him, out of love, but the unyielding look in his eyes told her that whatever she might say would be disbelieved.

Instead, quietly, she said, "I will only be a few moments." She began to move toward her bedchamber.

He blocked her path. "Oh, no, you're not leaving my sight."

Heat flooded her cheeks. The last thing she wanted was to undress before this man in the mood he was in. She swallowed. "Then could you at least turn around, please?"

He touched her cheek, then cupped her chin in his hand, but the gesture was a mockery of his tenderness from the night before. His lips—those beautiful lips—curled in a cold smile. "Surely, you must be accustomed to undressing before men. Why the sudden modesty, *Marguerite*?"

His touch and that name cracked her composure. Tears filled her eyes. One spilled down her cheek. He responded to that with a cruel chuckle.

The sound made anger flare within her. What right did he have to mock her, to belittle her feelings? He knew nothing. Nothing!

Jerking away, she stomped to a chair where she tossed down the dress and began to unfasten her clothes. She turned away from him as she struggled with the buttons down the back of her gown. Her fingers were clumsy, and two buttons defied her. He brushed away her hands and undid the buttons for her. Then, she felt his hands smooth across her back before he pushed the dress from her shoulders.

She could not see his face, but his touch had been gentle. Perhaps she had imagined it, but she thought his hands had lingered for just the tiniest moment on her shoulders before he pushed the gown from them and moved away. Did he still feel some fondness for her? The thought gave her a spark of hope that they might salvage something positive from this terrible nightmare. She quashed that idea immediately. Cameron was too furious to forgive her, and she was still tied to Pinard.

Stepping out of her gown and the petticoat beneath, then pulling her chemise over her head, she could feel his eyes on her back. This time, she felt no answering throb of desire. Instead, she felt exposed, vulnerable, shamed. Quickly, she pulled on the black silk chemise and the green satin dress. Turning finally to face him, she discovered that being clothed did not make those feelings go away. His gaze swept over her with crude vulgarity. She never thought she could feel so humiliated just from a glance.

"Here, put these on. You might as well complete the costume." He tossed the green satin slippers at her.

She fumbled to catch them. One fell to the floor at her feet. Sluggishly, like an old woman, she bent to retrieve it, and moving like someone ancient and sapped of all energy, she sat in the chair to do as he commanded. This was her penance, she told herself. This was what she deserved for helping to destroy Ian. It did not matter that she had been forced to it, that her father would have died if she had disobeyed Pinard. It did not matter that she had to keep the existence of Luc a secret. Whatever Cameron had planned for her, she would accept. Despite the pain, despite the fear.

"Stand up," he ordered when he saw she had finished. "Take down your hair."

Arianne did as she was told, then stood quietly while she waited for whatever he would do next. He gazed at her in silence a moment. Cold fury showed in his eyes, and something else — sorrow, pain. His suffering touched her, and she wanted to reach out to him, to make it go away. She wanted to take back the moment when she had forced a cruel laugh at Ian West's declaration of love. She wanted to take back her words when she told him he was a fool for wanting to marry her, that he was not good enough for her. She wanted to murder Henri Pinard for forcing her to do such a terrible thing.

"So, *Marguerite*, is this how you looked the night you seduced my brother?" His tone was mildly curious, but Arianne sensed the rage barely leashed beneath the surface of his words.

That name, the one Ian had called her, knifed into her heart. Wordlessly, she shook her head in denial.

"No? You did not look like this? How then?" He strode forward and grabbed the front of her dress in both hands. "Maybe you stood before him like this." With a jerk and the sound of rending cloth, he tore the front of her dress apart. Arianne was too shocked to move. "Or maybe, it was like this." With another jerk, he ripped her chemise down the front.

"No!" she cried.

Grabbing the pieces of her clothing together, she tried to spin away from him. He caught her by the arm. With a tug and a twist, he yanked her up against his hard chest. He forced her to look up at him.

"Then how did you seduce Ian, Marguerite?" He murmured the words, inches from her mouth, like a lover might murmur endearments.

Arianne stared up into his dark eyes, wanting the feel of his lips on hers, knowing that would never happen, realizing she had lost something precious. "I never — I didn't — " Somehow, she could not find the words to deny his accusation.

"No? You didn't seduce Ian? Then I must have made a terrible mistake," he mocked. "You did not touch him like this?" He trailed his fingers around her ear and down her throat. "Nor like this?" His hand traced across her shoulder and down her back to her buttocks. "Nor like this?" Gripping her hard, he ground against her.

"No!" she sobbed, feeling shamed by his touch, so different than the night before.

So different from his brother. She had never loved Ian. She had liked him and been fond of him. But she had never given him her body, only her charm and empty promises. Promises, then cruel rejection that had destroyed him.

Guilt, that loathsome serpent, writhed within her.

Cameron spat out one vulgar, vile word. Swinging away, he stalked to the other side of the room. She sank into the chair. With his back to her, he stared out the window into the night. She heard his breathing, great gulping breaths, as he fought with his rage. He was turned away from her and all the way across the room. If she moved very quietly and very quickly, she might be able to escape. But she remained stuck where she was. Where would she go if she escaped? To Pinard, to have Cameron follow her to his death? To Luc, to have Cameron discover his existence and use her son against her? Both of those options appalled her. Besides, if she escaped, Cameron would only hunt her down.

Cameron stared out the window, but he did not really see the moonlit buildings, the starlit sky. His rage and pain twisted together inside him like twin snakes until he could think of nothing else. He had wanted to kill her. He knew how, quietly, deadly, with his hands. That was a skill he had learned for his own protection, working with his friends, Wyndham and Dunbary. But he had a conscience, and that prevented him from following through, despite his rage. And he knew that killing her would not bring Ian back. But something else had halted his hand. He was not sure what that something else was. Perhaps it was what they had shared the night before. Or perhaps it was the emotional pain that he saw in her eyes. Maybe she had a conscience, too. He nearly laughed at that. If she had a conscience, why had she done what she had to his brother?

When he brought his emotions under control, he turned to look at her. She sat and gazed warily back at him. Her eyes held the sheen of tears. He was too angry to care that she cried. He raised a curious brow.

"What? No attempt to escape me? Or to murder me while my back is turned? But then, that type of murder is not your style, is it, Madame de Vouvret? You prefer to bind a man to you until he has no will of his own, and then cut him free to fall into despair, despair so great that he does your dirty work for you. *So that he kills himself.*"

She shook her head, her coppery tresses catching the light, then falling back into darkness. "No! I didn't—I never meant—"

He leaned his hip against a table, crossed his arms, and glared at her.

She drew a breath and finished, "I never meant for him to d-d...I never meant for that to happen."

"Then what did you mean to happen? Suppose you explain that to me." He made his tone deceptively gentle. This was not the time to frighten her into silence. For some reason, he wanted to hear her explanation. He *needed* to hear it.

She pulled her bottom lip between her teeth. Even now, when he knew her for what she was, that small action aroused him. He could still taste that lip, could still feel it, plump and sensuous, beneath his. Forcing himself to remember that she was a Circe, a Jezebel, a woman who knew all the tricks of seduction, he focused on his anger.

"I—I don't know what I meant to happen," she said. She shook her head. "But not that. Never that."

He banged his fist on the table beside him. The candlestick and vase of flowers on it jumped. "You lie! What did you expect Ian to do? He lost a fortune, his reputation, and the woman he thought he loved betrayed him. Why? Why did you want to destroy him?"

"I didn't want to destroy him. I never wanted to do that." Tears flowed down her cheeks.

Something in the inflection of her words made him ask, "Then who did?"

Her eyes widened, and her lips parted in surprise at his question. She stared at him a moment, then pressed her mouth closed and lowered her head. "No one." Her answer was muted.

Striding forward, he tossed the scrap of dress design he had received from Dunbary into her lap. Even though she made no move, he heard her quick intake of breath.

"I know this is yours," he said. "I think it is somehow connected to Ian's death. I don't know yet what the connection is, but I'll find out. I can use that scrap to have you arrested for smuggling, or for being a traitor. I will take you to London myself and turn you over to the authorities. Or you can tell me why you did what you did to my brother and who was the man who aided you."

She looked up at him. Her face was pale, and torment clouded her eyes. "I can't. There was no one else."

He was torn between wanting to strangle her and wanting to gather her in his arms to ease her pain. Doing neither, he turned and walked away.

Arianne watched him turn his back and stand before the window again. Hurt so sharp she nearly cried out sliced through her. She could have absorbed his anger, accepted it as her due, for at least then she would have known he felt some emotion toward her. But his cold dismissal was too much to bear. She wanted to call out to him, to tell him about Pinard and de Pagière and the others, to tell him of her father and little Luc. But she could not. Once he knew, he might do something to endanger her father's life or alert Pinard to the knowledge of Luc's existence. Having de Pagière know about her son was precarious enough, despite their agreement.

His voice came then, calm, distant, from across the room. "When did I become your next victim, Arianne?"

She would not, could not, answer that.

"Have you ever heard of the black widow spider?" His question was conversational. He did not wait for her answer. "She weaves this wonderful, beautiful web, then sits in the middle of it and lures her mate to her. When she has taken what she wants from him, she eats him."

An inarticulate sound, partway between a sob and a groan, escaped her throat.

He swung about to face her. "Amazing, isn't it, how nature is reflected in the human race?"

172

"Please, don't do this." She wrapped her arms around her middle, trying to block the terrible pain. "I didn't know. I didn't know."

"Perhaps not then, but you do now. Now you know exactly what you did to Ian. And you were going to do it again to me." He strode forward to stand over her.

"No! That's not true! Last night—" She stopped, swallowed, and tried to steady her voice.

"Ah, last night," he mocked.

"Last night, I was trying to save you." She flung her words at him like a challenge.

He laughed contemptuously. "How? By seducing me? By luring me into your web? By making me believe you had not lain with any other man besides your dearly departed husband?"

She shot to her feet, despite the anger spiking off him like dangerous blades. "It's true! I did not lie to you."

His silence felt like a heavy weight as he stared at her. Then he said, "Perhaps you can tell me why you decided to so honor me. Am I that much of a prize that you felt the need to play the whore? Or perhaps that's not the reason either. How much of a reward were you to receive for offering yourself to me?" As she opened her mouth to reply, he interrupted by slicing his hand through the air. "Don't bother to answer that. I'm not sure I want to know."

Arianne searched for words to convince him that she was trying to save him. She couldn't tell him she loved him. He would only laugh at her. Finding no words, she bowed her head. Her gaze fell on the scrap of parchment in her lap. It was from the message she had sent to Pinard after Cameron had first appeared at her door. She wondered how Cameron had acquired it and how long he'd had possession of it. Courcy had told her that the fisherman who sailed her dress designs across the Channel had been stopped by the naval patrols. Only someone connected to the government would have access to anything they had confiscated. Did that mean Cameron was a spy? Had he come to Bath specifically to find her? Or had he come for some other reason? Had he known she was Ian's Marguerite all along? Had his charming pursuit of her been a sham?

She felt a crushing, heavy feeling in her chest at the thought. His invitation to walk, his ardor, his gift of the dress had all been tools in his search. They had not been for her because of who she was, but for what she was: the instrument of his brother's destruction.

Frustration at what had been done to her by Pinard, by what he had forced her to do, by what she had just learned about the man she loved turned into wild, primal rage. Catapulting from the chair, she took one step toward him and shook the bit of parchment at him.

"How long?" she demanded. "How long have you had this? How long have you been stalking me? You talk of me being the whore. Ha! It's not just women who can lay claim to that title. You seduced me, made me believe that you were attracted to me. Liar. Rogue. *Bâtard. Cochon. Animale.*" She threw the bit of parchment at him, then stalked to the shelves against the wall. Pulling out the copy of *Pride and Prejudice*, she flipped the pages open upside-down until the single daisy petal she had hidden there fluttered out. Snatching it up, she held it out to him in her open palm. "'For the fairest flower of them all,'" she quoted. "Lies. All lies. Last night meant nothing to you except a roll in bed. How you must have laughed with glee when you saw me in your house last night. Oh, I was so stupid, so blind. You want to know who helped me destroy Ian? No one. I did it myself. Everything. So, go to hell, Monsieur le Duc!"

Closing her fist around the flower petal, she held it to her breast, then she stalked to her bedchamber, and slammed the door behind her. She did not care what Cameron did. He could break the door down and strangle her. He could go collect the authorities and have her arrested. At least then, she would be finished with Pinard. She was tired of fighting, tired of hiding, tired of walking the sword's edge between truth and lies. Going to her bed, she flung herself down on it and curled up as small as she could get.

Later, she would deal with her broken heart. Later, she would push the love she felt for him into that dark corner where she kept the rest of her feelings. Later, after he had gone. After he had walked out of her life.

Dry-eyed, she waited to see what he would do. She felt a stab of guilt, for her father was still in Pinard's clutches. He was innocent in all this. He had done nothing to deserve Cameron's rage. Perhaps, before Cameron had her arrested, she could convince him to try to rescue her father. But her son would remain a secret. Nothing would make her reveal his existence. George and Bess Inglis would keep Luc safe. She would warn them of de Pagière. They would take her son away, raise him as their own, and eventually, Luc would forget her. She tried to convince herself that he would be better off that way.

Finally, after what seemed like a very long time, she heard the bedchamber door open and swing back to bump the wall. Unmoving, she listened to his silence, then his footsteps crossing the floor to the side of the bed. When he spoke, his voice, although quiet, made her jump.

"You almost had me convinced." He paused, perhaps waiting for her to respond. When she did not move or answer, he went on. "You almost persuaded me that you were doing this by yourself, but I know that's a lie. You see, I know what a spy is, how a spy works. And I know a spy never works alone. You have acted precisely as a spy would, so I know you are not working alone." He leaned on the bed and loomed over her. "Who are you working for, Arianne? Who are you protecting?"

She remained silent, unmoving.

He curled his fingers around her shoulder and pulled her onto her back, so she was forced to look at him. "Who, Arianne? Who is it?"

She wanted so much to tell him, to blurt out her whole story. But she could not. Not now, not yet. The safety of her son and her father demanded her silence. He was so filled with rage that she didn't know how he would react. He might help her save them. Or he might feel he was exacting his revenge by leaving them to Pinard. His eyes were dark with emotions she dared not name. She wanted to erase that turmoil of emotions, to have only one, focused only on her. But that was impossible. So she pressed her lips together and turned her head to stare at the wall.

He straightened and began pacing around the bed, down one side, across the foot, up the other side, to turn and start another round. "You have told me often that I know nothing about you. That is not quite true." He passed through her field of vision, then out again. "I know you work hard at your profession of modiste, and you are very good at it."

He stopped before her line of sight when he said that last. His expression was sincere. A small glow ignited in her at his words, but it was too little too late. She could only watch him and wait.

He began pacing again. "A woman who works so hard and is so successful must have some integrity. Otherwise, her customers would leave her. Your customers are loyal and sing your praises. You must be honorable and decent for all those women to come to you. For a woman like that to do what she did to Ian…it just doesn't make any sense." He stopped before her again. "Why did you destroy Ian?"

She whimpered in frustration and rolled onto her side away from him. The anger, the accusation, the plea for an explanation that was in his eyes was more than she could bear. With a growl like an angry wildcat, he pounced on the bed. Straddling her on his knees, he pushed her onto her back.

He glowered down at her and snarled, "Why? Why did you destroy my brother? Who helped you? *Who helped you?*" He shook her with each word.

His angry persistence, her frustration at being unable to answer him, fueled her anger. She would fight for her father, for her son, for herself. Pushing against his chest, she tried to get him to move. "Get off me." She felt as though she were shoving against a stone building. "I don't have to tell you anything."

"Oh, yes, you do. And you will." His eyes narrowed with his confidence. "I know ways to make you tell me everything I want to know." His fingers trailed from her shoulder to the crevice between her breasts. Leaning down, he tickled her ear with his tongue. "Everything," he whispered.

Arianne swallowed convulsively. Her skin flamed where his fingers touched. Her pulse raced at the caress of his tongue. Even now, when she knew he despised her, when she feared his threat, her traitorous body craved him. She wanted to lay beneath him—open, compliant, yielding. Willing herself not to give in to temptation, she closed her eyes to gather herself. With a single motion, she brought up her knees, heaved him off her, and scrambled from the bed. She expected him to come after her, and she stood ready to flee. Knowing he would never let her completely escape, all she wanted was to be away from his body, the touch of him, the scent of him. If she could keep some space between them, then she might be able to keep her sanity — and her secrets.

She was surprised when he did not chase her. Clutching the front of her dress together, she watched him lithely slip from the bed and stalk toward her. She retreated until she came up against a small chair in the corner of the room.

"You won't escape me," he informed her.

"I know." But even as she acquiesced, she defied him with her eyes.

"You'll stay here until you tell me what I want to know," he stated flatly.

She shook her head in denial.

"Oh, yes. You will." Glancing out the window, he sighed. "It's late. Are you tired, Arianne?"

Yes, she was very tired. Tired of hiding, tired of lying, and tired from lack of sleep. When she followed his gaze, she saw the faint line of dawn beginning to appear above the buildings. She had been awake for almost twenty-four hours. In a few hours, she should be on her way to visit Luc. Panic grabbed her at the thought. She had to go to him, protect him. But the man standing before her would not allow her to leave her rooms. Somehow, she had to escape.

He turned back to her. "When are your servants coming back?"

The question startled her, but it also gave her some hope. Her maid would be returning later that day. Marie and the other seamstresses would not be back until the next day, but he did not have to know that.

"They'll all be coming back soon," she said. "You'll have to leave."

He laughed at that. "Why would I want to leave? I have the woman who destroyed my brother. Wouldn't it be fitting for her servants to discover she is not the paragon of virtue they believe her to be?"

The blood drained from her face. She knew the ordered life she had created would not go on forever, but the reality of its demise and the reality of her confinement made her knees quake. How would she be able to support Luc and herself? How would she be able to save her father? Somehow, she had to strike a bargain with this man of midnight eyes and dazzling smile.

Wetting her lips, she blurted, "I lied."

CHAPTER 12

His bark of cynical laughter made her cringe. "Why doesn't that surprise me?" He crossed his arms over his chest and raised his brows expectantly. "Well?"

Arianne flicked her tongue across her lips again. "Not all of my staff will be returning. Only my personal maid. The rest will not return until tomorrow."

"Is that all?" He seemed disappointed that she had not laid out the whole evil truth all at once.

"Yes," she said, her tone level.

"You don't have anything else to tell me?" A single brow curved up.

"No." She forced herself to meet his gaze.

"Well, then, we'll just stay here until you decide that your reputation has been dirtied enough for you to confide in me. We'll have your maid turn away anyone who comes to your shop today."

A tiny twinge of relief passed through her. "No one will come today. My shop is closed for the day."

"All the better. When your maid begins to talk to her friends about the gentleman who has stayed in your rooms for a night and a day, tongues will wag about the well-respected Madame de Vouvret. Do you think the upstanding ladies of Bath will come to you for their gowns after that?"

She swallowed in a dry throat. "Please, don't force my maid into this. She knows nothing about—. She knows nothing about any of it. Let me talk to her, give her the day off."

His eyes narrowed. "If I do this for you, will you tell me who else is involved?"

Arianne chewed on her bottom lip as she considered her options. Finally, she jerked her head in a nod. She would tell him only one name, a name that would convince him that she was not lying and would satisfy him that no one else was involved. She could not tell him about Pinard and her father, nor about Luc. If she told him, he would do something to alert Pinard. Her father would be killed. Luc would be taken from her. They would be lost to her forever, and then *she* would be lost.

From below, Arianne heard the sound of the door being unlocked, heard her maid, Lizzie, enter and quietly close the door behind her. She was a good girl, a dependable and conscientious maid. The girl's parents worked on an estate somewhere between Bath and London and had been in service all their lives. Lizzie could visit them now, for at least several days, for she was going to give the girl an extended leave. She wanted no one around while Cameron threatened her with exposure.

Cameron had heard Lizzie, too. "Your maid?"

"Yes. Please, may I go down alone to speak with her?" she entreated.

"And let you slip away?" He huffed a cynical laugh. "I think not. Ring for her. Have her come up. I will stay out of sight."

Arianne sent him an annoyed glance. "I said I would tell you who else was involved. If I run away, how would I do that?"

His smile was cold. "Exactly."

Arianne shivered. She was not sure whether her chill came from his expression or the coolness in the air.

He glanced at her hand clutching the green satin and black silk together. "Put on something else. I'm beginning to hate that gown." As she moved past him to her armoire, his hand wrapped about her wrist. "Don't try anything foolish when you speak with your maid. I won't hesitate to dirty your reputation."

Arianne jerked her wrist free, glared at him, and stalked across the room. After pulling a dressing gown from her armoire, she stripped off the green satin rag and its black silk companion. She gave no thought to the fact that her naked back was exposed to his view for a moment. This was no time for thoughts of seduction. This was a time for battle, a battle of wits, a battle of wills. She had to win this or her father's life would be forfeit, she would never see Luc again, her whole world would be lost.

Tying the sash of the gown about her waist, she turned back to him. "All right?"

He nodded and motioned to the bellpull beside the bed. Arianne obediently walked over and jerked it. Almost immediately, she heard Lizzie's footsteps on the stairs, and a light rap came at her sitting room door. Cameron hid in her bedchamber just as the girl stepped across the threshold

"Ooh, madam, I didn't expect ye t'be up an' about so early," Lizzie exclaimed as she bobbed a curtsy. The girl, still in her street clothes, had not even had time to tie on an apron.

Arianne forced a calm smile, then explained about the days off.

Lizzie's face lit up. "There's a post-chaise t' London, leaves in about an hour, goes right past me mum's and dad's. I can get a ticket an' be off on it if I hurry. That is if ye don't need me an' all."

With a wave of her hand and a smile, Arianne dismissed her. "I will send a message in a few days when I need you to return. *Bon voyage*, Lizzie."

Lizzie bobbed another curtsy and flew out the door and back down the stairs. Arianne breathed a sigh of relief as Cameron emerged from the other room. He had kept his promise and not revealed himself. Now it was her turn to keep her promise.

They both remained silent and unmoving while they waited for Lizzie to leave. After only a few moments, they heard the door open and close. Lizzie was gone. They were alone.

Arianne did not move as she prepared herself for the coming battle. She could feel Cameron behind her as he waited, like a predator studying its victim, gauging the best time to pounce. Reluctantly, she turned to face him.

"Rathbone," she said. "Mr. Clifford Rathbone. He is the other person involved. He must have offered you a chance to invest in some scheme by now."

Cameron's eyebrows lifted in mild surprise. "As a matter of fact, he has. A venture into India for diamonds."

"Don't invest in it," she advised with a shake of her head. "The venture is a sham. He'll swindle you out of every shilling."

"How kind of you to warn me." His tone was sardonic. "What was your part in the scheme?"

Arianne laughed, but it came out brittle and forced. "Why, I was to make you fall in love with me. You were to become so infatuated that you would not be able to think straight. You would let Rathbone handle the investment. When you were completely hooked, I was to break off our relationship, and at the same time, Rathbone would tell you that all the investment funds were lost."

An odd expression crossed his face. Arianne thought it might be pain, but it was gone swiftly, replaced by the suspicious, guarded look he had worn since she had arrived home.

"I see." Cameron nodded. "What would you get out of this?"

"Why…" Arianne was a bit flustered by his question, and she searched frantically for an answer. "Why, Rathbone and I would split the money."

He stalked toward her. "And what was I expected to do? Slink away to lick my wounds? Didn't it ever occur to you that I might go to the authorities?"

"Well…" Arianne fell back a step.

He followed. "You've been a modiste in Bath for over four years. I checked. Were you going to give up your business for a few banknotes?"

"I…" Arianne did not know how to answer.

"Why me?" he demanded. "Why was I the target? What did I do to make you hate me so much?"

Arianne's emotions roiled through her in a tangle. Unable to tell him the truth, fearful of what he might do if he learned it, she found her brain numb and her tongue paralyzed.

He persisted. "What did my brother do to you to make you hate him so much?"

Guilt finally made her cry out, "I didn't hate him! I didn't!" Fear for herself, guilt at her actions, terror for her father and son made her tremble. Every inch of her seemed to shiver, harder and harder. Her hands, usually so steady with a needle, were like fluttery birds. Her teeth chattered in her head. Her knees vibrated beneath her weight. "I d-didn't h-hate him. I d-don't hate y-you." She took a breath, then whispered, "I had to do it. I had to."

Gazing at him, at this man who could make the earth disappear beneath her feet, she willed him to believe her, to stop pressing her for answers. She had no more answers to give—at least, none that she could tell him. Her secrets had to remain silent, hidden. Her father and her son depended on her silence. Hugging her arms about her, she held in her secrets and, at the same time, tried to warm herself. She was cold, so cold. Her guilt, that familiar, writhing serpent, sat like a hard rock of ice in her middle. It spread its icy tentacles along her nerves, freezing her, making her brittle and hard, shaking her until she thought she would break apart and shatter into a thousand pieces.

Then he spoke. "Ian thought he loved you, Arianne."

And she did shatter. "No-o-o!" The single word was a wail of deep, wrenching distress.

She had known that Ian thought he loved her. She had been fond of him but had not loved him in return. That did not matter. She never should have been as cruel, as vicious to him at the end. If Pinard had not held her father captive, if she had not had to keep Luc's existence a secret, she never would have treated Ian like she had. But she had to. She had to. She had to keep her father alive. She had to keep Luc a secret. She'd had no choice but to destroy Ian West.

Panting, she tried to drag air into her lungs. She could not breathe. She gasped for air like a landed trout flopping about on the bank of a stream. Great, dark spots blossomed before her eyes. Cameron's face moved in and out of focus. Death was coming for her. Death would be her release from this torment. Death would enclose her in his clawed fist and sweep her away into eternal forgetfulness. Her only regret was not seeing Luc and Papa once more before she died. But it was too late now. Blackness covered her eyes. Her knees crumpled beneath her. Oblivion claimed her.

Cameron caught her as she fainted. Cradling her in his arms, he carried her to the bed and laid her upon it. Her skin was pale and nearly as white as the pillow covering. Dark circles smudged beneath her eyes. Her lips, usually so rosy and full, had paled to a colorless hue. She looked so helpless, so innocent, so wretched.

After covering her with the counterpane, he sat beside her on the bed and took her cold, lifeless hand in his. He wanted to take her in his arms and hug some warmth back into her, to kiss life back into those pale lips, to bring color back to her cheeks, but he resisted the urge. This woman had helped destroy his brother. She had been attempting to do the same to him. He would not allow himself to be beguiled by her harmless appearance. She was not a vulnerable victim but a sly seducer. He must remember that.

He had watched her distress, watched her try to drag air into her lungs. He hated what he was doing, revolted against the cruelty he was inflicting on her. He could see her remorse, and he wanted to reach out and soothe her. Yet, he sensed she was holding something back, hiding information. No matter what it took, he was determined to discover what those secrets were. He would find out who was behind his brother's destruction.

Her fingers twitched in his hand, and she took a deep breath. A bit of color came back to her cheeks and lips. With a sigh, she turned her head on the pillow. Her eyelids fluttered open a moment, then closed again. He waited a moment, then heard her even breathing and realized she had fallen asleep.

A wry smile twitched his lips at her momentary escape from his questioning. He had known she was exhausted by the dark circles beneath her eyes and the way her skin was stretched taut across her cheekbones. Something besides late nights and long hours in her shop had been keeping her awake. Something he would discover before he left her rooms.

Laying her hand down on the bed, he stood and stretched. He was tired, too, and he decided to take advantage of Arianne's little nap to refresh himself with some sleep. Taking an extra pillow from the bed, he walked out into the sitting room. He saw a small settee that would do nicely as a cot. Placing it across the doorway to the stairs, he tossed the pillow to one end, then he went back to the bedchamber to check all the windows to make sure Arianne had no other means of escape.

He walked to the bed once more and watched as she slept. The lines of worry between her brows had smoothed out, and the tightness about her mouth had relaxed. Tendrils of coppery hair lay across her cheek. With a gentle touch, he smoothed them back. Sorrow and hurt filled him as he realized this woman who dazzled him was a conniving Jezebel. He had thought at first that she might be something more than a casual liaison, that she might even consent to be…. He closed off the rest of that thought before it formed in his head. This woman had helped to destroy Ian. She was trying to destroy him. Allowing his anger to sweep through him again, he turned and left the room to stretch out on the settee and try to get some rest.

Arianne awoke slowly, swimming up through layers of sleep before she opened her eyes. A heavy, thick sense of guilt and depression sat like a shapeless monster in her chest, and at first, she could not remember why. Then, as her gaze roamed the sunlit room, she remembered.

Cameron had come last night to accuse her, demand answers. He had wanted to know who had helped her destroy his brother.

She was a bit surprised he had left her alone, that he had allowed her to sleep. From the position of the sun shining through the window and onto the wall, she realized it must be late afternoon. She had been asleep for a very long time. Suddenly panicked, she sat up. She should have been with Luc hours ago. Mr. and Mrs. Inglis must be very worried about her. She had to go to Luc, to reassure herself that he was all right. But first, she had to make sure that Cameron was gone.

Swinging her feet to the floor, she slipped from the bed, hurried across the room, and flung open the door. She stopped short when she saw him sitting contentedly by the window and reading the newspaper. Having removed his coat, untied his stock, and unfastened the neck of his shirt, he looked like he belonged in just that position in her sitting room.

"Oh. I didn't think you were here." Even to her, the words sounded stupid.

He peeked at her around the edge of the paper. "Did you really believe I would leave you so that you might run to your accomplices and warn them?" Folding the paper, he placed it on the table beside him and stood up. "I'm glad you slept. You seemed rather worn out." He motioned to the table where a plate of cheese, a basket of bread, a few pears, and a pot of tea stood. "Would you care for something to eat?"

Pulling her dressing gown closer about her, tying the sash tighter, she raised her chin and started forward. She would not let on that she should be in the country with her son. Cameron was not to know. Luc would be safe with George and Bess Inglis. Somehow, she would get word to them that she was safe, too. Even if it was a lie.

"I'm not very hungry," she said.

"You should have something to eat to keep up your strength." He held her chair as she sat down. "I think we are going to be here for quite a while." Putting his fingers beneath her chin, he tilted her face up. "I intend to find out everything there is to know about you, Arianne de Vouvret."

A shiver slipped down her spine at his words. Before, he had made that promise teasingly, seductively. Now, his words were threatening, for they jeopardized her safety and the safety of her son and her father.

He picked up the knife and deftly sliced the pear. Placing the pieces on the plate before her, he added a few chunks of cheese and a small slice of bread. Watching him, Arianne was reminded of the small dagger she kept in a drawer of the table near the door. She did not want to hurt this man, but if she were forced to threaten him in order to save those she loved, then she would not hesitate. He poured tea into her cup, then sat down across from her.

She looked down at the food on her plate. "I'm not very hungry," she repeated.

"Guilt has a tendency to take away one's appetite." He leaned back in his chair and toyed with the fruit knife. "Fear will do that, too."

"I am not afraid of you." She knew her words were false.

"No?" He chuckled, then became deadly serious. "You should be, you know. You should be terrified of me."

She was terrified of him. Not physically. She could not be afraid of the man who had made love to her so tenderly, so passionately.

He would not harm a hair on her head. But he could destroy her life and the lives of those she held dear. She had discovered this man was not all dazzle and beauty, that a dark side lurked somewhere beneath the surface. His next words confirmed that.

"I have not lived the comfortable, soft life of a country gentle-men for the past several years as my brother did," he said as if telling some storybook tale. "I have been in the worst sections of many of the great cities of the world. I have roamed with cutpurses in Venice, bargained with pirates in Tripoli, traveled with Mongol slavers, escaped from a hellhole in Calcutta, ridden with Cossacks on the Steppes of Russia. I have stolen secrets in Madrid and Paris and sold them again in Copenhagen and Prague. I have done some despicable things, *but I have never killed an innocent man.*"

His confession shocked and frightened her. But now she knew the reason for that dark side that cracked through the charming exterior. Her hands shook, and she clasped them together in her lap as she made her protest. "I didn't—"

He held up his hand to halt her words. "I know. You didn't kill Ian. You didn't put the noose around his neck and shove him off into thin air. But you might as well have. You manipulated him—you and your accomplices." Leaning forward, he stabbed the knife into the chunk of cheese. "Who are they, Arianne?"

She jumped at his violent movement and ferocious tone. Swallowing, she reminded herself to stay calm, to keep her secrets to herself. "I already told you. Clifford Rathbone."

His eyes narrowed. "He's not the only one. Who else? Why are you protecting them?"

"There is no one else." She tried to look him in the eye when she said that, but somehow her gaze stuck on the hollow of his throat, revealed by his open shirt.

Leaning back in his chair once more, he turned to look out the window. He appeared to accept her answer, for he was silent for a moment. Then, his voice came again, casually, as if they had only been speaking of the weather. "You had a visitor while you slept."

Arianne tensed, wondering who had come to her door. Edouard Courcy perhaps? Monsieur le Marquis de Pagière? Or an innocent customer?

"He was quite concerned about you." Cameron turned those midnight eyes on her again. "He thought something terrible might have happened to you. I informed him I was watching out for your safety."

Arianne felt hysterical laughter bubble up at his statement. Cameron would keep her safe only as long as she told him nothing, only as long as she held her secrets from him.

He pulled the knife from the cheese and casually twirled the blade between his fingers. "He seemed relieved when I told him no harm had come to you. You see, he wondered why you had not arrived to visit your son."

Her whole world seemed to explode at his statement. Mr. Inglis had come. Cameron knew about Luc. Cameron knew, and now he would use that knowledge against her. She had to escape from him. She had to escape and go to Luc, to hide him away someplace safe, someplace where no one would never find him. Her foot jerked at the urge to bolt, but that little knife in his hand halted her.

"Why didn't you tell me you had a son?" he asked, sounding both merely curious and hurt by her omission at the same time.

"I couldn't." She remembered the dagger in the drawer by the door and stood. "I couldn't tell you because he is a secret." Cautiously, she edged toward the table. "No one knows I have a son." That, too, was a lie. The Marquis de Pagière knew, but he would keep that secret as long as he could use the information as leverage to get what he wanted.

Turning her back to him, she eased the drawer open. The dagger lay there, glinting dully. She closed her fingers about the handle, swung around to face him, and held the knife before her. "I'm leaving. Don't try to stop me."

Amusement flickered in his eyes. "Do you really believe you can best me with that little blade?"

"It's small, but it can still do damage." She stepped toward her bedchamber. "I'm going to dress and then I am leaving."

He grinned and folded his arms. "Let me know if you need help with your lacings."

"Damn you!" She lunged at him. Rage blotted out all coherent thought. She was furious with him, with his attitude. Did he think he could keep her captive, take over her life, with no thought of the consequences? She had two very dear people to protect. She would escape him and go to Luc. She would force him to let her go.

He jumped to meet her rush. With ease, he caught her wrists and held her arms still. The dagger waved uselessly in her hand.

"Let me go!" She struggled to free herself, but his grip held her fast. "Let me go!"

"Not until you tell me everything." His warm breath fanned her cheek.

She ignored the pull of him, the scent of him. The feel of his fingers curled around her wrists, firm but gentle. "I have told you everything. There is nothing more." She tried to wriggle free, a useless exercise.

"I think there is more." Using his superior strength, without hurting her, he turned her about and forced her to sit in the chair at the table. He pulled the dagger from her fingers and tossed it out of reach. "I have already discovered two interesting bits of information — about Rathbone and your son."

She glared at him and tried again to wrestle free. His hands held her like iron manacles.

"You don't have to be afraid for your son, Arianne. He is safe. I will not harm him." His words sounded sincere.

Turning away, she stared out the window. She could not trust him. She could not trust anyone. Pinard might find Luc, and then what would happen?

"Arianne, look at me." His calm tone demanded obedience.

Tentatively, she turned back to him.

"I promise you," he said, "on my brother's grave, that I will do nothing to harm your son, nor place him in any danger. Do you believe me?"

She gazed up at him, into those midnight eyes, into that face that made the ground disappear beneath her feet. She wanted so much to believe him. She wanted to love him, to trust him. She wanted to have his arms around her forever. She wanted — no, she could not have what she wanted. That was impossible after what she had done.

"Arianne, do you believe me?" His question snagged her attention.

God help her, she did believe him, this man with the smile of an angel, the eyes of the Devil. She jerked her head in a nod.

Releasing her, he squatted before her. "You must miss your son very much. I can fetch him and bring him back to Bath."

"No." Her word was adamant, edged with fright.

His brows curved up in surprise. "No? Then I can take you to him."

"No." She turned away again and refused to say any more.

She wanted to go to Luc more than anything, but she suspected de Pagière watched her. Even with Cameron beside her, she did not want that creature laying eyes on her child. He might go to Pinard and reveal Luc's existence. De Pagière and Pinard—two monsters who might prey on her son.

When she said nothing, he released a frustrated sigh and sat across the table from her. "Eat." His single word was clipped and short.

She shook her head. "I'm not hungry."

"Eat, damn you!" His fist came down on the table. The dishes jumped. "I do not intend to have you faint on me again."

At his outburst, she cast an apprehensive glance in his direction. His mouth was an uncompromising line. Deciding she should do as he commanded, with shaky fingers, she picked up a slice of pear and nibbled on it. The sweet, ripe fruit tasted like old wool in her mouth. Somehow, she finished the pear and washed it down with tea. Cameron watched her every move, and when she stopped eating, he motioned impatiently for her to continue.

Not a word passed between them. She felt his gaze on her like a pall. But in the silence, she had time to think. He had promised to keep Luc safe. And she believed him. Those places where he'd been were quite dangerous, and he'd come out alive. She suspected he was proficient in every sort of deadly skill. What if he could help her rescue Papa?

When she had eaten everything he had put on her plate, he sat back, apparently satisfied she had obeyed. The food she had consumed sat like a lump of unleavened dough in her stomach. But she had come to a decision.

She would tell him.

Everything.

Almost everything.

She met his gaze.

"My husband," she began, "was murdered five years ago."

CHAPTER 13

Arianne told him about her father, forced to decode secret messages during the revolution in France, about her marriage to Jean-Paul, and hiding on the tiny farm. About being discovered, then their mad flight in the middle of the night, and her husband's murder. She even told about her arrival in England and the Countess hiding her during her pregnancy and then helping her hide Luc. She told him about the Countess's assistance in establishing her as a modiste in Bath. And finally, she told Cameron about the elaborate plan to destroy Ian West.

"I was supposed to be charming to Ian," she said. "I never expected him to fall in love with me. I didn't know —" She swallowed, the words stuck in her throat. "I didn't know that they planned to kill him. Courcy pushed him from the roof." She covered her face, unable to look at him in her shame.

He sat silent through her story. He knew it all now. He knew for certain she was a spy and that she was responsible for his brother's death. He would arrest her, send her to prison. She would never see little Luc again. And Pinard would murder her father.

Grief held her in its smothering grip. But she had no tears. What she had done was too enormous for tears. Instead, a heavy weight sat in her chest, a weight she would carry with her until the end of her days.

"Who forced you to do this, Arianne?"

His soft-spoken question made her drop her hands. She swallowed in a dry throat. "A man named Pinard."

Cameron froze. He focused on her like a bird of prey on its next meal. "Pinard? Henri Pinard?"

Surprise that he knew of Pinard widened her eyes. She jerked a nod.

He stabbed the little knife down into the table and ruined the smooth, satiny finish.

Arianne felt the stab wound as sharply as if he had thrust the knife into her. He was furious, disgusted with her. He might be able to keep Luc safe, but now that he knew of Pinard, Papa's life was lost. No one, not even this man across the table from her, could save her father from Pinard.

He jumped up and paced across the room. Raking his hand through his hair, he kept his head down as he stalked twice to the far wall and back again.

"I should have guessed," he mumbled. "I should have guessed."

He stopped before the table and stared out the window, but his eyes were focused on something far beyond what was visible through the glass.

"He wants me dead, doesn't he?" His voice was a monotone, and he spoke like someone in a dream. "He wants to destroy me like he destroyed my brother."

Arianne was compelled to answer. "Yes. In the end."

"And you would have helped him." His accusation was a mere statement of truth.

"No." She spoke the word with as much honesty as she could.

He focused on her, those midnight eyes drilling into her. "Why not?"

"Because—" She wanted to tell him the real reason, that she loved him, but she knew he would never accept that truth. So she chose an answer that would make her sound convincing. "Because I saw what happened to Ian, and I couldn't allow that to happen again."

A distant, mocking smile curved his lips. "I almost believe you."

Her curiosity overcame the pain of his distrust. "Why would Pinard want you dead?"

His brows rose up in astonishment. "You don't know?"

"Pinard does not confide in his servants," she said with a twist to her lips.

"You, a servant?" He chuckled at that. "You could never be a servant, Madame de Vouvret, especially not for Pinard."

Arianne's cheeks heated at his statement, but she was not about to examine the reason for that. "Why does he want you dead?" she prodded. "What did you do to him?"

Her question tore a laugh from Cameron. "Nothing," he said. "I have never even met the man."

"Then why?"

Cameron studied her as he contemplated her question. He had no reservations about revealing any of his story. If she wanted to know the truth, he would tell it. If nothing else, they had Pinard's cruelty in common. He sat across the table from her, pulled the knife from the wood and turned it over and over as he considered how to begin.

"When my father was a young man," he said, "he collected information for the Foreign Office."

"He was a spy?" she asked.

Amused at her forthright label, he shrugged and smiled. "If you wish, yes, he was a spy." At her nod, he went on. "He was in France during the Revolution. During the Reign of Terror, he helped many noble families escape the guillotine. One of these families had a beautiful daughter, and he fell in love with her. There was another man who desired her, a Frenchman who worked for the secret police. He had been trying to capture my father for a long time, so not only were they rival spies, they were rivals for this young woman's affections. But what the Frenchman really wanted was her father's estate and the wealth and prestige it would bring him. He was charming and seductive in his suit for the girl's hand, and she became enamored of his false front. When she discovered the true reason for this man's pursuit of her hand, she rejected him. He became enraged and accused the family of treason. He told the daughter that he would save them from the guillotine if she married him."

Arianne gasped. "This man was Pinard?"

"Yes, Pinard." He nodded. "My father tried to smuggle the family out of France, but Pinard betrayed them. The family was captured and sent to their deaths, but my father and the young woman had already gone ahead to the coast to make arrangements. Pinard caught up with them. There was a sword fight, and my father cut Pinard's face."

Arianne drew a breath. "His eye."

He raised a brow. "His eye?"

She nodded. "Pinard wears a patch over his left eye. And he has a scar." She dragged a finger down the left side of her face.

One corner of Cameron's mouth lifted. "Interesting. And distinctive. Hard to hide such a disfigurement," he mused.

"He hides on his vast estate," she mumbled.

Cameron tucked that bit of information away. He knew exactly what estate and where it was located.

He continued his story. "My father thought Pinard was dying, so he left him and sailed for England with the woman he loved. They married shortly after."

"And then you were born," she added with a tiny smile.

"No." He shook his head. "I'm not a product of their union. They are my adopted parents. My father told me I am the son of some other aristocratic family sent to the guillotine. He brought me back on that last trip from France. But I was raised as if I were their own blood, and heir to the title, even after my brother was born." He glanced away. She did not need to know of the secret negotiations and legal bargaining to make that happen. He always felt as if he were a bit of a fraud for assuming the title after his father's death. "Everyone always commented on how much my eyes resembled my mother's." He shrugged. "Our resemblance is a coincidence."

"Didn't you wonder who your real parents were?" she asked.

"I didn't want to know," he said quietly. "It was too painful to think of their suffering in prison and their death at the guillotine."

He drew a breath and turned to gaze out the window. "My father fell from his horse six years ago and broke his back. He was an invalid for several months before he died. My mother died about a year later from influenza." Even now, he could still feel the pain of their deaths.

"I am so sorry." She reached across the table and covered his hand.

Her gentle touch and her sympathy angered him. He didn't want compassion from this woman who had helped destroy his brother. Snatching away his hand, he leaned back, out of her reach. He would not allow himself to be swayed by soft feelings. Hardening his heart and cooling his gaze, he watched her hand drop into her lap.

Arianne looked into his eyes and saw no softening of his feelings, despite having told her his background. But he had revealed that he was not the natural son of the previous duke. She had no idea if that was common knowledge, but it was certainly a weapon she could use against him. He had left himself vulnerable. He had given her a gift.

She dropped her gaze to her hands in her lap. She had to give him something in return. He already knew about her husband's murder and Luc. The only thing left was to tell him about her father. If she revealed that, she would have to tell Cameron why Pinard held her father hostage. She would have to reveal that not only was she a spy for the French, but her father was as well. What would he do when he learned that?

She drew a breath. She had no choice. He held her prisoner, and she knew he wouldn't release her until he learned every sordid detail about what she had done and why. Perhaps she could prevail upon him to take pity on her father and try to rescue him, but that was asking a great deal. He would have to travel to France, find Pinard's estate, and confront the monster. She had no doubt about Cameron's ability, but he would be in danger. Pinard was cruel and cunning. Cameron might lose his life. And that was one thing for which she could never forgive herself.

"You've left something out of your story," he said. "I can understand why you wish to keep your son a secret, but I think you could easily disappear from those who keep watch over you. Why don't you escape them?"

Arianne startled at his words. Her gaze flew to his face, to those dark eyes, that beautiful mouth. The air seemed to grow thin, and she felt that void open beneath her. No, she couldn't faint. Not now. She grabbed the edge of the table and dragged air into her lungs. If she told him, Pinard would somehow learn of it. He would murder Papa.

"Arianne." Her name snapped out as if he had spoken a command.

She could not refuse him. "My father," she gasped out and closed her eyes to hide from the pain. "Pinard holds my father."

Silence came from across the table. She waited for him to say something. Time clicked past. She couldn't look.

"How long?" he finally asked.

"Five years." She still couldn't look.

She heard him shift in his seat. The noise prompted her to peek beneath her lashes. He was leaning back in his chair, focused on the small knife that he twirled between his fingers. She dared to look at him fully. His brows were drawn together. His mouth was a flat line. He finally raised his eyes and met her gaze.

"Pinard has been holding your father hostage for five years," he said. "And you have been hiding your son from him."

Arianne gave a short nod.

"You have been communicating with Pinard through your dress designs." His statement was more of a question.

Arianne gave another affirmative nod.

"God's teeth," he muttered.

Cameron listened to her story with growing horror at the evil machinations of Pinard. The man's drive for revenge told of insanity. And now that he knew of Pinard's plans, he could foil them. The woman sitting across from him had been very brave. She had been forced to play her role in order to keep her father alive, and she had kept her son hidden and safe. While he hated that she'd had a part in his brother's death, he understood that she'd had no choice.

He studied her as he absently toyed with the little knife. Her face was pale, and tight, tiny lines around her eyes testified to her distress. Her lips, those plump sensuous lips, were nearly colorless. Her shoulders slumped, and her hair was tangled and wild. Despite all that, she was the most beautiful creature he had ever seen. And the most tragic. For some reason, regardless of what she had done, he wanted to help her. And he wanted to destroy Pinard.

Leaning forward, he said, "How soon can you be ready to travel to France?"

Her eyes widened, and her lips parted. "France?" Panic replaced her surprise. "No, I cannot go to France."

Her resistance angered him. "Don't you want to rescue your father? Don't you want to destroy Pinard?"

"*Oui.* Yes, of course, but—" She looked everywhere except at him.

"What?" he demanded. "What is holding you back?"

She met his gaze. "My son. Luc. I cannot leave him."

"I have met Mr. Inglis," he said. "I believe he can keep Luc safe while we are gone."

She swallowed. "But what if we don't come back?" she whispered.

He allowed himself a tight smile. "We'll come back."

She nodded, and her gaze slipped away again.

His eyes narrowed. "What else, Arianne? What aren't you telling me?"

She sat silently, staring out the window. He thought she wasn't going to answer him. Finally, she spoke very quietly.

"De Pagiére," she said.

He frowned. "He can't hurt you if you are with me in France."

She swallowed again and still would not look at him. "He knows about Luc. He said he would tell Pinard about him unless I granted him a favor."

Anger rose up in him so fast he nearly choked. "What did he demand? Did he want you to lay with him?"

She looked at him then, her eyes stark. "No. I must dress his lover, a young man, a boy." She swallowed and said, "I tried to refuse, but…. If word gets out about this, no one will come to me for their frocks. My business will be ruined." She drew a shaky breath. "I'm afraid he will prey on Luc."

Cameron wanted to pummel the weaselly predator. His hand curled into a fist. "When is he coming?"

"Tonight." Her word broke in the middle.

He reached across the table and covered her hand. "Then we will meet him tonight. I will take care of this. He'll not bother you again. And tomorrow night, we will sail for France."

Hope flashed through her eyes. It was gone just as quickly. But that light created a warm glow in his chest. He shouldn't be pleased with her reaction, at the faith she had in him, no matter how fleeting.

But he was. And he wanted to gather her close and comfort her. That confused him. So instead of doing what he wanted, he sat back and laid out a plan for the meeting with de Pagière.

CHAPTER 14

The knock came at Arianne's back door just before midnight. When she opened it, de Pagière stepped through accompanied by a smaller cloaked and hooded figure. The marquis had his hand curled possessively around his companion's arm.

"You are so kind to receive us at such an hour, madame," he said with a smile.

Arianne ignored his courtesy. She closed the door behind them. "This way," she tossed over her shoulder, and led them to one of the private rooms where her customers were measured for their frocks.

Only a few lamps were lit, and the drape was firmly closed across her front window. She wanted no one alerted to what she did this night. She had sent her seamstresses home, and Lizzie was enjoying her parents' company. She stepped into one of the smaller spaces. This room had no mirror. It held two simple armchairs with a small table between them and a changing screen decorated with painted roses and exotic birds in one corner. After de Pagière and his companion entered the room, she firmly closed the door behind them.

"Let us see," she said, as she motioned for de Pagière's companion to remove the cloak.

The marquis stepped in front of his companion and blocked her view. He pushed back the hood and unclasped the cloak. With a flourish, he stepped back and whipped away the garment.

"Voilà!" he said as if uncovering a priceless work of art.

A youth stood before her, perhaps twelve or thirteen years old. He was dressed in a simple white shirt and brown linen breeches, no stockings, and shoes that looked several sizes too big. The clothes were well-worn but clean. He held his arms crossed tightly at his chest. His shoulders slumped, and his head drooped. With his gaze focused on the floor, he obviously did not want to be where he was. Arianne's heart flipped over, and her chest tightened. She had no idea de Pagière's companion would be so young.

"What is your name?" she asked in a gentle voice.

The boy mumbled something.

At the same time, the marquis said, "He is Apollo."

Arianne hissed. "That is not his name."

"Of course, it is." De Pagière placed a finger under the boy's chin and forced his head up. "Look at him, Arianne. He is a young Greek god."

He was a beautiful boy. Piercing blue eyes looked at her from beneath thick lashes. His dark, wavy hair curled just below his ears and flopped over his brow. His nose was straight, his skin was clear, and his mouth was well-formed. His chin held a tiny cleft.

"What is your name?" she asked again and sent a hard glance at the marquis to keep him quiet.

"Jacky," the boy said, barely above a whisper, and lowered his eyes again.

"Do you want to be here, Jacky?" she prodded.

Fear flickered in his eyes before he ducked his head. "Y-yes, ma'am."

With a scowl, Arianne turned to de Pagière. "How much did you pay him?"

The marquis placed his hand to his chest. "Madame, you wound me. I would never—"

She glared at him.

De Pagière dropped his pretense. With a charming smile and an airy wave of his hand, he said, "Enough to keep his dear papa happy and bring tears to his mama's eyes."

"Jules, you are a pig," she said in French. "A monster."

The marquis's eyes narrowed. "You may call me anything you like, Arianne, but you will perform your task as I requested. Remember, I know your sweet little secret."

Her teeth clenched so hard her jaw ached. She glanced away as she swallowed her revulsion and fear. Reminding herself she had Cameron's promise to protect Luc, she motioned to the changing screen.

"You may disrobe there," she said to Jacky. "You will find several frocks of different sizes. Try on the one that looks closest to your size."

Jacky gave an obedient nod and headed toward the screen.

"Apollo will change clothes here before me," de Pagière said as he sat in one of the chairs.

Jacky halted halfway to the screen.

Arianne ground her teeth. Taking a breath, she forced her tone to remain level. "Don't you wish to be surprised at the transformation, Jules?"

He cocked a suspicious brow at her. "Do not think you can spirit my young friend away, Arianne. You know what I will do if you trick me."

She forced a laugh. "How am I supposed to do that? Do you see any other door besides the one where we entered? Do you think I am a conjurer and can make him disappear?" She shook her head. "You are very distrustful. Or fanciful."

De Pagière studied her a moment, then waved a dismissive hand. "Very well." He jerked his chin at Jacky to proceed. As the boy disappeared behind the screen, he called to him, "Choose well, Apollo. Take my breath away."

Arianne sat in the other chair and waited. Normally, she would engage in conversation with her customer and offer refreshment, a cup of tea or stronger spirits. Instead, she sat stoically silent with her hands clasped primly in her lap. The marquis sat equally quiet, merely tapping a finger on the arm of his chair. The rustle of clothing, the thud of a shoe, and various gasps and grunts came from behind the screen.

With an impatient sigh, de Pagière called out, "What's taking so long, Apollo? Should I come back there and help?"

A pause, then the boy answered, "No, sir. I'm ready."

The marquis expectantly watched the screen.

Instead of a boy transformed into a girl, Cameron stepped from behind the screen.

De Pagière stiffened, remaining perfectly still, but Arianne saw his hand twitch in shock. Then he turned to her with a crooked smile.

"I believe you are a conjurer, Arianne," he said. "You send a boy behind the screen, and a full-grown man appears in his place." His lips pursed thoughtfully as he regarded Cameron. "You are a very attractive man, Lythmore, but I do like my lovers a bit younger."

Cameron's mouth twisted in disgust. "You'll not prey on children any longer, de Pagière."

The marquis jerked to his feet. "I'll do what I wish, Lythmore. Send out the boy. We will leave."

"I'm afraid I can't do that," Cameron said.

The marquis turned on Arianne. "You will regret this, Madame de Vouvret," he snarled. "You have made a grave mistake. One day, you will find your sweet little secret has vanished."

Despite the chilly fear that ran through her at his words, Arianne rose to her feet and raised her chin. "You don't frighten me, Jules. My son is safe, hidden away from you."

With a growl, he pushed her back into her chair and surged toward Cameron. "Get the boy out here. We are leaving."

Cameron stood his ground. He stopped de Pagière's headlong rush with one hard hand gripping the lapel of the marquis's elegant coat. "Jacky is remaining here."

"I paid for him. You have no right to keep him," the marquis said as he tried to pull Cameron's hand loose.

Cameron showed his other hand holding a dagger. "This gives me the right."

De Pagière released an insulting laugh. "Do you expect me to be afraid of that?"

With a cool, raised brow, Cameron said, "I really don't know, but I have killed with less."

The marquis snarled and grabbed for the knife. Arianne gasped. The two men swayed in their struggle, but she could not see the weapon. De Pagière punched Cameron in the ribs, but the blow did not seem to affect him. Another blow, and another, but the blade remained hidden between them as they struggled. Suddenly, they froze, locked together. Arianne gasped. Had Cameron been stabbed? De Pagière lurched back, hunched over, holding his arm across his middle.

"You have unmanned me!" he screeched. "I'll have you arrested for this!"

Bright spots of blood dripped onto his shoes.

"I think, rather, that you'll be arrested for being a spy," Cameron said.

With a growl, de Pagière spun around. Arianne clapped her hands over her mouth when she saw the knife sticking from his groin. De Pagière yanked out the dagger with a scream of pain and threw it down. Blood seeped across his fashionable attire. He staggered to the door. As he pushed past Arianne, his handsome face twisted in a snarl. Then he disappeared down the hall.

"He's getting away! Go after him!" she urged Cameron.

"There's no need," he said. "I have men waiting outside. They'll arrest him, provided he doesn't bleed to death first."

Arianne sank into a chair, relief weakening her knees. She heard men's voices challenging from the alley and de Pagière's pathetic whine in response, then some commotion and feet shuffling off.

Cameron beckoned to Jacky. "You can come out now."

Jacky stepped from behind the screen, still dressed in shirt and breeches. Apprehensive, he looked from Cameron to Arianne.

"Can I go now, sir? Ma'am?" the boy asked.

"Where do you live, Jacky?" Arianne asked.

His gaze shifted left and right. "I…ah…on Ware Street."

Arianne met Cameron's gaze and gave her head a little shake. She knew of no street by that name in the city.

"Are your parents alive?" Cameron probed gently.

Jacky hung his head, remaining silent for so long, Arianne thought he wouldn't answer. Finally, he mumbled, "No, sir."

Cameron met Arianne's gaze again, then asked, "Who did the marquis pay for your services?"

Jacky did not answer immediately. Then, barely above a whisper, he said, "Me aunt and uncle. They was happy to be rid o' me."

Arianne caught her bottom lip between her teeth. Her heart wrenched for the child. Cameron took her by the arm and guided her out the door. "We'll be back in a moment, Jacky," he said over his shoulder. When they had walked a few steps away, he said, "We can't just send him away. I don't think he has anywhere to go. Do you think Mr. and Mrs. Inglis would take him in?"

Arianne's eyes widened at the thought. That was a wonderful idea. But she could barely provide them with enough for Luc's care.

Before she could put her thoughts into words, he said, "I will take care of the expenses. Do you think they'll do it?"

She gave a vigorous nod. "Yes, I'm sure they will."

"Then it's settled, provided Jacky agrees." He turned back to the changing room.

Arianne stopped him with a hand on his arm. "You are a very generous, kind man."

"Only when it pleases me," he said shortly, then slipped away from her and returned to the room.

Arianne's hand fell to her side. He hated her, could not stand her touch. Her heart twisted painfully. How ironic that the man she had come to love detested her. She bit down on her bottom lip, shoving away the pain. They had saved Jacky from a predator, and now, with the help of the Inglises and Cameron's generosity, the boy had a new life ahead of him.

At least she had done something good before she went to jail. Straightening her spine, she headed back into the changing room to face whatever decision Cameron might make for her future.

CHAPTER 15

Two nights later, Cameron stood at the prow of the fishing boat that was heading for the coast of France. The sky was overcast, so no moon lit their progress across the choppy water. Near the port rail, he could see the huddled form of Madame de Vouvret. Arianne. She was a darker shadow against the shapes of the nets and fishing tackle that were stacked neatly around the deck. The hood of her cloak was up, hiding her face, but even in the dark, he could sense her apprehension. Her fear. She had hidden it well when they had visited Mr. and Mrs. Inglis, when they had asked them to look after Jacky, when she had hugged Luc to her and kissed him goodbye. But now, as she gazed across the Channel toward France, her hands clutched her cloak close around her, and her shoulders slumped.

He wanted to ease that fear, to tell her she would be safe, that her father would be safe. He wanted to tell her he would protect her from anything that might harm her. From Pinard. He wanted to put his arms around her, hold her close, whisper his longing into her ear. He wanted to trace his fingers up her delicate neck, tangle them in her hair. He wanted to breathe her in, her spicy-sweet scent, like peonies. He couldn't. Not yet. Perhaps never. Too much had happened.

He turned away to stare across the water. His honor, his duty demanded that he follow the law. His anger, his grief demanded he seek revenge. His compassion demanded that he forgive her. The conflict of emotions roiling inside him kept him in thrall, paralyzed, not allowing him to move in any direction. What was he going to do about her once they had confronted Pinard and, hopefully, destroyed him? The indecision churned inside him. Because one truth had become clear.

He loved Arianne de Vouvret.

How could that have happened? She was the woman who had helped destroy his brother. She was Ian's Marguerite. Before he met her, he had thought of her as a scheming, cold-hearted Jezebel. Instead, he had discovered she was talented, intelligent, and a loving mother. She was courageous. And she was passionate. His muscles tightened at the memory of the glorious night they had spent at Shipley Hall. When he was away from her, all he wanted was to be near her.

He couldn't dwell on that now. He must focus on the task ahead of him. In the distance lay the coast of France. The black water stretched out before him. Chilly spray landed on his cheek. The dark night concealed the land ahead, but he could smell it—the pungent dank of the salt marsh and a trace now and again of wet earth and vegetation. Rain had fallen recently. They were close. His heartbeat kicked up as it always did when he embarked on a new assignment for the Foreign Office. But this time, the task was personal.

He had no plan, and he had never taken on a task without a plan. All he had done this time was to make arrangements to be met when they reached France. His anger at what Pinard had done to Arianne had driven him to act impulsively. He would let circumstances guide him. Several times, serendipity and coincidence had helped him in the past. He'd always had a good instinct for doing what needed to be done in order to have a favorable outcome. He hoped this time, the gods of chance would look kindly on him.

From the shore, a light winked, then was gone. He squinted, searching to see it again. There. It came twice more, fast, appearing like the light from a secluded cottage behind tree limbs swaying with the wind. But it wasn't.

He picked up the dark lantern beside him on the deck and held it high. Its panel was closed, shutting out the lit candle within. He opened and closed the panel twice, waited, then repeated the action. From onshore, a light twinkled once, then went dark. His contact had seen his signal.

Cameron pointed out the direction to the captain of the tiny sailing vessel and told Arianne they would soon be arriving. She acknowledged him with a silent nod, then turned back to her contemplation of the dark shore. Cameron's hand twitched, nearly reaching out to comfort her, but he refrained. Better that he keep his distance until he could uncoil the knot of emotions inside him. He returned to his station near the prow.

Less than an hour later, they scraped hard against the sandy bottom only a short distance from the beach. They had timed their landing perfectly with low tide. It would turn soon and, within a few hours, would refloat the fishing boat, allowing the captain to sail away.

Cameron slipped into the knee-high water. Arianne came to the rail and looked down. He held out his arms.

"Climb over and jump," he said. "I'll catch you."

She hesitated a moment, then sat on the rail, threw her legs over and jumped into his arms. He saw a flash of breeches beneath her skirts and smiled to himself as he caught her. Clever lady. She would be able to disguise herself as a boy if the need arose. As he held her above the water, the weight of her against him, the suppleness of her body made him want to snuggle her close and kiss her. Instead, he waded to the dry sand, where he placed her on her feet.

A dark figure emerged from the low brush at the head of the beach.

"You're late," the man said.

"I was unavoidably detained." Cameron responded with the correct response that indicated he was friend, not foe. He peered closer at the man. "Edward? Edward Johnson?"

The man, who used to be Wyndham's second in command when the duke was the notorious spy Le Chat, dipped into an exaggerated, courtly bow. "At your service."

"Good God! I had no idea Wyndham and Dunbary would be sending you to meet us." He strode forward and clasped Johnson's hand.

Edward grinned. "I was already in Querqueville. I'll be embarking on my wedding trip as soon as I return."

"Wedding trip! Best wishes to you." Cameron tipped his head. "I can't believe your new bride allowed you to perform this clandestine task."

Edward's grin grew broader. "I'm returning on the fishing boat that brought you here. She's waiting for me across the Channel."

"*Pardon, monsieur,* but here in France this body of water is called La Manche," Arianne said.

Cameron laughed. "She's right." He held out his hand to Arianne and drew her forward. "This is Madame de Vourvret. We have come to rescue her father."

Arianne offered her hand to the handsome man, whom Cameron seemed to know quite well. As Mr. Johnson bowed, she wondered about the men's connection and why he was there to meet them. Her question was answered with his next words.

"The inn is located just this side of the village, a couple of miles down the road. I have horses for you on the other side of the dunes," Mr. Johnson said. "Beware of the patrols. I was nearly spotted just a short while ago, and I heard they have been more vigilant of late."

Cameron nodded his understanding. Arianne suspected that Pinard most likely had something to do with their vigilance.

Concern crossed Mr. Johnson's face. "Are you sure you don't want me to contact our man in Paris? He can be here in a day or two. Then you won't be on your own."

Cameron shook his head. "I need to do this alone. There are delicate circumstances." He cast a quick glance in Arianne's direction, then drew the other man aside.

As the men spoke for a few more minutes, her attention wandered to her surroundings. The moon broke through the clouds for an instant, and the beach stretched away on either side. She was reminded of that night five years ago when she had tried to flee this country with her father and Jean-Paul, when she had just discovered she was with child. They had never made it to the beach. Pinard and his men had caught them.

She watched Cameron and Mr. Johnson converse in low tones. Like Pinard, Cameron had men, too. He had been able to gather the authorities to capture and arrest the Marquis de Pagière. The arrangements to smuggle them into France were made very quickly. And now, he had someone to meet them and provide horses. He had influence in England. Besides being a duke, he was something else besides, something more. Remembering the story he had told about his parents, about the dangerous places he had been, she knew what that something else was. He was a spy. And as soon as they found and released her father, he would take her back to England, where he would arrest *her* for being a spy. She would never see Luc again. Her chest constricted painfully at never hugging him close or watching him grow. But she could not think of that now.

The moon hid behind the clouds again, turning the landscape dark. She glanced up at the sky. One tiny star twinkled, then snuffed out. She wanted to be like that star, visible for now, but then disappearing, escaping from Cameron West, Duke of Lythmore, who sought revenge for his brother. She wanted to sneak to Pinard's chateau and free her father, return to England, collect Luc, and all together, they would hide someplace where Cameron could never find them.

And bury the love she felt for him deep within her heart forever.

CHAPTER 16

Very early the next morning, Cameron knocked on the door to Arianne's room. From the floor below, he could hear the cook and a few maids in the kitchen, but the rest of the inn was quiet. After rousing the innkeeper the night before, he had been able to procure two rooms with a generous bribe of coins. When he left Arianne at the door to her room, she had looked exhausted. The trip across the Channel and the ride to the inn had made for a very long night. They'd also had to hide from one of the patrols that Johnson had mentioned, an anxious moment. He regretted having to rouse her so early, but he needed to ride to Pinard's chateau and keep watch, to learn the rhythm of the place and decide the best way to sneak inside. For her safety and his peace of mind, he was not going to leave her unguarded while he was gone.

Getting no response from her, he knocked again. Still no answer.

"Madame de Vouvret," he called.

Nothing.

"Arianne."

Silence.

Concern furrowed his brow, then a wave of suspicion swept it away. Had she fled? He tried the knob. Locked. Of course. The silence from the other side of the door was too deep, too complete for anyone to be there.

He pulled a small case out of his pocket and selected two small, thin, metal picks. Inserting them into the lock, he twisted and jiggled them. The lock released and he threw open the door. The room was empty. The bed had never been slept in. The gown she had worn on the crossing was in a heap on the floor. A chair lay on its side. The window was wide open. He strode to the opening and looked out. A trellis covered in a thick vine stopped just below the sill. Someone could have easily climbed up and forced the window open. A scattering of leaves and twigs on the ground confirmed his suspicions.

A rush of emotions engulfed him. A flame of anger. A clutch of fear. He knew without a doubt that she had been taken by Pinard. How had the man known she was here? And how had he slept through the commotion of her kidnapping? He pounded his fists on the sill. He should have slept in the same room as her. But he couldn't trust himself not to reach for her, hold her in his arms, kiss her…. He had been too complacent in their anonymity. And too arrogant. Of course, Pinard had spies in the surrounding countryside. Of course, they would have noted a man and woman arriving quite late at the inn. They might have even seen their boat beaching and the meeting with Johnson. He hoped the man got away safely.

He hurried out of the room and down the stairs to the common room. The innkeeper, a friendly fellow since Cameron had paid him triple for the rooms and stabling the horses, was wiping down the small bar where he poured the ale and brandy and other spirits.

"Bonjour, monsieur," he called. "Did you pass a peaceful night? You are up and about very early for having retired so late." He reached under the bar and pulled out a folded parchment. "This was left at my door before the sun rose with a note to give this to the English gentleman. A note within a note. Very secretive, n'est-ce pas?"

Cameron's heart stuttered as he accepted the note with a nod of thanks. *Monsieur West* was scrawled across the front. He had not given his name to the innkeeper. Edward Johnson and his contact who had left the horses knew better than to reveal who he was. He ripped open the wax seal, pressed with an intricate coat of arms. The note was short and to the point.

My dear Monsieur West,

I am entertaining the delightful and lovely Arianne de Vouvret. Please call at my Chateau du Vainqueur at your earliest convenience so that you may be reunited with her before I kill you.

Regards,
Henri Pinard

Cameron crushed the note in his fist. Besides the blatant arrogance of Pinard, the fact that Arianne had been captured made him want to tear apart the inn. A black haze hovered before his eyes.

"Monsieur! Monsieur West, is everything all right?" The innkeeper's voice brought him back to his surroundings.

Cameron forced a smile. "Yes. Quite. I will be leaving earlier than I expected. Please have the horses brought round. And I will need the direction to the Chateau du Vainqueur."

As soon as he mentioned the chateau, the innkeeper's mouth pursed, and he frowned. "That is not a place you wish to go, monsieur," he said. "There are stories…" His voice trailed off, and he shook his head.

Cameron could imagine what rumors flew about Pinard's chateau, all of them vile, no doubt. His mouth flattened with determination. "I have business there. Perhaps, after my visit, those stories will end."

The innkeeper studied him a moment with shrewd eyes. "Perhaps they will. Very well, monsieur, this is how you will go."

After receiving the directions, Cameron flipped the innkeeper another coin, but the man refused, saying that he only wished him godspeed. As he set out, worry about Arianne's safety sat next to anticipation at meeting Pinard. Finally, he would gaze upon his father's nemesis and end the villain's life. And he would free Arianne. He urged his horse into a gallop and leaned over its neck. The decision about what to do about Arianne once they returned to England could wait.

Arianne paced the length of the bedchamber inside Pinard's chateau, the Chateau du Vainqueur. The Chateau of the Winner. She snorted in disgust. Of course, Pinard would consider himself victorious. He had sent the original owners to the guillotine so he could win the lands that had been theirs for generations. She paced another length of the room. It was a lovely space, airy and light, with walls of creamy ivory painted with delicate pink roses. The canopy bed was draped with miles of pink and white lace and satin. The floor she paced was covered with a cushiony Aubusson carpet. But she might as well have been in a damp and dreary cell of stone. She had been locked in this beautiful room for hours since she had been taken from her room at the inn just before dawn. Two men had snuck through the window, bound and gagged her before she could utter a sound, and brought her to this room. Stopping in the middle of the floor, she puffed out a breath of frustration, using her anger at her situation and herself to tamp down her fear.

She had escaped from Cameron, but not in the way she had envisioned. She had been afraid of what Cameron thought of her, afraid of the punishment at the end of this journey, afraid of never seeing her father again. But now she was in Pinard's clutches, and Cameron most likely thought she had run away. Would he come after her? She could only hope he would. Despite her apprehension at what awaited her when this was finished, she knew, deep in her soul, he had devised a plan to rescue her father and return them all safely to England. He would have kept her safe. At least until they reached England.

When her captors had brought her before Pinard, he had greeted her with undisguised glee. She had demanded to see her father, but, of course, her puppeteer had denied that request. Pinard had told her that her father was hard at work deciphering a message he had just received. And then she had been locked in this room.

She had passed the time by trying to unlock one of the windows to escape. They had been nailed shut. Even if she had succeeded in breaking one, the ground was three stories down. And the patrols passed at regular intervals. The only door in the room was the one that led to the hallway, and a guard stood on the other side. So, she paced.

216

A knock came at the door. She did not bother to answer, for whoever was on the other side held the key and could enter whether she wished them to or not. The lock clicked, and the door opened. A young maid stood in the opening with an armful of purple satin, blue silk, and frothy lace.

"Pardon, madame," the girl said as she bobbed a curtsey, "the master invites you to dine with him, and he sends this frock for you to wear."

Although Arianne had eaten nothing since the night before on the fishing boat, when Cameron had unfolded a napkin-wrapped parcel on her lap to reveal a chunk of cheese and loaf of bread, she would starve before she dined with Pinard. "Tell your master I am not hungry."

Panic flashed through the girl's eyes. "I—ah—of course, madame. Not hungry." She bobbed another curtsey, this one a bit wobbly.

As she turned to leave, Arianne called to her. "Wait. I've changed my mind. Will you help me dress?" She surmised the girl would feel the brunt of Pinard's anger if his wishes were not carried out, and she did not want the maid to suffer on her account.

The girl smiled, relief allowing her shoulders to drop. She stepped into the room and laid out the frock across the bed. The dress was old-fashioned with many petticoats. A split overskirt of blue satin showed off a purple silk underskirt embroidered with rosebuds. Heavy lace flounced at the edge of the elbow-length sleeves. The maid also laid out a beautifully embroidered chemise and silk stays of padded whalebone, along with a hoop petticoat. The quality of the material and the workmanship was very fine, and she wondered if the gown had belonged to one of the women who had previously lived in the chateau—a woman who had been sent to the guillotine or fled for her life.

Arianne traced her fingers lightly over the satin. Sadness tinged with a sense of connection for that woman filled her. She, too, had been caught. And if she did not don this garment, then Pinard would find some cruel way to punish her. So, she allowed the maid to help her dress and fix her hair.

As the girl helped her, Arianne tried to elicit some information about her father, but the maid either claimed ignorance or refused to answer. As before, when Arianne had said she wasn't hungry, the girl became very anxious. Arianne stopped probing and allowed the maid to finish dressing her.

The maid pulled her before a cheval mirror. The woman who looked back at Arianne was someone from another era. Her hair had been piled high on her head and decorated with a white plume. The dress, with its yards of fabric, snugged about her upper torso and flared widely over her hips and legs. It had belonged to someone who had been a few inches shorter, so the hem only reached her ankles and showed off her boots, a sharp contrast of styles. The bodice was tight, so her breasts were in danger of spilling from the neckline.

"Monsieur Pinard will be pleased, I think," the girl murmured.

Arianne's mouth twisted in distaste. She hated the dress. She hated the way it made her feel, all trussed up and barely able to breathe. She hated the eerie sensation of wearing a dress that had belonged to someone who might have been beheaded. She hated that Pinard had forced her to wear it and that the maid had been forced to help her. She wanted to tear it off.

But she did not, and she did not say any of those things. She merely nodded.

She followed the girl out the door, past the guard standing in the hall, and down the wide, curving staircase. As she descended, she wondered how Cameron had reacted when he found her gone. Would he think she had escaped from him? Would he figure out where she was? Would he come after her? As she entered the salon, the idea of being Pinard's pawn and plaything for the rest of her life landed in her middle like a spent cannonball.

Pinard was standing before the fireplace. "My dear Madame de Vouvret," he said as he came forward to take her hand. "You look exquisite."

She gritted her teeth at his touch and was about to tell him to keep his hands to himself when she happened to glance across his shoulder to the portrait hanging above the mantle. It was of a young woman. And she was dressed in the exact gown that Arianne was wearing. A gasp escaped her throat.

Pinard smiled. "Ah, you have seen Yseult. She was a beauty, was she not?" He lifted her fingers to his lips. "You are quite her match, Arianne."

Arianne jerked her hand from his grasp. "Did you send her to the guillotine, Pinard? Are you salving your conscience by pretending that I am her?"

His eyes narrowed dangerously. "I did not send her to the guillotine. Do not presume on my good nature. I can find different quarters for you that will not be quite so comfortable." He took her hand again, this time crushing her fingers. "And do not ever pull away from me again," he said in a menacing murmur. Then he smiled. "But come, it is time to dine, and I do so want you to meet my guest." He tucked her hand into the crook of his arm.

As he led her across the hall and into the dining room, she swallowed down her revulsion, most likely the only thing she would be able to get down her throat.

Cameron drummed his fingers on the dining table before him. Three elaborate settings of porcelain china and heavy silver cutlery had been laid out, one before him, one to his right at the head of the table, and one across from him. He had arrived at Pinard's chateau several hours ago and had surveyed the grounds to learn how well-guarded it was. He saw guards patrolling, and he was sure Pinard had other men ready to ward off any intruders, men who would not think twice about killing anyone they thought suspicious. Cameron decided the best way to gain entrance and discover where Arianne was being held was to knock on the front door. After all, he had been sent an invitation, but he planned to foil Pinard's final intent. He was not sure how he would do that, but he had improvised many times in dangerous situations. This was no exception.

He passed three men patrolling the grounds, but they merely scowled at him as he approached the huge double wooden door. His knock was answered by a dour-faced majordomo who left him in the entry hall without a word, then returned with two men holding pistols. The guards locked him in a small room just off the kitchen where candles and other sundries were stored. He did not fear for his immediate safety, for the guards had not searched him for weapons, and he was quite sure Pinard wanted to gloat before he tried to kill him. He would allow Pinard to gloat. As for the other, he would do everything he could to foil Pinard's final intent.

After a very long wait, the door was unlocked, and his two armed guards escorted him to the dining room, where they made him sit at the table and trained a gun on him. He sat back and waited again.

After quite a while, the door finally opened. Arianne stepped through, and Cameron caught his breath. She was dressed in an old-fashioned gown of blue and purple satin. It turned her eyes a vivid blue. A white plume curled down from her intricate curls and curved around one ear. She was stunning. He was not sure what he had expected, but it surely had not been Arianne dressed as if she were heading off to a ball. His heart, which had been squeezed by anxiety, eased at the sight of her. Although she appeared unharmed, anxiety etched fine lines around her eyes and her tight lips.

His gaze swept over her again. Something about that gown nagged at him. Besides the fact that it had no doubt belonged to the lady who had once lived in this chateau, the sight of the gown opened a dark void in the pit of his stomach. He didn't know why he should feel such despair, but he would never let on that the gown disturbed him. Instead, he pasted a cool smile on his lips.

"Madame de Vouvret," he greeted. "What a surprise finding you here and looking quite beautiful. Pardon me for not rising to greet you." He gestured to the guard. "It seems our host is most anxious for my company."

Arianne stopped short in the doorway. She never expected to see Cameron sitting so comfortably at Pinard's dining table. She swung around to face Pinard.

"What is this?" she hissed. "What game are you playing? Let him go."

Pinard's brows rose in surprised confusion. "Let him go? Why ever should I do that? No, no, no. Letting him go would ruin all my enjoyable plans. Besides, I sent him an invitation, and he accepted. We will all dine together. Monsieur West and I will get to know each other. You will have a final conversation with him. And then he will die." He shrugged as if his last statement had no evil consequence. "It is as easy as that. Now, come, Arianne, you are keeping our guest waiting."

She sent a desperate glance over her shoulder at Cameron. She wanted him to do something, but he merely sat, calmly waiting beneath the guard's vigilance. The tick in his jaw showed his fury. Perhaps he was not so calm after all. But he was as trapped as she was. Hope for her escape deflated like an empty sack. But she would do everything she could to save Cameron's life.

CHAPTER 17

They dined as if nothing evil hung in the air. Pinard spoke of the damp weather, of the difficulty in raising sheep, of the surliness of the peasants, and of Napoleon's brilliance. Servants offered tureens of vegetable soup, platters of chicken, mushrooms, and onions in a brandy sauce, baked sole, and fried potatoes. Cameron nibbled at the food, listened to Pinard's false chatter, and occasionally offered a comment. He noticed Arianne pushed the food around on her plate, kept her eyes lowered, and remained silent. Her fingers shook just the tiniest bit. The sight made his own fingers clench on his fork. He could use that fork to kill Pinard, but the two guards remained watchful, and the footmen were in and out of the room as they served. Too many people around who could foil his attempt and prevent their escape. He would bide his time and find a better opportunity.

He had to concentrate on staying alive in order to bring Pinard to justice. And he had to save Arianne. As Pinard played his little game of being the perfect host, Cameron responded as the perfect guest. The man would kill him as soon as he tired of his toying. So, he took note of exits and possible weapons.

The meal finally ended with Pinard's pronouncement that they would now adjourn to the salon.

"I have something I wish to show you," Pinard said as he led the way.

Cameron braced himself, not knowing what to expect. Arianne hesitated in the doorway, blocking him as if she did not want him to enter, but Pinard took her hand and drew her forward.

"Come, come, my dear," he said. "You must let our guest see."

Cameron stepped into the room. At first, he saw nothing unusual. It was a well-appointed salon like one might find in any wealthy man's chateau. Panels with gilded swags adorned the walls, and in the center of each was a painting of a bucolic scene. Armchairs and sofas were placed around the edge with a grouping near the fireplace. Two gilt chandeliers hung from the ceiling. His gaze caught on the portrait of a woman above the mantle. She wore a gown the exact color as the one Arianne now wore. On closer inspection, he realized it was the same gown. He glanced at her, then at Pinard. Arianne would not meet his gaze. The Frenchman's single eye danced as if he were hiding a wonderful surprise. Cameron looked more closely at the portrait. His heart froze. It was a painting of his mother!

"What is this?" he growled. "Why is this here?"

"Isn't it lovely?" Pinard sighed as he gazed at the portrait. "She was so beautiful. A delicate rose." He shook his head regretfully. "We were to wed, you know. Then she met that Englishman. Bah! She thought she would marry him instead. I told her that she risked the life of her parents if she did not marry me. She refused to listen. She was quite willful." He sighed. "I had to punish her. I had to prove to her that I was better than Lythmore. So, I sent her parents to Paris to meet Madame Guillotine. And then I showed her how much better I was than that English fop. I showed her several times. In the stables. In the dining room. In her father's bed. I believe I even showed her here in the salon." He smiled, and his single eye half-closed in ecstasy as he remembered. "She was delectable. Sweet and soft."

Horror crawled up Cameron's throat. He could barely breathe. "You defiled her!"

Arianne gasped. Her hands flew to her mouth, and she stared from Pinard to Cameron and back again. "Oh, mon Dieu! He is your father!"

White-hot rage clouded Cameron's vision. He lunged at Pinard, and his hands clamped around the cur's neck. They landed in a heap on the floor. Pinard cried out and clawed at Cameron's fingers choking him. But Cameron held on tight. He wanted to squeeze the life from him. All he could see was that one gloating eye, as soulless as a snake.

Hands grabbed at him. They annoyed him like gnats. He squeezed and squeezed. His single focus riveted on crushing the life out of the monster. Somewhere in the distance, he heard Arianne's voice. A sudden blow to the back of his head created exploding stars before his eyes. His fingers went slack. Then blackness.

Arianne watched Pinard stomp back and forth from one side of her bedchamber to the other. She sat rigidly, her knees clamped together and her hands clasped tightly in her lap. As soon as Cameron had been dragged away, unconscious, she had run to her room, ripped off the extravagant gown, and pulled on her breeches. She had planned to discover where he had been taken, find her father, and some-how escape with both of them. That had been a wild and foolish scheme. Before she had a chance to think it through, Pinard barged into her room.

"He tried to kill me!" he ranted, his voice hoarse from Cameron's attack. "How could he?" He grabbed a candlestick from the mantle and flung it across the room. "I am his father!" Next was a delicate figurine that smashed on the floor. "I made him!" He swung to her. "I loved his mother!"

Arianne flinched at his vehemence. But her horror at hearing what he had done to Cameron's mother had turned to rage. And that rage made her brave. She swallowed and sat up straighter. "Did you? Or did you just lust after her? And this chateau?"

Pinard's single eye narrowed. She thought he might strike her. He glared, then swung away. With a wave of his hand, he muttered, "It is the same. He is my son. And he tried to kill me!" He rubbed his throat where bruises had begun to purple. "I should kill him!" He stopped abruptly. "But he is my son." He paced some more.

Before he could work himself into another round of frenzy, a ser-vant knocked on the open door. With a growl, he strode to the door and listened to the servant's murmur. He waved the man away and turned to Arianne with a delighted smile.

Apprehensive at that expression, she leaned back in her chair.

"Arianne," he said. "We have a surprise guest. Come and greet him."

Reluctantly, she followed him to a small drawing room. Edouard Courcy turned at her entrance. And a small voice cried out, "Mama!"

Little Luc popped out from behind Courcy and ran to her. With a gasp, she dropped onto one knee and caught him up in her arms. She cuddled his warm little body close as emotions tumbled through her. Relief and surprise and love at seeing him. Fear that Courcy had found him. Terror that now Pinard knew about him.

"What a delightful surprise," Pinard said. "And such a touching scene at the reunion of mother and child. Arianne, you have been keeping secrets."

She glared at him. "You will not touch a hair on his head, Pinard."

"I will have no reason to harm him if you do as you are told." Pinard paused and looked from Arianne to Luc and back again. He smiled and his eye twinkled cruelly. "I have just thought of the most marvelous solution to my dilemma. It is brilliant. I cannot believe I did not think of it before. *You* will kill Mr. West for me."

Horrified, she gasped, "No!"

He motioned to Courcy. "Take the boy."

Courcy wrenched Luc from her arms despite her protests and Luc's cries.

As her son slipped from her grasp, Arianne bolted to her feet. "He's just a little boy, Pinard. You can't take him. Please."

"Then you will do as I tell you, and he won't be harmed," Pinard said.

She looked at Luc, who was sobbing in fright. Her heart twisted painfully in her chest. How could she murder anyone, and especially the man who had slipped beneath her defenses and captured her love? How could she protect her son from the monster who held her life?

"Arianne, I'm waiting for your answer," Pinard said as if he only waited for her to tell him how she drank her morning chocolate.

She had no choice. She nodded her agreement. Somehow, she would find a way out of this. Somehow, she would save Cameron and protect her son and her father. Somehow.

And she vowed that, somehow, she would make Pinard pay.

Cameron awoke to a pounding head and someone poking him on the shoulder.

"Wake up," a man urged. "Please, monsieur, wake up."

Cameron groaned and gingerly opened his eyes to slits. He was lying on the floor of a bare little room with a tiny window high in one wall. The air was stifling hot. His hands had been bound behind him. An older man crouched over him and worked at his bonds. When he had been freed, Cameron dragged the heels of his hands across his eyes and attempted to sit up. Nausea roiled through him. He flopped back, swallowed hard, fighting it down, and tried to get his bearings.

"Where am I?" he bit out. "Who are you?"

"You are in the attics of the Chateau de Vainqueur, a prisoner of Henri Pinard," the man said as he helped Cameron to sit upright. "I am François Chiasson. Who are you?"

"Lythmore," Cameron said, then shook his head. His brain sloshed around inside his skull, and he dropped his head to his hands. No, that name wasn't right. His memory flowed back. That monster had raped his mother. Pinard was most likely his father. He was not the Duke of Lythmore. "West," he croaked. That was not right, either. He couldn't claim the family name. He wasn't sure who he was. "Cameron," he finally added. "Just Cameron."

Chiasson nodded. "Ah, yes. I believe you know my daughter, Arianne."

Cameron raised his head and studied the man. He was about Pinard's age, and of slight build. His clothes were well-worn and a bit musty. Gray hair, receding at the hairline, was pulled back in a queue. Deep wrinkles were etched around his mouth and eyes. Those eyes, the same hazel as Arianne's, shone with intelligence and determination behind spectacles.

"She came here to rescue you," Cameron said.

"She is here?" Pleasure flashed across his face, then a sudden sheen of tears glossed his eyes. He swallowed back his emotion. "I had no idea." He shook his head. "She should not have come."

Cameron did not tell him she had little say in the matter. "How did you know I was here?"

"I heard them bring you up and lock you in." He waved at one of the walls. "I live in the next room." He paused and studied Cameron. "Pinard likes to play at being the courteous gentleman, even with his enemies. What did you do to make him lock you in here?"

Cameron felt the back of his head where a large lump throbbed. "I tried to kill him."

Chiasson grinned. "That must have annoyed him." He stood and held out a hand. "Come, we must find Arianne and escape here."

Cameron dubiously accepted the man's help to stand and found him surprisingly strong. After the floor stopped tilting beneath him, he turned to the door, which was standing open. "I thought you said that Pinard had locked me in," he said.

"I decipher codes for him," Chiasson said with a shrug. "A little lock is not going to stop me." He stepped into the hallway.

Cameron followed, intrigued, and just a tiny bit in awe of Arianne's father. Something clicked in his head. "Codes? What sort of codes?"

"All sorts," he flung back over his shoulder. "Number codes, letter codes, even some I have made up myself."

Cameron thought of the scrap of parchment with its swirl of colors and random letters that had been taken from the French fisherman. "Codes that might be incorporated into a dress design?" he asked.

Chiasson chuckled. "Yes. That is one of my best. No one besides myself has any idea it is even code. No one other than Arianne, of course. And Pinard." He spat out the name, then stopped and defiantly faced Cameron. "We have been forced to work for Pinard, monsieur. I do not know what my daughter has told you, but she has lived in danger to protect her son and me. And I do not know why you have come, but I will help you only as long as I think you can help my Arianne. If I think you will betray her, then I will turn you over to Pinard. Am I clear?"

"Quite," Cameron said.

With a nod, the older man stepped into the room where he indicated he lived. A narrow pallet stood against one wall, and against another was a desk where pens and papers and books were scattered and piled across its surface. Several candlesticks lined up at its back edge, and two lamps were suspended from the wall. A wall hook held a faded robe.

Chiasson put his finger to his lips and dropped his voice. "We must be quiet now, for we will be going through passageways that no one knows about."

He swept aside the robe and pushed against a barely visible panel on the wall. It stuck. As he pushed and pulled and muttered under his breath, Cameron heard footsteps in the hallway.

"Hurry," he whispered. "Someone's coming." The panel finally swung open. Cameron gently pushed the older man through into the darkness beyond, then grabbed one of the lanterns from the wall and shoved it at him. "Escape," he said. "Take my horse and ride to the inn at the edge of the village. Give them my name. The innkeeper will take care of you. Hurry." He pulled the panel closed on a whisper of sound before the older man could protest. Just in time. Pinard appeared in the doorway.

"Monsieur West," he said. "You have recovered. That was quite a nasty fall you had."

Cameron knew very well that he had not fallen, but he allowed the monster to have his charade. He was happy to hear the rasp in Pinard's voice from the stranglehold he'd had on the man's throat.

Pinard glanced around. "Where is the chevalier? Have you spirited him away?"

Cameron made note of the title Pinard gave Chiasson. So, the older man was a royalist from the old regime. Casually, he stepped away from the wall panel to draw Pinard's attention and shrugged. "He was not here when I entered." He poked at some papers on the desk. "Is this where he decodes information for you, Pinard?"

"That does not concern you," Pinard snapped and stepped farther into the room.

Arianne stumbled in after as if she had been pushed. Courcy followed, holding Luc by the arm with one hand, and a pistol in the other.

Pinard grinned, the movement twisting his scar. "We have come to kill you," he announced. "Or rather, our dear Arianne has come to kill you. Because, you see, if she does not, Courcy will kill the little boy."

Cameron glanced at Courcy, who held a pistol against Luc's neck. He wanted to throttle the ogre, but he didn't want to risk the boy's life. His gaze swiveled to Arianne. Her eyes were wide and dark, her face pale, and she looked as if she might shatter at any moment. She was caught in an impossible situation. Did she hate him enough to kill him? Did she think he hated her for what she had done to his brother? He had at first. All he'd wanted was revenge. But not now.

Regret twisted inside him. He should have realized that a woman with such courage, who loved her family enough to do the unthinkable, could not be the cruel Circe he had first thought her. She had not been heartless.

He had.

A true product of his true father—Pinard.

Perhaps he deserved to die.

Arianne stared at Cameron as Pinard's words washed over her. She barely heard what was said. The conversation was merely a blur of sound. All she could think of was little Luc's sniffles of fear behind her and what she had to do to save him.

Kill Cameron. The man she had come to love.

His gaze was steadfast, but she saw a bleakness in those blue eyes that had never been there before. She wanted to wipe that away, to tell him that he was not Pinard and never would be, that she would never hurt him. But she already had hurt him terribly with what she had done to his brother. But to kill him? Never, never, never.

"Arianne!" Pinard's voice cut through the haze in her head.

She dragged her gaze away from Cameron and stared at her tormentor.

"Take the pistol, Arianne, and shoot him," Pinard instructed.

"But—" Courcy protested.

"Good God!" Pinard yelled. "You have a knife. Use it. Or break the brat's neck. Now, give her the damn pistol!"

Courcy shoved the pistol at her. Like an automaton, as if her hand did not belong to her, Arianne wrapped her fingers around the grip.

With two hands, she aimed the pistol at Cameron. Dear Cameron, with those blue, blue eyes.

No, no, no, no, no. She couldn't.

Cameron held his breath. His glance slipped from Arianne to Pinard to Courcy. He could attack Pinard, but Courcy now held a knife to the boy's throat. He could attack Courcy, but Luc might get hurt, and Pinard remained a threat. Frustrated, he realized he could do nothing. His life was in Arianne's hands.

He tried to meet her gaze, to let her know he understood. But she stared at the space beyond his shoulder. What was she thinking? Her son was her world, and she would do anything to protect him. But would she murder?

A commotion far down the hall distracted him. Footsteps approached, one set determined, punctuated by the click of a cane, and another, scurrying to keep up.

"But, madame…Countess," a young man's voice entreated, "you can't be up here. He does not wish to be disturbed."

"Get away from me," an older woman ordered.

He heard the whack of a cane landing hard on the floor.

The scurrying footsteps receded down the hall.

And then she appeared in the doorway, a commanding figure, her back steely straight, her gaze chilly and imperious. She banged her cane on the floor.

"What have you done, Henri?" she demanded.

Pinard's face paled. His mouth opened, then closed, then opened. "Mother," he croaked.

If Cameron did not hate him so much, he might have felt sorry for him. If the situation were not so monstrous, he might have laughed. Instead, he wondered where this woman had come from and why she was here. In a flash of insight, he realized that if she were Pinard's mother, then he was meeting his grandmother. He had trouble processing that, so he tucked it away to examine later.

The woman's gaze swept over them all, taking everything in, then landed on him. Her eyes narrowed. She glanced from Pinard to him and back again. Her mouth pursed. She gazed at Luc, weeping silently in Courcy's grip. Then she focused on Arianne with the pistol, shaking in her hand and pointed at Cameron.

"You have done some vile things, Henri, but with this," she nodded at the gun, "you have outdone even yourself."

Pinard's lip curled in a sneer. "Go back to your ivory castle, mother, where you can shut out the world. You know nothing."

"I know that a little boy has been kidnapped. And I know that a mother has been living in fear since he was born," she snapped.

Luc whimpered and sniffled.

"Get rid of her, Pinard," Courcy said as he shook Luc into silence.

The woman turned on him. "You would do well not to provoke me."

Pinard snarled. "Go away, you old baggage. You abandoned me when I was young. I don't want to lay eyes on you again."

"And I don't wish to lay eyes on you," she said coolly as she reached into her reticule. "Did you think I was unaware that you sent your own father to the guillotine? Did you think I did not know that the reason your sister drowned herself was because of you? Did you think I fled to England because I wanted to be there?" She pulled out a small pistol and aimed it at Pinard.

He scoffed. "What are going to do with that, mother?"

"I'm going to right the wrong I committed by bringing you into this world," she said with a sniff and pulled the trigger.

Everyone stood motionless in the echo. Shock hung in the air. Pinard gasped into the silence.

Cameron watched a splotch of red bloom on Pinard's white shirt and seep into the monster's yellow brocade vest. The man's mouth opened as if he would speak, but no words came out. His single eye was wide in surprise. Without another sound, he collapsed to the floor.

Cameron leaped forward to grab Luc away from Courcy, but before he could snatch the boy away, the man spun Luc out of reach and pressed the knife closer to the boy's throat. A bead of bright blood dripped down the child's neck.

"I will kill him," Courcy said.

Cameron backed up a step and held up his hands. "Don't hurt him. Release him, and we'll let you go."

Courcy grinned. "Let me go? No, monsieur. I am in charge now. All I have to do is call out, and Pinard's men will come running."

Before Cameron had a chance to answer, Monsieur Chiasson appeared behind Courcy. With his teeth bared, in a blur of motion, a crash and exploding glass, the older man attacked Courcy with a lantern about his head and shoulders. As Courcy tried to fend off the blows, Cameron slipped Luc from his grip and pushed him into Arianne's arms. Courcy shoved Chiasson away, and Cameron jumped into the fray. He grabbed the arm holding the knife, but Courcy was strong and wily. He twisted, slicing the dagger through the air. Cameron felt the chill of cold steel on his upper arm. He clamped onto Courcy's wrist and wrenched, but the Frenchman was strong and brought the dagger between them. Cameron strained to hold the dagger away from him. If he weakened, the point of the dagger would pierce his gut. He stomped on Courcy's foot. As the man faltered, he thrust the dagger deep into soft tissue.

Courcy froze and backed a step. He looked down at the dagger protruding from his middle. Wrapping his fingers around the hilt, he pulled it out. Blood burbled from the wound. He looked at Cameron, then at Arianne, who huddled with Luc in a corner.

"You win, Madame de Vouvret," he said. Then he slashed the knife across his throat, dropped the weapon, and collapsed. Blood gushed from the slice across his neck. His gaze went blank. He was dead.

"Well!" the Countess said. "That's finished."

Cameron glanced at Monsieur Chiasson, who was hovering in the doorway. "Thank you, sir, for your help."

"It was only a little help," the older man said modestly.

The Countess sniffed her disagreement. "More than a little."

Cameron nodded his agreement. "But you did not ride for the inn, sir."

Chiasson smiled sheepishly. "I did not wish to miss the excitement."

"Oh, Papa," Arianne scolded. "You might have been killed."

The older man drew himself up. "I am not helpless."

"Certainly not," the Countess agreed.

Cameron hid his smile, then looked at the two bodies on the floor. "We must hurry. Someone will be coming to investigate the noise."

Monsieur Chiasson crooked his finger. "This way." He stepped into the room, avoiding the bodies and blood, and pushed open the secret panel. "This will lead us outside, but remember, we must be quiet."

Cameron waved him on. "Lead the way, sir."

Chiasson took the other lantern from the hook on the wall and ducked through the opening. Cameron motioned for the Countess to follow. Arianne sent Luc after them. As she passed Cameron, she stopped with a little gasp and lightly touched his arm.

"You're hurt."

"Only a scratch, madame," he said, shrugging off the throbbing pain and the blood running down his arm beneath his coat.

"More than a scratch, I think." She paused and caught her bottom lip between her teeth. "Thank you for saving Luc."

Cameron's lips twitched. "Thank you for not shooting me."

"I think the Countess took care of that," she said with a tiny smile.

"Hurry!" her father whispered.

They had no more time. Arianne entered the secret passage. Before Cameron followed, he grabbed one of the candles on the desk and lit the papers lying there. One of them was a dress design. His candle flame hovered over it for a moment as he considered taking it with him, then he lit the corner. He wanted no one to find any of the secrets that had been passed to Pinard, no matter how encoded they might be. No matter how much he wished to take a reminder of Arianne. Then he turned into the dark passage.

As he trailed behind the others, he sent up a silent prayer of thanks. The woman he loved was safe, along with her family. For now, that was enough. He would decide what to do with his undeserved title and the woman who was his grandmother later, and figure out his life when he had time to think. What he had to do was get them safely to the coast and across the Channel to England.

Monsieur Chiasson led them through a labyrinth of narrow passages and stairways that snaked behind the decorated walls of the chateau. They passed numerous small doors that opened into rooms on all the floors. Cameron surmised the passages had been incorporated into the chateau to allow servants to pass unseen between rooms, and perhaps for clandestine nighttime visits between the inhabitants.

He had one more task to accomplish. As they reached the bottom floor, he opened a hidden door that led into one of the grand rooms of the chateau. It was the salon where the portrait of his mother hung. The room was dripping with elaborate decoration — carved reliefs on all the wall panels, a mythical scene painted on the ceiling, a huge gilt chandelier, brocade silk covering the chairs and sofas, and miles of damask drapery at the windows. The room was empty. He slipped in, smashed several oil lamps near the drapes, and set the oil on fire. A young maid stepped into the room, gave a gasp, then turned and fled. She would no doubt alert the other servants. He was relieved that the alarm would be spread because he wanted the chateau to burn to the ground.

His final act was to smash another lamp against the portrait. He could not take it with him, and he did not want anyone ogling it, least of all Pinard's lackeys. With a nod to his mother, he returned to the others. No one would inhabit the Chateau de Vainqueur. Its history was too tragic, despite its beauty. Setting it afire eased some of the pain in Cameron's heart.

CHAPTER 18

They came to a door on the ground floor. Chiasson pushed it open to reveal a tangle of vines. Moonlight poked through the leaves.

Chiasson put his finger to his lips, indicating silence, shoved the lantern at Cameron, then slipped between the vines.

"Papa!" Arianne whispered urgently, but he was gone.

Annoyed at the older man for his recklessness, Cameron pushed the foliage aside. He saw him running across the lawn and waving his arms.

"Help! Help!" Chiasson cried. "Trouble! Tragedy! Fire!"

Two men ran to meet him. Chiasson spoke to them as he waved his arms and indicated the upper floor of the chateau. Then he bent in half and clutched his chest as if the exertion was too much. The two men ran off. Chiasson straightened and hurried back to where they waited.

"Come," he said. "The stables are this way."

"No," The Countess said. "I came in that." She used her cane to point out a cabriolet waiting on the drive. A boy held the horse's head. "I did not expect to be leaving with a crowd. I will meet you at the inn."

She pushed past Chiasson and strode across the lawn as if she owned the property. Since the vehicle only held two persons, Cameron swept Luc up into his arms, then hurried Arianne and her father to the stables. As he saddled their two horses, he cursed silently when his bloody fingers slipped and fumbled with the cinches. His wound would have to wait. He tossed Arianne and Luc on one horse, then mounted his and yanked Monsieur Chiasson up behind him.

"Whatever happens," he said to Arianne, "don't stop. Keep riding until you get to the inn. Promise me."

She looked as if she were about to argue. Before she could say anything, he slapped the rump of her horse. As it galloped off, he urged his horse to follow. The cabriolet was already gone.

Behind them, servants spilled from every door of the chateau as flames danced in the windows. They milled about in disarray. Glass shattered as the heat built. The fire roared. In the confusion, Cameron and Arianne raced down the chateau's drive as shouts erupted behind them. Two shots exploded. Cameron felt a ball whizz past his ear. Ahead of him, Arianne turned onto the road, and he breathed a bit easier. As he trailed her, their pursuers seemed to give up. But he did not take a complete breath until they skidded into the inn's courtyard.

Cameron stared down into the courtyard from his solitary room. The Countess had arrived safely and was ensconced in a room at the end of the hall. Arianne, her father, and her son were settled in the next room. He did not worry that she would try to run from him, for she would stay to protect Luc and Monsieur Chiasson. The innkeeper had seemed relieved when Cameron mentioned trouble and the fire at the chateau. He wondered what brutalities Pinard had imposed on the villagers.

He could hear conversation and laughter from the common room where the local people gathered for conversation and a pint before retiring for the night. No one seemed to be rushing to help at the chateau, and the noise reaching him sounded celebratory. When he turned his head, he could see down the road, where an orange glow lit the night sky above the trees. The chateau was being consumed, and with it, all of Pinard's evil.

Satisfaction washed through him, followed by a twinge of regret that he was losing a bit of his mother. But too much wrong had been done there. It needed to be expunged.

On the other hand, he seemed to have gained a grandmother. The twists of fate befuddled him. He wondered if he would get to know this forbidding woman who had abruptly appeared in his life. Who had killed her own son, the man who was his father. His mind stumbled over that. He was not who he thought he was.

A soft knock sounded on his door and interrupted his musings. He had told the innkeeper he did not wish to be disturbed. With a sigh of annoyance, he went to answer it. Arianne stood on the other side. Behind her was a maid holding a tray with a bowl of water, cloths, bottles, and other items.

"I came to take care of your wound," she said. "It must be stitched."

"It is nothing. There's no need." Now that he'd had a bit of quiet, the wound had begun to sting and burn. He flexed his fingers, crusted with dried blood that had seeped down beneath his sleeve. He'd merely tied a handkerchief around his arm to stop the flow, but it had become soaked through. He'd had no inclination to clean himself up.

She pushed past him into the room. "You do not want an infection set in." She sounded as imperious as his grandmother. She told the maid to place the tray on a small table next to the bed, then dismissed her. "Please," she said as she waved to the bed. "Come, sit."

Cameron hesitated. The bed was where he most wanted to be with Arianne. He wanted to kiss her, touch her, taste her, feel her softness beneath his fingers, hear her sighs and gasps. He wanted to make love to her. But this was not the time. That time might never come again.

"Your son and your father," he said. "How do they fare?"

She fiddled with the items on the tray. "My father was telling Luc a story when I left them. Luc was falling asleep in his grandfather's arms. They are happy to get to know each other."

"The Countess has retired as well. It seems she brought her maid to attend her," he said.

She shook her head. "It's a wonder she can sleep after what she did. I can't imagine…" Her words choked off.

Cameron wandered farther from the bed. "I think she felt she was righting a wrong."

"Perhaps." She turned to him with a threaded needle. "You have not sat down. Are you delaying? Do you fear my needle piercing your skin? I assure you, your grace, I've had quite a bit of practice using that tool."

"I have every confidence in your expertise, madame," he said. How could he tell her that he had been so wrong about her? How could he tell her how horrified he was to be the son of a monster? Before the words could fall from his lips, he chose the easiest route and sank to the bed.

Arianne helped him remove his coat, sat beside him, then tsked when she saw the makeshift bandage he had wound around his arm. When she tried to remove it, he flinched at the pain. The handkerchief and his shirt beneath had become glued to his wound with dried blood. She soaked it with a wet cloth to dissolve the blood, then delicately peeled away the bandage and his shirt sleeve. With an abrupt tug, she ripped his sleeve apart and tsked again.

"I have come here just in time. If you had left this longer, it would have become poisoned. You must have a care," she scolded. She reached for one of the bottles and poured something into a glass, then handed it to him. "Here, drink this. The innkeeper told me it is his best brandy."

Like a dutiful child, Cameron took it and drank. It was very good brandy. It burned all the way down and hit his stomach with a jolt.

"*Merci,*" she said. "Now, I will begin."

Cameron concentrated on her gentle touch. Her fingers felt like butterfly wings against his skin. But when she poured some of that precious brandy on his wound, he hissed between his teeth. Determined not to show any other weakness, he clamped his teeth together when she pierced his flesh with her needle. By the time she had finished and rebandaged the wound with clean strips of cloth, he was feeling quite relaxed. He suspected she had put something into that glass besides brandy.

"I think we need to remove your boots, your grace," she said briskly.

He obediently held out one foot, then the other as she tugged them off. Leaning back on his arms, trying not wince at the pain from his wound, he gazed up at her. He had to tell her. He felt compelled.

"Arianne," he said. "I am not a duke at all. I am an imposter. I am the son of a monster." His eyelids started to droop, but he shook off the drowsiness.

"You are the bravest and most honorable man I know, Monsieur le Duc de Lythmore. You are *mon loup*. My wolf. Now you must sleep." Her fingers trailed across his cheek.

The sensation was sweet and soft. His eyes closed as he savored her touch. She pressed him back onto the bed, then covered him with the blanket. Sleep beckoned. He tried to ignore its call and forced his eyes open.

"And my brother…" he mumbled. "Foolish…Selfish to do that."

"We'll talk later," she said.

"But—" he protested.

"Shh. Close your eyes," she commanded gently.

Obviously, he had to obey. But he needed to tell her something else. What was it? He could not find it in his brain.

"I love you, Cameron West," she whispered.

Did she truly say that? Or had he dreamt it?

Her lips touched his in the lightest of kisses.

He smiled. If all his dreams were like this, he would sleep forever.

CHAPTER 19

Cameron stood at the rail of the luxurious yacht that was taking them back to England. The Countess had hired it to bring her across. She evidently did not skimp on her comforts. He'd been relieved that he'd not had to make arrangements for their return, for his brain was crowded with questions and doubts. He'd felt off-balance since learning he was not who he thought he was.

The moonlight on the water created a path as if illuminating the way home. He would be glad to be back on English soil, even though it would most likely feel as unbalanced as being on the sea. His identity had been swept away, turned to ash as surely as his mother's portrait hanging in Pinard's chateau. How could he face his friends and peers after what he had learned about himself?

The sound of footsteps punctuated by a cane approached across the deck. The Countess. His grandmother. She stood beside him in silence a moment, contemplating the same scene as he did. Then she spoke, that chilly voice modulated into a warmer tone.

"My son," she said, "was cruel from the time he was a child. He delighted in pulling the wings from butterflies, strangling frogs, and drowning kittens. He tormented his nannies, and there were many. Some requested to leave, but others merely fled. He was uncontrollable, even as an infant. I resolved never to have another child.

"He left for Paris after a rather violent disagreement with his father and was gone several years. When he returned, he seemed calmer and to have given up his cruelty. He was courting a young woman, the daughter of a marquis. I heard her parents had been sent to their deaths. And then one day, he appeared with a horrible wound on his face. He fell into a fever, and in his delirium, he ranted about the young woman and the man who stole her. I was able to piece together the horrendous thing he had done. While he was ill, the soldiers came to arrest his father, for he had already put that into motion."

She stopped and drew a deep breath. "I could no longer stand the sight of him. Afraid that he would also have me arrested if he recovered, I left him to the servants and the physician and fled to England. Years passed before I heard from him. He wished me to help a young woman. I did not respond, but she appeared on my doorstep. And then I realized she was desperately afraid and with child."

She stopped again. Appalled at the story she recounted, Cameron could find no words. Where did such a monster come from?

Turning to him, she said, "You are nothing like him. You are like your mother, the daughter of the marquis. Perhaps, if you would like, we could become better acquainted."

For the first time since learning who his father was, Cameron felt as if he finally had a toehold on solid ground. "I would like that," he said.

The Countess—his grandmother—nodded.

Sensing she was a bit more approachable, he said, "If I may, I have a question."

She gave an assenting wave of her hand, all of the many generations of nobility in her blood appearing in that single gesture.

"How did you know to come to France?" he asked. "Your appearance was quite serendipitous."

The tiniest twitch at the corner of her mouth indicated her amusement. "I have always been aware of my son's activities. He thought everything he did went unnoticed, but I had placed my spies in his house long ago. I had heard one of his plans was nearing fruition. Then Mr. Inglis came to tell me that the boy had been taken. I knew immediately where the boy was. I was done with watching my son play his evil games." She looked away across the water.

Although she showed no sign of grief, Cameron sensed her deep emotion at what had taken place inside the Chateau du Vainqueur. "I am sorry," he said.

She turned to look at him. "*Merci*. But it is done." Then she gestured at the figure standing in the bow of the boat. "She is lovely, don't you agree? And quite courageous." Without another word, she went below.

A bit bemused, Cameron watched her go, then he glanced at the bow of the boat. Arianne's silhouette stood limned by the moonlight. Her father and son were below, sleeping. She no doubt thought he was going to arrest her for passing secrets. He had no intention of doing that. He'd been a complete and utter fool. She had done what she had to in order to keep her family safe. He needed to speak with her, tell her how he felt.

She turned and saw him, as if his glance had called her. He could feel her gaze assessing, perhaps a bit fearful. Then she left her spot at the bow and approached. He met her halfway.

"We will be in England soon," she said.

He glanced across her shoulder. The Dover cliffs were a smudge on the horizon. "Yes. In a little more than an hour."

"I wanted to explain about your brother." Her words were quiet, but steady, as if she had rehearsed them.

Cameron was not sure he wanted to hear what she had to say. He'd had enough emotional blows in the past couple of days to last a lifetime. But she seemed to need to talk, so he nodded for her to go on.

"Your brother," she said, "was murdered by Courcy. I already told you that. But I feel responsible for his death as well. Pinard had ordered me to…to…seduce him. I tried to avoid that, but de Pagière introduced us at a house party at Shipley Hall. It was part of Pinard's plan. Your brother became very attached to me, but when I tried to discourage him, he would not listen." She looked away, out over the water.

"He lost heavily at cards one night," she continued. "De Pagière mocked him, and your brother blurted something about knowing secrets because his brother was a spy. He thought he had betrayed you. That night he sent me a note to meet him on the roof. When I got there, he said he loved me. Because I had been ordered by Pinard to break his heart or he would hurt my father, I laughed at Ian's declaration. He ran to the edge and put a noose around his neck. I told him I did care for him, and I would explain if only he would step away. I begged him not to jump. I almost had him convinced when Courcy came up behind me and pushed him. The last thing I saw was his hand reaching out to me."

245

She turned back to Cameron, her cheeks wet with tears. "I'm so sorry."

Cameron drew a breath. Let it out. His need for revenge was gone, burnt to nothing in the ashes of the Chateau de Vainqueur. De Pagière was in prison or dead. Courcy was dead. Pinard was dead. His grief for his brother still hurt, but it was a dull ache instead of the sharp pain he had been living with. His brother had been young and foolish. Because of that, Ian had allowed those men to manipulate him. Arianne had not caused his brother's death.

The woman before him was alive. Courageous. Honorable. Beautiful. Seductive. The words she had whispered the night before as he fell into his dream sang through him.

Her lashes swept down. "I know you will arrest me when we get to England. I just want you to know that I am not the wicked person you think I am."

"Arianne." He pushed back the hood of her cloak and cupped her cheeks. "Arianne, my sweet, I don't think you are wicked. I am not going to arrest you."

"You're not?"

He shook his head. "No. Do you know why?"

"Why?" she whispered.

"Because I think you are the bravest woman I know."

A tiny line appeared between her brows. "That's no reason."

"Because you didn't kill Ian. I don't blame you for what you did."

"You don't?"

"No." He smiled, took both her hands and nestled them against his chest over his heart. "Pinard would have found some other way to kill my brother if he hadn't been able to use you and your father."

"But—" she began, her eyes troubled.

"Shh." He placed a finger across her lips. "No arguments."

"But I could have done something to dissuade Ian," she persisted.

"Arianne, you have my forgiveness. Ian was foolish and impulsive. You did the only thing you could to protect your family." He drew a breath. "I have another very good reason not to arrest you."

Her eyes widened. "You do?"

"Yes." He nodded. "Arianne de Vouvret, I love you. I want to marry you. Will you? Marry me?"

246

Her mouth dropped open. "I beg your pardon?"

He laughed. "I love you. Will you marry me? Will you have me, a man who has no idea who he is?"

She softly touched the corner of his mouth, then traced her fingers over his cheek. "I know who you are. You are *mon loup*, my brave wolf of a duke. The man I love." She smiled. "Of course, I will marry you."

His blood bubbled with happiness, and drawing her into his embrace, he kissed her to seal the bargain. He might have to discover himself again, but for now, he knew exactly who he was—a man in love with the most glorious woman he had ever known. Instead of finding the Jezebel who had destroyed his brother, he found the woman who made his heart sing. Together, when the passion of their kiss had faded to a promise, they looked toward the cliffs of Dover and their new life.

I hope you enjoyed tucking into *CONFESSIONS OF A DANGEROUS DUKE.*

And now, here's the moment I ask you to share your thoughts about the book.

I welcome all reviews — the good, the bad, and everything in between.

Click here to leave a review for *CONFESSIONS OF A DANGEROUS DUKE.*

Thank you,
Patricia Barletta

PATRICIA BARLETTA'S BOOK LIST

ON HIS MAJESTY'S SECRET SERVICE

The Duke Who Loved Me
Book 1

Desperate for money, Lady Jessica Carlton risks it all at the most notorious gaming hell in London and loses to the handsome Damien Trevor, Duke of Wyndham. A spy for the king, Damien suspects the dark-haired beauty of passing traitorous secrets to the French. As danger deals them a deadly hand, can they trust the truth in their hearts?

The Duke's Dangerous Kiss
Book 2

Jillian St. Clare is happily wiggling her aching toes behind a potted fern at a society ball when a tiny scroll flies into her empty shoe. A spy's secret message! Trouble! The notorious Duke of Dunbary appears and asks her to dance. He wants the note! Can she trust him? Or will she lose herself to the duke's dangerous kiss?

Confessions of a Dangerous Duke
Book 3

Arianne de Vourvret, the most sought-after modiste in Bath, hides a terrible secret. Caught in the clutches of a sadistic and powerful Frenchman, she's forced to lure in his enemies as he plots their demise. But when she meets the dashing Duke of Lythmore, she can't resist his beguiling pursuit. Can she keep her dangerous double life disguised?

AURIANO CURSE SERIES

Moon Dark
Book 1

Venetian Prince Alessandro is cursed, forced to live half his life as a shadow, losing all sense of touch. When he saves an Englishwoman from an assassin's blade, he's captivated by her beauty and shocked at his ability to feel her. Could she be the key to unlocking his family's tormented existence?

Moon Shadow
Book 2

He is a duke of shadows. A man with a curse upon his head. She is an alluring and mysterious thief who will do everything she can to protect her brother. Fate thrusts them together. Passion entwines them. Danger stalks them. But when evil forces seek to destroy them, can they trust in each other to escape their doomed darkness?

Moon Bright
Book 3

Allegra D'Este, Princess of Auriano, lives under a deadly curse invoked by the evil sorceress, Nulkana. Only the magical Sphere of Astarte will break the curse and enable her to live a life free from danger. Fleeing to Bath, England, she meets the devastatingly handsome Earl of Hawksmoor who presents a different kind of danger to Allegra—one that could break her heart.

Coming in 2021…*Moon Gold*

Sign up for Patricia's newsletter at patriciabarletta.com

Follow Patricia Barletta on BookBub
Follow Patricia Barletta on Amazon
Like Patricia Barletta's Facebook Page

ABOUT
PATRICIA BARLETTA

Patricia Barletta is an award-winning author of historical and paranormal romance fiction. After a fulfilling career teaching English Literature in high school, she decided to go back to school herself, and obtained a Master of Fine Arts in Creative Writing at Stonecoast (University of Southern Maine). When she's not at a yoga class doing her best downward dog, Patricia is usually tending her hydrangeas or hosting a brunch for her writing group. Patricia loves to travel, and often finds the inspiration for her dark heroes, feisty heroines, and romantic settings while on a research trip. At the end of each journey she loves going home to her cozy, historical old house outside of Boston where she weaves her magical tales.

Find out more about Patricia and her books on her website: patriciabarletta.com and on Facebook.

www.ingramcontent.com/pod-product-compliance
Lightning Source LLC
Chambersburg PA
CBHW020057180626
46812CB00006B/2364